# *Blaphaus Maximus*
# and the
# *Order of Blattodea*

### *By Jason Peverett*

*Names: Peverett, Jason, author*
*Cover artwork: Victor Langlois*
*Title: Blaphaus Maximus and the Order of Blattodea*

*Description: First edition*
*Summary: A story about a galaxy that is about to but change not for the better... all because of who is Galactic President.*

*Also in the series... Blaphaus Maximus and the New Galaxy Day*

*It was one week after New Galaxy Day...*

## CHAPTER 1

The House was covered with confetti pieces as well as streamers still from the New Galaxy Day that was a week ago. She wondered as she climbed the stairs why nobody thought of sweeping it up. Even the streets were still full of confetti and trash from the celebration. The streets used to be nice and clean on Launderington but now it looked like a mess. She went inside the building to be greeted by the House robot who scanned her from top to bottom.

"Hello, my memory banks don't know who you are, so who are you?" the robot asked in a pleasant female voice.

The woman with short blonde hair, wearing spectacles sighed. She was annoyed she got stopped, but also was more concerned that this robot was the only security the House had… as far as she knew. What about if someone wanted to come in and try to assassinate the Governors or the Galactic President?

"My name is Fami Tapperdau, I'm looking for Galactic President Blaphaus Maximus. Do you know where he is?"

"I'm not at a liberty to tell you that, Ms. Tapperdau. Galactic President Maximus is a very busy man…"

"Busy *man*? Don't you mean busy *Toob*?"

"Oh, if you say so." the robot said.

"Hmmmm. If he comes back here can you let him know I'm looking for him?"

"Certainly, Ms. Tapperdau. Anything else?"

"Yes, is Governor Noj Peezle here?"

"Yes, that I can answer. Would you like to speak to him?"

"Yes… I would."

"I will take you to his office. Please follow me. You don't have any weapons on you, do you?"

"No, no I don't."

And Fami followed the robot to the lift. This might be easier than she thought she guessed.

Cakerlak wasn't the nicest planet in the galaxy, and Blaphaus was not surprised. He was surprised when the Cyrakuse Joorg, who was the Governor of Cakerlak called for him to go there. Blaphaus was very hesitant, but when Noam said he'll also go as well as Haathee, who knew the Cakerlak and Joorg. Rüppell wanted to go to but Blaphaus said be didn't need an entourage. It has been a week since the big day when he announced on the top of the House steps that the 22 planets in the galaxy were all together. He still wasn't happy he had to wear the Toob suit, but he was half glad only a group of beings knew the truth about him. In week nothing really happened, and apart from going to Ceilingida to go home this was the first trip he made. For him again it was a new planet. He hated going to new planets, especially one where someone came from

that tried to kill him. The four walked down the ramp of Space False One, the yellow shuttle that now had those words painted on the side. They were greeted by a round fat Cakerlak with a red shell that had black dots all over it, and a vest and pants in front.

"Hello, Governor Joorg, Galactic President Maximus, I hope your trip to Cakerlak was fine." she said.

"It was." Joorg smiled, "Thank you, Laterille. This is Governor Noam from Homunculus."

"Hello, Governor. You're mighty short."

"And you're round." Noam remarked.

"Of course you know Governor Haathee from Phytnes."

"Yes, always good to see you, Governor."

Blap saw they were outside, outside a castle looking building on the top of  a very tall cliff.

"So, we are here to see you?" Blap asked.

"Oh, no, not me, Planet Mayor Coleoptera."

"Planet Mayor? This planet still has a Planet Mayor? Wot for?"

"Why not?" Joorg asked, "I stay off planet and he stays on. You'll like old Cole, he's a solid Cakerlak."

"Terrific. So, we're just going to stand around or get this bloody trip over with?"

"Follow me." Laterille smiled.

She led them through the door that was carved into the rocky wall.

"This is one way to build a place to live and work in." Noam said, "And no steps, Blaphaus."

"No one should have steps." Blap remarked.

They were led into the room where the black, six armed Cakerlak sat, wearing a black jacket. He had short antennas and compounded eyes. It was hard to tell where his clothes and black shell started and ended and he looked more menacing then he actually was.

"Wow, you actually brought him here, Joorg. I'm impressed." smiled Cole.

Joorg said, "I told you, Cole. Blaphaus is a good Toob."

Cole shook Blap's hand, looking up at him.

"It's a pleasure to meet you, Galactic President Maximus. I never met a Tooberosum before."

"You didn't come to a Launderington for New Galaxy Day. You could've met me then."

"Oh, I don't like leaving this planet. I'm old, you know."

"Cole, this is Governor Noam and you know Governor Haathee."

"Governor Haathee? You're not Planet Mayor anymore?"

"No, P.M. Coleoptera. I was 'promoted.'"

"So was I. As soon Joorg here became Governor he asked me to be P.M."

"That's great. So, why are we here?" Blap asked.

"Joorg didn't tell you?"

"Uh, no. Should he have?"

"Well, not really. We had a good relationship with Traf when he was G.P., you know."

"So good that this planet wasn't part of the Cabinet." scoffed Blaphaus.

"We liked to keep things 'underground' so to speak."

"Or on top off a bloody cliff." Blap said.

"This is the highest cliff on Cakerlak, G.P. Maximus."

."Wotever. So, why did you call for me to come here?"

"Traf would give us dosh to keep us protected from any invasions, or attacks. As you said on New Galaxy Day you have been to other galaxies. We wouldn't want to be left armless in case a hostile invasion happened. And as the Toobs and the Cakerlak did not get along a long time ago, I was hoping you'd still protect us by giving us dosh so we can protect ourselves."

"Wait a minute." Blap said, "One of your species is sitting in jail because he tried to assassinate me..."

"That's nothing to do me. What he did was on his own."

"But he had a weapon." Noam spoke up, "There's only one species with weapons and an army..."

"That is part of the Cabinet... we had to defend ourselves alone."

"That was your bloody choice, Cakerlak. And you have nothing to worry about now. The Xenarthra will protect you if you ever need to be protected..." Blap remarked.

"Can you guaranteed that, Galactic President? The Illiger Governor is not here with you to agree. Instead you brought this little man and these two..."

"Who are you calling little?" snapped Noam.

"If I knew wot you're be asking I wouldn't be here. You don't need dosh or anything to protect anything. You definitely don't need weapons." Blap turned to Joorg, "Did you know this?"

"Yes. I heard Traf took care of the Cakerlak, I assumed you would too."

"Well, you assumed wrong. Maybe if one of this ugly race didn't try to kill me I might have a different thought."

"It's an agreement that Traf promised, Maximus." Cole said seriously.

"Which ended when he dropped dead from a heart attack. Noam, did anybody on the Cabinet know about this shadyness?"

"Uh, it's news to me. Maybe Peezle knows."

"Great. Then I'll ask Peezle. Cakerlak, you're not getting any help from me or the Cabinet until I figure this feces out."

"Well, I just hope an invasion doesn't come." Cole said crossing his six arms.

On Launderington, Peezle sat behind his desk playing Yerkal's holo-recording on the fob. Ever since Yerkal left and Peezle found the fob in his kitchen he pretty much played it over and over. The House robot stood at the doorway with Fami. Peezle quickly turned the holo-recording off and put it in the pocket of his multi-colored jacket. He stood up quickly when he saw them.

"Oh, hello." he walked around the desk and shook her hand. "I'm Governor Peezle."

"I'm Fami Tapperdau, can we talk?"

"Oh, sure. House robot 1, you can go back to your post."

"Yes, Governor Peezle." the robot scooted off.

"Take a seat, Ms. Tapperdau."

He sat behind the desk and she sat in front of it.

"House robot 1? That's an odd name."

"Yeah, we'll, it's the first House robot."

"So, anyone can walk in and assassinate any of you or the G.P. when the robot took me up in the lift?"

"No, she would've been replaced with House robot 2. We are always protected. We had two security guards who once led me out this building. I have fired them."

"I see. If someone would come in here and try to do you harm you'll be safe?"

"You'll be surprised. Is that why you're here, Ms. Tapperdau, to talk about our safety?"

"Kind of. So, you're the fourth Governor in less than a month for Ceilingida, is that right?"

He nodded, "Yes, ma'am. There was definitely a few of us. But I guess it'll be me for a while."

She smiled, "Wasn't your husband Yerkal Peezle the last Governor?"

Peezle nodded, "Yeah, I was his successor."

"And weren't you G.P. Traf's Assistant and was there when he passed?"

"Yes, I was. If you don't mind me asking what's with all these questions? Are you a reporter?"

"No, I'm not. I'm just someone who is trying to figure out a few things. So, the new G.P. is a Tooberosum, a species that's hardly ever seen..."

"Unless you go to their planet, Ms. Tapperdau." he smirked.

"And you've been there? To Tooberosum?"

"Yes, all the Governors have." he lied.

"And they didn't want to be part of the Cabinet I take it."

"Correct. We settled with the 22. That's pretty good though."

"Do you believe there's other galaxy's out there and other planets, Governor Peezle?"

"Ummm... it's possible."

"G.P. Maximus said he's seen other galaxy's last week, do you remember that?"

Peezle sat back, not liking where this was going.

"Yeah..."

"Did you believe him?"

"If G.P. says he's been to another galaxy then it must be true."

"And do you believe that a species from that galaxy can come to this one?"

"I doubt that's likely, Ms. Tapperdau..."

"But the G.P. managed it..."

"If what he's saying *is* true. So, you're not a reporter, you sure sound like one..."

"No, I'm an individual looking out for the safety of this galaxy."

"We have the G.B.I. for that and the Cabinet..."

Just then Governor Gillian, the Giraffeidae appeared in the doorway.

"Sorry for interrupting, but you are needed in the meeting room, Governor."

"Okay, I'll be right there." he stood up and walked around the desk. "Are we done, Ms. Tapperdau?"

She stood up as well and nodded, "For now, but I'll be back. I want to talk to the G.P. "

"Well, whenever he gets back I'm sure we can arrange something. Gillian, can you show Ms. Tapperdau out?"

"Yes, follow me." Gillian nodded with her tall long neck.

"Hang on." Tapperdau whispered into Peezle's ear, "I know your secret."

She smiled and followed Gillian out the office and down the hallway. Peezle frowned, wondering what the secret was. He didn't have any secrets... except for the one where Blap is really a human from another galaxy wearing a Toob suit.

He walked into the meeting room which now had a new longer table to fit 21 Governors around. All were there seated but Gillian and the three that were with Blaphaus, who was actually there but in holo-call form on the middle of the table.

"Peezle, where were you?" Blap demanded when Peezle walked in.

"I had a visitor... sorry."

"A visitor? Your missing husband?" Southington, the tall blonde female human Governor asked, "Any word from him?"

"Nope, nothing yet. So, what's up?" he took his seat. "How is everything going on Cakerlak?"

"You tell me. The Planet Mayor, which none of us knew bloody existed says that Traf used to fund weapons and food and things to that planet. Joorg confirmed it. Do you know anything about it?"

"No. Why would I?"

"You were Traf's Assistant." Thaw said besides him.

"Yeah, but I didn't know everything he did. Like the meeting with Tostone for example. Did he fund the planet from his pocket or the House budget?"

"We should know if he funded the planet through." the other human female named Dawber said. "You'd think."

"Pity he's not here to question." Penya said calmly, under his triangle shaped straw hat.

"Nope. So, I don't want to stand around in this castle waiting." Blap said, "Do we fund this six armed lot or do I say no?"

"We need to find out how Traf funded them." Thaw said. "So, tell them to wait."

"Okay. You got it." Blap's holo-call ended.

"So, how do we find this out?" Bodie asked, "Who is in charge of accounting for the House?"

"Tostone." the Cyrakuse Zucaritas replied, "And with everything else happening we never had anyone take over that job."

"Where is Tostone now?" Jaboney asked.

"Working for the King on Cyrakuse." Zucaritas replied.

"I say we contact Blaphaus and have him go to Cyrakuse on his way here." told Thaw.

Zucaritas stood up, "I'll head there as well. As Governor for that planet I should be there."

"You heard the Leetric." Blap said to Cole, "We will let you know."

Haathee explained, "If the House funded this planet then we will continue..."

"If we vote for that." Noam interrupted, "But if it was out of Traf's own pocket then you can just get the same as the rest of the planets. Is that clear?"

Joorg said, "That's understandable. Right, Cole?"

"It'll have to be. Thanks for visiting, G.P. Maximus."

"Yeah, yeah. Wotever. Can we go now?"


In his sky blue suit the skinny unshaven dark haired man watched the Cakerlak walk out through the jail building's gates and walk to the curb. The dark haired man walked across the street, and up to the Cakerlak.

"Oh, it's Governor, I mean *Solicitor* Peezle. You look like a mess, human. I would not want to be seen looking like that in public."

"Neop, where are you going?" Yerkal asked firmly.

"Back to Cakerlak. I was let off, the judge said I only threatened the Toob, which is true. You're not going to run and tell GNN or the Toob, are you? I really want to just get to the spaceport and get off this planet."

"I'm coming with you." Yerkal said.

"Why is that, Governor?"

"I'm not a Governor anymore. I want to learn about the Order of Blattodea and the Toobs. And I want to find out which member of the Cabinet is on it."

"No you don't."

Yerkal looked into Neop's large eyes. "Oh, yes I do."


Zucaritas' holo-call stood before the other Governors and Blaphaus on Space False One.

"So, head towards Cyrakuse, we have to talk to Tostone about the House accounting..."

"Wot?" Blap asked sitting.

His Toob suit was piled in a corner of the shuttle. The only thing he was wearing was the Toob feet, and his black skintight outfit. Even the data-pad that he used to control the Toobs eyes, mouth and arms and legs was sitting on top of the pile.

"I just got out the bloody Toob suit. And I said I'll agree to go to Cakerlak but I said nothing about Cyrakuse."

"Tostone was in charge of accounting." Noam explained. "He would know if the House funded the Cakerlak or if he did it out of pocket."

"So, who is the accountant Governor now?" Haathee asked.

"No one." Noam replied.

"We need someone good at maths." Zucaritas' holo-call said.

"I know exactly who then." told Blap, "And it's not going to be none of you idiots."

"Then who?" Noam asked.

Blap winked at them.


The Gink Governor went into his office which had green lights giving the room and eerie green glow. He sat at his desk and turned on his info-pad. The holo-call of the Great Weta, the big Cakerlak appeared on the desk.

"Yes?"

"Great Weta, did you know that the Toob and some Governors were on Cakerlak to meet with Coleoptera?"

"A lot doesn't get passed me on this planet. I am well aware. Joorg will be spoken to and dealt with."

"They are trying to work out who funded the planet. Do you know anything about it?"

"Yes. Traf funded the planet."

"What should I do?"

"Nothing, Gink. Let them spin their wheels working it out. You don't say a word. Understood?"

The green Gink nodded, "Yes, Weta."

"Just concentrate what you need to do."

The Gink nodded.


The King and Lady Gerda stood holding hands in front of their palace on Cyrakuse as the yellow shuttle came down to land on the green in front of it. Four Cyrakuse soldiers stood with them, holding spears. The ramp descended and Blap and the three Governors walked down it. They walked over and Joorg and Haathee bowed before the King.

"Welcome back!" the King smiled. "I wondered how long it'll take you to come back to this planet."

"Me too." grumbled the Toob.

"Zucaritas said he's on his way, but you are a Cyrakuse as well." the King said to Joorg. "I saw you at the celebration on Launderington but we didn't meet."

"I'm Governor Joorg."

"Governor of what planet?"

"Cakerlak."

Lady Gerda gave an odd look to the King.

"What was that look for?" Joorg asked.

"That's a rough planet. I have no idea why another species would want to govern them." she replied.

"Somebody has to do it." Blap said, "Where's Tostone?"

"He is working for me on doing P.R. Come on into the palace. He'll be surprised to see you."

The G.P. and the Governors followed the King and Lady Gerda towards the palace.

"That was one hell of a celebration last week." told the King, "A lot has changed in such a short time."

"Yep." Blap commented.

"So Tooberosum didn't want to be part of the Cabinet?"

"Nope. And I knew they wouldn't." Blap said, "They're a boring lot."

"Ha! If you say so."

They went into the palace to be approached by Blake, who helped the King. Blake was a black Cyrakuse that they met before.

"Galactic President! How have you been?" Blake asked.

"I'm alive."

They went down the hallway to the closed wooden door. The King knocked it and a few seconds later it opened up to reveal Celley Tostone.

"Oh, it's you." she glared at Blap.

"Did you like the party last week?" Blap asked.

"No. I didn't want to go back to that Creator-damned planet, but Charcat insisted."

"Well, he is to blame for this whole thing... me being G.P. that is. Where is he anyway?"

"If you're going to offer Governor again..."

"Peezle is Governor."

"Noj? Ha. That's good."

Noam said, "Is Charcat here? We have to ask him something. It's kind of urgent."

"Okay. Charcat!!!!" she yelled.

Just then Tostone appeared behind his wife, putting his arms around her.

"Galactic President! I thought I heard your voice. How has it been? New Galaxy Day was amazing. Pity your own planet didn't want to be part of the Cabinet."

"It's for the best." Blap said.

Tostone looked at Joorg and frowned, "Which planet are you Governor of, fellow Cyrakuse?"

"Cakerlak."

"Oh. I see. That's odd that a Cyrakuse is a Governor for Cakerlak."

"It's better than having one of *them* being a Governor." Blap replied.

"And you are?" Tostone asked Haathee.

"Haathee, Governor of Phytnes."

"Nice. Hello, Noam. So, what brings you here to visit?"

"Can we sit and talk?" Noam asked.

"Oh, of course. Come in,"

He led them into the apartment in the palace and Noam sat down. Across from him sat the King and Lady Gerda. Tostone sat with his wife and Haathee stood next to Blap.

"So, what's up?" Tostone asked.

Noam replied, "We went to Cakerlak to meet with the Planet Mayor and he mentioned that Traf used to fund them with supplies and weapons. Do you know anything about this?"

"Hmm. No, Joorg, did you know about this?"

"Yes, I promoted him."Joorg said.

"Wait a minute." Lady Gerda said, "Cakerlak has a Planet Mayor and Governor?"

"Yes, Planet Mayor Coleoptera."

"I thought only the Canis had both." the King said.

"He said he was P.M." Haathee replied, "He was promoted when Joorg became Governor."

"That's odd." mused Tostone.

"Wotever. This P.M. Cakerlak said that Traf funded them... was it the Cabinet or himself?" Blap asked. "Because I'm not agreeing on finding a species whose member tried to kill me."

"He threatened but that's it." Celley said, "Don't exaggerate."

Tostone said, "He could've succeeded if it wasn't for the GBI. No, the Cabinet never funded a planet that wasn't part of the Cabinet. But now they are, the Cabinet has to find them."

"Why would Traf fund them then?" Noam asked.

"He was too nice or a sucker." Blap said, "Maybe he wasn't as useless as you all thought."

"I wonder if his wife knows about it." Celley remarked. "Us women know a lot about our men, right, Lady Gerda?"

Lady Gerda nodded, "Yes, I know all about the King."

Blap glanced at Haathee, he bet Joorg still didn't know his wife was at Haathee's house that one day when he met them.

"Joorg, tell your planet P.M. the House will give them wot they want as far a dosh, but not for weapons. We only need one planet with weapons... not two." told Blap.

Tostone clapped, "Yay! You're starting to sound like a real G.P., Blaphaus! Well done!"

## CHAPTER 2

Yerkal did not like what he saw on Cakerlak. The spaceport was all dark and dingy, and crowded. And he had a hard time to catch up with Neop who was walking fast through the spaceport.

"Can you slow down?" Yerkal called out right before he was sent sprawling onto the hard floor. No one stopped to see how he was, the Cakerlak of different colors and shapes stepped either over him or on him. He moaned, thinking he would be killed at that spaceport. He was yanked to his feet by a black and yellow striped Caterlak, who seemed to have a long sharp sword looking device sticking out the bottom of his jacket.

"Thank you." Yerkal said, brushing himself down, trying to straighten his jacket.

"Don't thank me. I did not want to put a humans death in my report. What are you doing here?"

"I was following..."

"Humans don't come to this planet, not through this spaceport anyway."

"Like I said, I was following someone."

"Who?"

"I don't see them now. He didn't stop."

"Maybe he didn't want to be followed, human."

"We flew here together. Forget it." Yerkal sighed.

"Well, if I were you I'd either get out of here before you get knocked on your human ass again or get on the next shuttle to wherever you came from."

"But I'm here to find out about the Ord…"

Just then Neop stormed back up to him hastily.

"Solicitor! What are you doing? Let's go." "Um, okay. This is who I'm with."

"Okay, you better go."

"Thanks for saving my life!" called out Yerkal as he was dragged off.

The other Cakerlak shrugged, wondering who the Coleoptera was or what the Coleoptera was.

The green hand with the skinny fingers waved over the door buzzer. The door of the pretty big house on Ceilingida opened to reveal Ten, who was painted over his cream colored body. He was all in different colors now.

"What the bloody hell happened to you?" Blap asked.

"Galactic President Maximus, welcome. The children asked if they could paint me and I said 'sure.'"

"You are too nice, robot. Where are they? Where are their parents?"

"Mr. Belhopsa is on the Dook Energy space station but Mrs. Belhopsa is here. I am not sure you will be welcomed."

"I doubt it, but I need to ask the boy something."

"Come in." Ten motioned for Blap to walk in and he closed the door before he went off to the kitchen. Blap stood in the living room, wondering if he should tell them the truth about himself but decided this shouldn't be the time. Mal walked into the living room wearing a red dress, and Blap looked her up and down.

"Blaphaus! What are you doing here? Don't you have G.P. things to do?"

"I'm doing it, lady. This is official business."

"And you're alone?"

"Looks like it. So, where are the ankle biters? Especially the boy."

"He's in his room. Are you going to offer him your position or any other crazy thing today?"

"Wot? No. He's too young. But I do need his maths expertise. He's pretty bloody smart."

"Yes, he is. Okay, you can talk to him. I'm sure he'll be glad to see you, as well as Romana. We haven't seen you since New Galaxy Day."

"Nope."

She went to the bottom of the stairs and shouted up, "Nate! Romana! You have a visitor!"

Moments later the two children ran down the stairs.

"Mister Blaphaus!!" they cried out.

"We missed you!" Romana said, "Did you miss us?"

"Nope. I've been too busy. Being G.P. is busy work. You are smart to turn it down, boy."

"I didn't turn it down really."

"No, but you should if I ever offer it again. So, I have a question, how would you like to figure out some maths stuff for the House?"

"Really? Like what?"

"Yes, Blaphaus, like what?" Mal asked.

"Seems that we don't have an accountant, and we need to figure out some feces..."

The children giggled at the swear word and Mal scowled.

"Language, Blaphaus. What kind of maths problem?"

"Like how did Traf fund Cakerlak and did he fund anything else that no one didn't know about?"

"Traf did what?" Mal asked.

"Yeah, surprising, I know. No one thought he did anything. So, want to come to Launderington with me, kid?"

"Yes. Of course."

"Nate, you're not going anywhere. Not with Mr. Blaphaus anyway." Mal told him, "Why do you want him to go there, Blaphaus?"

"Because I need him to work out where the House's dosh went, and Traf's, because if he did some shady dealings I want to know because it'll be my bloody mess to fix."

"Can't he figure that out here?"

Blap said, "You always have to make things awkward. I liked you when you weren't so uptight."

"I liked you when you didn't put my son at risk."

"He didn't do that." Nate added.

"When Zalez comes here in a few days I'll have him get with you. Then you can work it out."

"Great." Blap said as he went to the front door.

"Where are you going, Mr. Blaphaus?" Romana asked.

"Launderington."

"We'll see you soon, Galactic President." smiled Nate.

"Yup." he opened the door and shuffled out.


The room that Yerkal was led into was all dark and smelt weird. He thought it was because it was high on top of a cliff. Laterille approached them and sized up the human.

"Who is this?" she asked.

"This is my Solicitor friend." told Neop. "He came with me to see Coleoptera."

"You mean Planet Mayor Coleoptera." Laterille chuckled.

"Planet Mayor? What happened to the Cyrakuse?"

"He is now Governor." explained Laterille. "A lot has happened since you got yourself locked up."

Yerkal looked so confused.

"A Cyrakuse is Governor of Cakerlak?" he asked.

"Apparently so." Laterille said unhappy. They went deeper into the dark area and Coleoptera stepped out the shadows.

"What is this? A human? You know we don't like humans here on Cakerlak."

"He's a Solicitor, saw me in jail."

"You let down the Order, Neop." Coleoptera said seriously.

"You wanted the G.P. dead?" Yerkal asked.

"Human, why are you here? Neop, why is he here?"

"He wants to know about the Order. I did warn him, Coleoptera."

"We will not talk about the Order to an outsider. You made a big mistake, Neop, in failing with the assassination and telling this human about the Order and then bringing him here."

"I did my best."

"That's not good enough. Take him away."

Two big Cakerlak that looked like the ones that Joorg had with him grabbed  both sides of Neop and dragged him off.

"You're making a big mistake!" he cried out before they were gone down a hallway.

"What's going to happen to him?" Yerkal asked.

Coleoptera stepped closer to Yerkal and said, "Go back where you came from. You will never know about the Order. The galaxy is going to be in a lot of danger... all because the Galactic President is a Tooberosum. Watch out, human, deaths are going to happen all because of him."

He turned and marched off back into the shadows. Yerkal just stood there, not knowing what to say. Just then they all heard a deathly scream.

"I think it's time for you to go." Laterille said. "Don't worry, everything will be okay."

Yerkal nodded and was led away. He still had to find a way to find out who if anybody was part of the Order that's part of the Cabinet. He knew he had to go back to Launderington and warn them... but how?

Mal's holo-call appeared on Zalez's desk on the Dook Energy space station.

"Mal! How are you? What's up?"

"You'll never guess who stopped by at the house today."

"Well, judging by your tone whoever it was you weren't pleased so that could be anyone."

"The Galactic President."

Zalez frowned, they haven't seen or heard from Blaphaus in a week since the celebration which was nice. Their lives were getting back to normal.

"Really? Why?"

"He said something about Traf funding Cakerlak and wanted Nate to do the accounting for the House. It's all pretty confusing really. You know I don't understand politics."

"I will try and reach out to him and see what's going on. But I doubt Traf funded Cakerlak as they weren't part of the Cabinet then."

"Like I said I don't understand politics. Blaphaus said he was heading to Launderington today."

"Then maybe I'll take a trip as well. Look on the bright side, at least Blap just offered accounting to Nate."

"Yeah, we'll put that on the list of all the other positions he offered our son." she said sarcastically. "So, want me to do one of my sexy dances? Do you have time?"

"I always have time for that." he replied, sitting back as she dropped her dress and started to dance in her underwear...

Rubyspears stood by the limo-vehicle waiting for the G.P. outside the spaceport. Blaphaus walked through the glass doors and spotted Rubyspears right away.

"Hello, G.P. Maximus, welcome back to Launderington. How have you been?" the bearded chauffeur asked.

"I'm alive, pseudo-Chordattian."

Because of his facial hair everyone assumed Rubyspears was a Chordattian but he was just a hairy human, which was rare.

This limo-vehicle was different than the other one. It was still black but the back area was big enough for Blap to stand up without sticking his head out the roof. He wished he was shorter, he would be if he wasn't wearing the Toob suit.

"So, there's a surprise for you at the House, G.P. Maximus, it's a lift they had built beside the steps for you to stand in and be raised to the top of the steps."

"If it was a bloody surprise why did you tell me?"

Rubyspears shrugged as he drove, "I don't know. I wanted to be the one to tell you. It was my idea after all."

"Terrific." Blap said, "So it it doesn't bloody work I can blame you?"

"Ummmm..." thought Rubyspears hoping it would work now.

Southington, Thaw and Zucaritas stood at the top of the steps when the limo-vehicle pulled up. Rubyspears got out, walked around to the other side and opened the door for Blap to get out.

"Hello, Blaphaus, we have a surprise for you." Southington called down the steps.

"Rubyspears already told me about it. Where is it?"

"Couldn't keep the secret?" Zucaritas asked annoyed.

"No, I was excited. And the G.P. doesn't like surprises." Rubyspears remarked. "I'm sorry."

Thaw walked to the left side, where the lift was. It was a basic thing, built pretty quick. All Blap had to do was stand on the small platform, press the red button and it would go up the side of the steps to the top level where the front door was, and where Blap did the NGD speech. It worked and he got off the platform. He noticed the confetti and steamers were still not swept up.

"Doesn't anybody clean up this mess?" he noticed the street wasn't cleaned either. "Wot kind of feces is this? Get this mess cleaned." he waved his arms.

"The cleaning robots will be ordered soon." Zucaritas commented.

"How did you like the lift?" Thaw asked.

"I'd prefer not to be G.P. or deal with any of this. But here we are. So, all you idiots here?"

Thaw nodded, "Yes, we are all here. Try not to insult us all the time."

"Ha! All right, slimy."

Zucaritas held in a laugh and Southington just rolled her eyes.

Inside the House all the Governors sat around the long table and Blaphaus stood at the end of it.

"Well, this is actually a first." Zeb smiled, "The first time that we are all here and you with you, Blaphaus."

"Do you like the lift?" Jaboney asked.

"We were concerned about your weight but then we realized you're not as heavy as you look." Rüppell remarked.

"Well, you lot easily could pick another G.P. and put me out of my misery." Blap said.

"How do you suppose we do that?" the white furred tall Kordiack asked.

"I could 'fall down the steps,' 'have a heart attack'..."

They all stared at him.

"Wot? Too soon? The best thing to happen to this galaxy is the Traf passing away and you lot finding me."

"So, Joorg, tell us about the Cakerlak." Southington said, "There's another Planet Mayor?"

"Why is that?" asked Jaboney.

"I figured it's good for the planet, putting someone in charge while I'm not there." Joorg replied.

"But you're a Cyrakuse, and I thought it's not good to have a Cakerlak in charge of anything." Kordiack said.

"It wasn't completely my idea." Joorg said seriously.

"Okay, so, what's the deal with that planet?" Blap asked. "Something *bugs* me about it."

"Why?" Dawber, the other female human asked.

"Because one of that species wanted me dead and have you been there?"

Dawber shook her head.

"They have six arms..."

"You're a human hiding in a suit." Jaboney said.

Blap stuck up his middle finger. "So, Tostone knew nothing about the House funding the planet before they became part of the Cabinet, so Traf did it himself. The question is why? If I were you lot I'd get the GBI involved and have them investigated."

"Having the GBI getting involved is the last thing we want to do."

"We can go see the one in jail and see why he wanted to threaten and shoot you." Lluhdor, the skinny necked feathered Governor asked.

"Peezle, you take Joorg to talk to him." Blap said.

"Why me?"

"Because I said so."

Noam said, "I think we should go talk to Thaw's widow. She might know something of why he would fund the Cakerlak."

Blap said, "You and Southington and long neck here will go speak to her."

"Gillian or I?" Lluhdor asked.

"Gillian."

"I think you should come as well, as G.P., Blaphaus." Dawber said.

"Wotever. So, I went and visited the Belhopsa's."

"Why?" Southington asked.

"Because the kid is bloody maths genius. He's going to look at the accounting, and be the accountant for the House."

Bodie said, "I think one of us..."

"Canis, I'm not trusting any of you lot. He's going to look at all the funding and I want him to look at Thaw's accounts as well."

"I doubt Mrs. Thaw would let that happen."

"That's why we're taking the kid. Who can say no to a kid?"

"Uh, Mal Belhopsa can." Thaw said.

"Not if Southington talks to her." Blap winked his yellow eye. "Woman to woman, it'll be fine."

Peezle said, "We might want to tell Zalez."

"Wotever." scoffed Blap.


Outside the House Yerkal got out of the vehicle and saw the mess that was everywhere. He shook his head and walked up the steps, going inside to be scanned by the House robot.

"Solicitor Yerkal Peezle, you don't look yourself." the robot pointed out.

"Thanks, are any of the Gover...?"

Peezle stepped out the lift and saw his husband standing in entrance.

"Yerkal!" he went running over to him, giving his husband a giant hug and kiss on the lips.

"You look like feces." Blap remarked, shuffling over.

"And you smell." Joorg commented, standing besides Blap.

"Who are you?" Yerkal asked.

"Governor Joorg."

"Governor or what planet?" Yerkal asked.

"Cakerlak. Why?"

"We need to talk."

Blap said, "It can wait. Go home, freshen up, change your clothes."

"Yerkal, we are going to the jail to talk to the Cakerlak who threatened Blaphaus."

"What? Don't bother, he's not there anymore, he's back on his planet."

"Wot? Terrific." Blap said, "He threatens me and gets off easy."

"How do you know this, Yerkal?" Noj asked.

"Noj, we have a lot to talk about. I think the G.P. is in danger, and Joorg, the Cakerlak are to blame."

Just then the three females walked out the lift to see the others standing in the House lobby.

"Yerkal! You're okay!" Gillian smiled.

Southington screwed up her face, "But you look bad and smell."

Blap said, "Peezle, find out wot your husband is babbling about. The ladies and I are going up Ceilingida."

A little bit later Yerkal stood in the shower that was for the Governors in the House, washing himself down. He knew Noj and Joorg were waiting for him to come out and tell them what he knew but he just wanted to stay in the hot shower forever.

***CHAPTER 3***

Yerkal walked into Peezle's office wearing the tan bath robe With "A.T." embroidered on the left side of the front. It fit him good but he was hesitant to wear it. At least it smelt better than his suit, which a House robot said would be washed. Peezle sat behind his desk and Joorg sat on the other side of it. Yerkal sat in the chair next to Joorg.

"Where did you go last week?" Peezle asked, "I was worried about you. I played your holo-recording every day."

"I'm sorry, Noj. I was sent to talk to the Cakerlak who threatened Blaphaus on the Canis-Cyrakuse treaty day to find out why he would threaten the G.P. Turns out he mentioned something about the Order of Blattodea."

"What is that?" Peezle asked, looking over to Joorg.

"Ummm... I don't know. Never heard of it." Joorg shrugged.

"Well, he said the Order and the Toobs have been at war for years."

"What Toobs?" Peezle asked, "Yerkal, we went to the planet that we thought was Tooberosum and it turned out to be a planet called Cantor. Apparently Tooberosum doesn't exist."

"The Toob has to come from somewhere." Yerkal replied.

"Yeah, another galaxy maybe. That doesn't explain why you went off and left me worried."

"Neop, the Cakerlak said someone in the Cabinet is part of the Order..."

"Not me." Joorg put his hands up in the air. "I'm innocent. I wasn't even Governor then."

"You don't know when this happened." Peezle said.

"Well, I went with Neop to Cakerlak when he was let free and I met this Cakerlak named Coleoptera who did not seem very nice, and who said he was Planet Mayor. He mentioned the Order... he was the one who ordered Blap to be assassinated."

"That's impossible." Joorg said, "I made Cole P.M., he's a friend."

"He also seems to be part of this." Peezle said. "When Blap gets back from his trip to Traf's wife's house... Wait a minute... Traf, funding Cakerlak. Oh, I feel really ill."

Yerkal and Joorg glanced at each other.

Rubyspears drove his limo-vehicle up the long driveway with Traf, and the three Governors in the back.

"I've been here before." Rubyspears was telling them, "When Mr. Peezle told the family that the Galactic President has passed away."

"Good for you." Blap said, "I could think of a hundred more things I'd rather do."

They pulled up to the nice big house and Rubyspears got out, opening the back door for them.

Southington told Blap, "If you want me to do the talking..."

"I don't give a feces."

Dawber said to Rubyspears, "Wait outside."

"Sure. If you say so. Tell the robot I said hi."

He remembered being aroused by the robot.

Southington buzzed the door buzzer and moments later the door opened to reveal a tall shiny purple robot.

"Hello, I'm 1-4-3, welcome. You are the new Galactic President..."

"Yup." he replied.

"And you are three Governors. Why are you here?"

"We are looking for Mrs. Traf." Southington smiled. "Is she here?"

"Yes. I will go get her." 1-4-3 turned and went into the house.

"Why does everyone have a bloody robot answering their doors?" Blap asked.

"Its what we do in this galaxy." Dawber explained.

"It's wot saves expenses." Blap said, "You don't have to pay for staff."

1-4-3 approached the door again with Mrs. Thaw standing besides her.

"Hello, everyone. This is a pleasant surprise. Last time I saw you all was when my husband's funeral was ruined by the inauguration of you, Toob."

"Wasn't my plan."

"Well, come on in."

They all went into the house and she led them into the living room.

"Would you want anything to eat or drink?"

"No, thank you." Southington replied.

"Well, take a seat." she looked over at Blap. "You can't sit I take it."

"Not right now." he replied.

The three Governors sat on the couch and Mrs. Traf sat in her chair.

"So, what brought you here today?"

"Wot did Traf do with lucre?"

"What? What do you mean?" Mrs. Traf asked. "Where did his lucre come from? I'm still waiting to be paid."

Southington gave Blap a look.

"What the G.P. is trying to say is do you know if Algar did anything charitable?"

"I still don't understand." Mrs. Traf replied. "Maybe Norab my son might understand." she clapped her hand three times and moments later her teenage son entered into the living room.

"Honey, this is..."

"I know who they are. Why are you here?"

"Turns out that your old man secretly funded Cakerlak with supplies and weapons and wotever feces. Do you know anything about it?"

"Why would he send money to a planet that wasn't part of the Cabinet?" Narob asked.

"Exactly." Blap remarked. "This is a bloody big house. Where did Traf get the dosh?"

"You don't know?" Mrs. Traf asked.

"Unfortunately we don't." Gillian said.

"Bet it's not being an Xtra driver." Blap scoffed.

"Father owned Dook Energy." Narob told them.

"And now Narob does." Mrs. Traf smiled.

"I thought Zalez owned Dook." Blap said.

"Zalez Belhopsa?" Norab asked, "He's in charge of the space station but he works for Dook. I don't know why father funded Cakerlak, which Dook doesn't do the energy for that planet... for now. And Old Eboracum and Gink and your planet, Toob."

Zalez meanwhile walked up the messy steps of the House shaking his head, wondering why the confetti and trash wasn't cleaned up. He went inside to be stopped by the House robot.

"Welcome, Mr. Belhopsa. What can I do for you?"

"Is G.P. Maximus here?"

"No, he is not."

"Do you know where he is?"

"I can't tell you for security reasons."

"Do you know when he will be back?"

"No, he never said. And if I did know I could not tell you."

Zalez sighed, "Okay. Are any of the Governors here?"

"Yes, except for three of them."

"That's good." he smiled, "Could I talk to them?"

"Yes. Follow me."

Narob opened the door to his fathers office.

"This is fathers office." Narob said, "No one has been inside it since he died."

The three Governors stood in the doorway and Blap walked into it. He saw the info-pad in the desk and turned to Narob.

"Can we take this? See if we can find out anything on it?"

"No, you're not taking it." told Narob.

"Okay. Dawber, contact the GBI, they might want to..."

"Fine." Narob Traf said not happy, "Take it."

"Long neck, come pick it up. We are going to Ceilingida next."

Peezle shook Zalez's hand and smiled.

"Hello, Zalez, good to see you again."

"Good to see you as well. So, where's Blaphaus?"

"He went to talk to Mrs. Traf."

"Really? Why?"

"Come into my office and we'll talk."

They went down the hallway and into the office. Sitting in there still was Yerkal wearing Traf's robe. Zalez looked surprised when he saw him.

"Yerkal, how are you? What's with the robe?" he sat in the other chair in front of the desk.

"My suit is getting washed. It was in bad shape. How are you, Zalez?"

"I'm okay."

"So, what brings you to Launderington and the House?" Peezle asked.

"I don't know if you know but Blaphaus showed up at my house to speak to Nate. He wants Nate to do some kind of accounting or something."

Peezle chuckled, "Yes, in fact he's going to be heading back there today to ask again. Apparently he got push back from your wife..."

"She's not a fan as you can imagine."

"None of us are fans of Blaphaus really." Yerkal muttered.

"Why is Blaphaus visiting Mrs. Traf?" Zalez asked.

"Well... he went to Cakerlak and apparently was told by the Planet Mayor that Traf helped fund the planet, and wants Blap to continue. As that planet is now part of the Cabinet we will fund them."

"So he's trying to find out why?" Zalez asked.

Peezle nodded, "Yes, and then he wants Nate to look at all the accounts to see what else Algar was up to."

"Did you know he funded Cakerlak?" Zalez asked.

"No, I was hardly told anything. It wouldn't be good publicity if it got out in the press either, so I wouldn't say anything."

"I won't." Zalez said, "It wouldn't be good for Dook either as Algar owned Dook Energy."

"He did?" Yerkal asked.

Zalez nodded, "Yes. Dook Energy didn't and still doesn't power Caterlak, you'd think we would if Traf gave the planet lucre."

"I've been to that planet, it's all torches... I don't think the planet has electricity."

"They have shuttles, they should have some kind of power." Zalez said. "Why were you there?"

"Zalez, have you heard of the Order of Blattodea?" Yerkal asked.

Zalez shook his head, "No, who are they?"

"That's why I went to Cakerlak to find out. I did find out that the new P.M. is a member of them and hired the assassination of Blaphaus."

"Are you sure?" Zalez asked.

Yerkal nodded, "And the assassin said someone in the Cabinet is a member. This has me so scared."

"Why are you scared?" Peezle asked.

"As I said, the Order and the Toobs had a war a long time ago. With Blaphaus being G.P. we could be on the brink of another war."

Peezle thought of telling them the truth about Blap but this wasn't the time.

"Noj, we need to tell Blaphaus."

Zalez stood up, "I'm going back home. If Blaphaus is heading there I need to speak to him." he went to the door, "Keep me posted."

Peezle nodded, "I will."


Back on Celingida, Blap felt like he was a driver all over again. He drove his white vehicle as the three Governors sat in the back seat. Gillian had the info-pad from Algar's office on her lap.

"It'll be nice to see the children again." smiled Southington.

"I'm not a big fan of children." Dawber replied. "Are you, Maximus?"

"Am I wot?"

"Fan of children?"

"Not really. No."

"But you like these children, don't you?" asked Southington.

"I put up with them. The boy has a better head on his shoulders than most adults I know."

"Do you have children back on Phulfortha?" Gillian asked.

"Rule number one, don't ever mention that planet to me or my former life. Got it, long neck?"

She nodded, "I get it. But do you regret telling and showing us the truth about you?"

"It was to save my bloody skin, and no. But don't let me regret it."

With that they pulled up to the house. The three female Governors got out the vehicle, Gillian still holding the info-pad. Blap stayed put, not getting out.

"Are you coming?" Southington asked.

"Twice in one day being here is a bit much. I'm staying out unless you need me."

Dawber mumbled, "That might be for the best."

Southington went up to the door and buzzed the buzzer. The door opened to reveal the multi-colored Ten.

"Oh, my! You look like Peezle." Southington said surprised. "All colorful and everything."

"Hello, Governors. Can I help you?"

Dawber asked, "Anybody home?"

"Yes, Mrs. Belhopsa and the children are here. Which one would you like to see?"

"Mrs. Belhopsa first." Southington said.

"I'll go get her." Ten turned and went into the house. He came back moments later with Mal.

"Lady Governors, hello. The G.P. was here earl..." she then saw he sat in his white vehicle.

"Ohhh... he's back. And he brought reinforcements."

"It's not like that." Gillian replied.

Dawber scowled, "It's very much like that. We have to ask you something. We have the late G.P.'s info-pad and want Nate to look at it, see if he could figure out Algar's old financing. See what he was up to."

"Is that legal?"

"We have a blessing from Mrs. Traf." Southington smiled. "Blaphaus wants Nate to be the official Cabinet accountant as well."

"I know. Okay, come on in. Have him come in as well. He shouldn't wait outside. He is the G.P. after all."

Dawber put two fingers in her mouth and whistled to Blaphaus to come.

"Wot am I, a Canis?" he muttered to himself.

They all went inside and Mal called up the stairs for Nate who came downstairs with Romana.

"G.P. Blaphaus! Governors!" Nate smiled. "Two times in one day?" he smiled up at Blap.

"Don't get used to it, kid."

Gillian put the info-pad on the table and Nate looked at it.

"What's that?"

"Traf's info-pad." told Southington. "Can you look through it for Traf's accounting?"

Nate nodded, "What's the password?"

The Governors all looked at each other blankly, then at Blap.

"How the bloody hell am I supposed to know?" he asked.

"Well, I can't get in without the password." Nate shrugged, "I'm sorry, G.P. Blaphaus, Governors."

"Blattodea." Ten said.

"Wot?" Blap asked, "Watch your language, robot."

"What does that mean?" Gillian asked.

"I do not know." Ten said, "My memory only tells me what I was told or programmed to know. And 'Blattodea,' I was told by Galactic President Traf that that is the password."

"And you never asked wot it meant?" Blaphaus asked.

"It was not my job to ask."

"Maybe Peezle knows." Southington remarked.

"In the meantime, kid, type in that bloody word." told Blap.

Nate sat at the table and pulled the info-pad over to him. He was about to type in 'Blattodea' when Mal held her hands up.

"Stop. Are you sure this is okay?"

"We got permission, lady. Do you have to be so annoying? I remember the days when you were attractive and nice."

"That's rude, Mr. Blaphaus." Romana said scowling.

"What should I do?" Nate asked.

"Type, kid." ordered Blap.

"We can't force you, Nate, but it might be good for the galaxy as a whole." Southington smiled, sitting at the table across from him.

"Okay, here goes." he smiled and typed in 'Blattodea.'

The info-pad came on and a holo-image of the Traf family appeared above it. It must've been taken years ago as the children looked younger in it. Traf looked exactly the same as they remembered and and his wife Lilly looked exactly the same as they saw her earlier. Nate played with the keyboard on  the info-pad and a bunch of words and numbers appeared above it. They tried to read it but it was all in some kind of code. Or so they thought.

"It's going to take me awhile to figure this out." Nate said, pointing to some words. "If these are planet names they are not planets in this galaxy. And there's more than this galaxy, right, G.P. Blaphaus? You said so in your New Galaxy Day speech."

"That might've been just talk, kid." Blap replied.

"But you said..."

"Just figure out wot that all means."

"Nate has school tomorrow, Blaphaus." told Mal.

"Yeah, yeah, yeah. This is more important than school." Blap told her.

"No it isn't." Dawber remarked, "After your homework can you try and work it out?"

"Yeah, and I have the rest of the evening." Nate smiled, "I can play around with it until I go to bed. Right, mother?"

She sighed, "I guess so."

Blap shuffled to the front door. "Good, I'll be back tomorrow."

"Where are you going?" Southington asked standing.

"Home. I'm done with this for today."

"Well, can you drop us off at the spaceport?" Southington asked.

"Wotever."

The Peezle's walked into their flat on Launderington and Yerkal took off his nice clean jacket and slumped down on the couch.

"You okay?" Noj asked, sitting besides him.

"Not really. I am trying to get this out of my head."

"Get what out of your head?"

"That one of your Governor peers belongs to an organization that wants to assassinate Blaphaus. And the P.M. of one of the planets ordered it. And who is this Order of Blattodea?" he rubbed his head.

"That's not for you to worry about, Yerkal. Tomorrow I will talk to Blaphaus about it. But I doubt he knows nothing."

"Well, he needs to know. And Governor Joorg might know something as well."

"I will talk to him as well. You should go to rest, Yerkal. You had a rough week."

Yerkal nodded, "I did." he kissed Noj on the lips. "Just I'm so worried about the galaxy and you. I will go to the House tomorrow to tell Blaphaus myself what I know."

Noj nodded, "And I'll be there with you."

Zalez walked into his house to see Ten standing besides Nate who sat at the dining room table going through the info-pad, taking notes on his own info-pad.

"Father! You're home!" Nate jumped up and ran over to his father, giving him a hug.

"Ten, what happened to you? New body?"

"The children asked if they could paint me. I said yes, sir."

"Well, you look very... colorful and original. Nate, where's your mother and sister?"

"Out back planting vegetables."

"And what info-pad is that?" Zalez asked, "What's all these numbers and words?"

"I think they are planets, but not sure, and how many dosh was sent to them. I think."

"Planets? Dosh?" Zalez looked closely at the holo-text. "Where did you get this?"

"It's G.P. Traf's old info-pad, father. G.P. Blaphaus and three Governors brought it here for me to go through it. I feel so important."

"He did what? I don't think you should be doing this."

"But mother agreed, father. Hesitantly but she did."

"I will talk to her about that." he made his way to the kitchen where the backdoor was.

"Father. One more thing..."

Zalez stopped snd turned around, "Yes, son?"

"What does Blattodea mean?"

Zalez dropped his bearded jaw…

# CHAPTER 4

On the rainy planet Siahl, Governor Thaw wondered to himself if Blaphaus liked the rain, especially when he wore the Toob suit. Thaw walked into the gray brick building, out of the rain to meet with Professor Phence. A dark black leathery skinned Olusegun species approached Thaw playing with its long whiskers.

"Hello, Governor. The Professor sent me down here to get you." the Olusegun female said.

"He is here, right?"

"Yes, he's here. Follow me. My name is Ade Ola by the way. But please call me Ade."


On Ceilingida, an unusually upset Zalez walked out to the backyard holding the info-pad that used to belong to Traf. Nate ran after him with tears in his eyes.

"Father! Don't be mad!"

Mal and Romana looked up from their gardening where they were kneeling to see Zalez standing there.

"Why didn't you tell me that Blaphaus already had Nate researching wherever he has him researching?"

Zalez's mad was a little different than when Mal got mad. When Mal got mad she shouted, when Zalez got mad, which was rare, he still spoke calmly.

"He came back a second time." Mal said standing up, "With three Governors..."

"Who? Which ones?"

"Southington, Dawber and Gillian."

"Three females. He used the female persuasion..."

"Not really. Well, maybe." Mal thought for a minute. "I think it's harmless anyway."

"You do?" Zalez looked surprised. "Why?"

"It's just boring accounting. Maths and all that."

"Hmmmm. And planet names that don't exist in this galaxy." Zalez remarked.

"That might not be true." Nate spoke up, wiping his face with his sleeve. "I think they are names of beings."

"Names?" Zalez asked. "What kind of names?"

"I don't know." Nate shrugged, "There's a lot of them though."

"And the word Blattodea, do you know what it is?" Zalez asked.

"It's the password." Mal told her husband. "To get into the info-pad."

"Really? And this is Traf's old info-pad?"

"Yes, from his house." Mal said. "The Governors and Blaphaus borrowed it."

"So, the password on Traf's personal info-pad is 'Blattodea'?"

"Yes."

Nate said, "Is it a grown-up word, father?"

"Yes. That's exactly what it is, son. How did you know the password?"

Romana smiled, happy to put her two stirling in, "Ten."

Ten was standing in the corner of the living room where he usually just stood until someone buzzed the door buzzer. He turned his round head to see Zalez approach him, holding the info-pad. He heard the conversation Zalez and Nate had, and knew eventually Zalez would come over to him.

"Ten, how did you know the password?"

"The late Galactic President Traf told me."

"Oh, yeah, you were his robot..."

"Yes, sir, for years. Now I'm yours."

"So, do you know what 'Blattodea' means?"

"No, sir. Maybe it's a made up word. But then again, all words are made up, am I right?"

"Ten, have you heard of the *Order* of Blattodea?"

"Order? No, sir, that makes no sense. How can that be in order? That is not the definition of Order."

"Do you know anybody that might know?"

"Well, Galactic President Traf's family, or Peezle, as he was the Galactic President's Assistant. Or Professor Phence might know. He knows a lot of things. It was his company that built me."

"Hmmm. Tomorrow, Ten, you are coming to Launderington with me."

"Why, sir?"

"We are going to figure this out."

Nate walked into the living room and asked his father, "Can I come to? And can I finish what I was doing?"

"You have school, so no. And we are going to look at it together."

"Okay." Nate smiled.


"Hello, Thaw. Welcome home." smiled Phence as Thaw walked into the office.

"It's always good to be back on Siahl, Professor."

Phence sat behind his desk and Thaw sat in front of it.

"At the celebration on Launderington the Toob said he's seen other galaxies. Did you notice or hear that?"

Thaw's leathery gray head nodded, "Yes, I heard that."

"Well, GNN haven't picked up on it... they seem to be over the whole Toob being G.P. thing. How does the Cabinet feel about that?"

Thaw shrugged, "It's good. For right now. Everything seemed to settle down. Media frenzy is over. Is that why you asked me to come here?"

"No. I went to Tooberosum and..."

Thaw gulped, "What did you find?"

"Nothing. There was nothing on it. It was empty. In fact it's not a planet at all."

Thaw hoped he didn't look confused, "What do you mean?"

"It's a big green moon."

"What's a moon?" Thaw asked.

"Something that has a thin atmosphere, and where nothing lives on."

"So, what does this mean?"

"There's 22 planets, and a few suns and a moon. So, I think either the Toob lied or he is from another galaxy."

Thaw sat back and didn't say a word. He wanted to tell the truth about Blaphaus but he had no idea if he could trust Phence.

Fami sat in her black vehicle with dark windows across the street from the Belhopsa house the next morning. She watched as Zalez Belhopsa walked out the front door with a child and a multi-colored robot who was carrying an info-pad. She knew the robot belonged to Traf at one time and she knew the child was Governor of Ceilingida for a short time. She watched as Mrs. Belhopsa stepped outside, hands on her hips, not looking happy. Fami couldn't hear what was going on but had a feeling. The robot and the other two got into Zalez's blue vehicle and drove off. She started her vehicle and turned it around in the street to follow Zalez's vehicle.

Blaphaus shuffled onto the yellow Space False One, which was the official shuttle of the Cabinet and Galactic President, thanks to Governor Jaboney. Blap took out his yellow eyes, then took off purple jacket, throwing them into a seat. He undid the back of his Toob suit and pulled it off. Under the suit he wore a black t-shirt and jeans, with the data-pad strapped to him. He pulled that off and put it down. He sat down in a seat, and smiled. No one else was on the shuttle, but the pilot, to tell him the trip was too short and he shouldn't take off the Toob suit if the pilot knew. But he didn't care. He looked down at his big green three toed shoes and chuckled. He couldn't really believe how his life turned out. He thought back for a moment to his life on Phulfortha, where he and his best friend were on the run. He did feel bad about leaving his friend behind, and wondered what happened to him. He knew he wasn't going to go back and find him, because he would be heading into a trap. There were beings out there somewhere looking for him.

"Welcome aboard, Galactic President Maximus, please remain standing and keep your seatbelt on. We are all clear to go in a few minutes."

Take your time, thought Blap. And remain standing... if the pilot only knew he was sitting, and not a real Toob.

"Mother is so unhappy with you, father." Nate said in the backseat of his fathers vehicle, sitting besides Ten, whose new legs could bend, so he could sit.

"I know, she doesn't understand politics. I barely understand politics."

"I understand it pretty well." Nate said. "Ten, you must understand it, right?"

"Little Nate, I do not understand beings at all or politics. I would not choose who would be Galactic President at all, or Governors."

"None of it makes sense." Zalez remarked.

"Well, I'm glad to be out of school for a day. Romana is not happy she still has to go."

Zalez nodded, "Well, after this trip you shouldn't be missing any more days of school. And I'm going to tell Blaphaus to keep away from you and the family. Unfortunately I have to deal with him on occasion."

"Father, I still think something is not right with Mr. Blaphaus. He said he's seen other galaxies, do you think he was lying?"

"You said he's not what he seems."

"I just have a weird feeling about him, father."

"Well, eventually we'll get to the bottom of it." Zalez said.

They approached the Ceilingida Intergalactic Spaceport, with the bigger black vehicle following. Fami cursed under her breath in her vehicle, she did not plan on leaving the planet yet. She didn't book a flight and she had no idea where they were going. She decided not to follow them anymore, and let them drive to the vehicle park. Wherever they go, she was sure they'd be back.

The Governors all took their seats in the House meeting room, except for the Gink Governor or Blaphaus.

"We're all here." Noam said, "But the Gink. Anybody seen him?"

Lluhdor replied, "I'm sure he'll be here soon. Should we wait to start the meeting with him? Or should we wait for Blaphaus?"

"We need to learn more about that man." Eastora, the bald human Governor with the goatee asked. "I don't like it he's a human. We have no idea his history or where he came from."

"Another galaxy my ass." Jaboney commented.

Rüppell, the orange upturned snouted Governor said, "I believe him."

Penya, the black and white furred Governor in the silky red robes rubbed his chin. "It is possible."

The Gink then walked in and took his seat quickly. "Sorry I'm late."

Zucaritas commented, "Well, Blaphaus isn't here, so you're good."

"Is everything okay on Gink?" Southington asked.

"What do you mean?"

"You were late so just making sure."

Joorg said, "The Planet Mayor of Cakerlak wants a definite answer on the funding."

The Toob then walked into the meeting room. "Cyrakuse, you're the bloody Governor of that planet, not the Cakerlak. He answers to you."

Zeb said, "Nice of you to join us."

"You're lucky I'm here, chubby Chordattian. There's no reason that planets have Planet Mayors, and that goes to your planet as well, Canis."

Bodie, the Canis who wore a patch nodded, "You want me to tell P.M. Losergram he's no longer P.M.?"

Dawber said, "Blaphaus, P.M.'s are elected. You can't just say it's not a thing anymore."

"Then they have no power, like the bloody King. He might think he has power, but doesn't. Joorg, yes, every planet that belongs to the Cabinet which is all now, except for the one planet I won't mention, so yes, Cakerlak will be taken care of. But no weapons. I want you to go there and tell them that the only planet to have weapons is tXenarthra. I don't want a bunch of planets to have weapons."

Joorg nodded, "I will let him know."

"Good. So, anybody heard of the word 'Blattodea'?"

No one said a word.

Zalez, Nate and Ten made their way through the spaceport on Launderington. Ten was carrying a black messenger like satchel with the info-pad inside of it.

"How are we going to get to the House?"

Nate asked as they stepped outside through the glass doors.

"I arranged something." Ten replied.

"Hello, Mr. Belhopsa, Nate... 10-E-C?" Rubyspears stared at the robot who was a painted a bunch of different colors, and had new legs.

"What happened to you?"

Nate grinned, "Romana and I painted him. He said we could."

"Oh. Well, you look very colorful, Ten, almost like Peezle's outfit."

"Thanks for coming to pick us up." Zalez said.

"It was my pleasure. It's the second time I've been here today. I picked up the Galactic President earlier."

"Oh, good, he's here." Zalez said, "I was wondering."

"Shouldn't you be in school today?" Rubyspears asked Nate.

"Yes, but I'm here on official business." Nate smiled.


At the House, Peezle found himself staring at Blap. How did he know that word? Blattodea. None of the Governors claimed to know it, or even blinked and eye. But one of them, apart from Peezle knew it... or at least heard of it.

"So, wot do you have to tell me?" Blap asked.

Peezle made sure his office door was closed, and they were the only two inside.

"A number of things." Peezle sat behind his desk. "First of all yesterday a woman stopped by named Fami Tapperdau and asked me a few questions about you. Do you know that name?"

"No. Was she cute?"

"Ummm... she's not really my type, Blaphaus..."

"Of course not. Your type is skinny little Solicitor types. So, wot did she want?"

"I don't know. She never said exactly. She said though she knows my secret..."

"Wot secret?"

"I don't know, I don't have any secrets."

"Except about me."

"Yes. Except about you."

"So, this it?"

"Well, no, you asked if anyone knew the word Blattodea..."

"Yep. Do you know it?"

"Yes, I heard of it. It's some kind of Order... the ones who sent the Cakerlak to assassinate you. Apparently the Planet Mayor you met knows about it."

"And you know this how?"

"Yerkal told me."

"He did, did he? Well, where is he?"

"Home. I hope."

"Then get him here." ordered Blap.

Just then one of the House robots knocked on the office door. Peezle stood up and went over to it, opening it.

"Mr. Belhopsa is here with the boy Nate and 10-E-C."

"That's surprising. Have them meet me in the conference room... or briefing room. Peezle, you need to get your husband here."

Blap walked into the conference room to see it was empty, except the Gink who sat at the table, his info-pad before him. As soon as Blap walked in Guoz shut it down.

"I need this room." Blap said sternly.

Guoz stood and picked up his info-pad and nodded.

"It's all yours, G.P. Maximus." he walked out past him. In the hallway outside he saw the House robot with Zalez, Nate and Ten. Gink's don't frown, or blink, because of their large round like eyes. But if he could frown he would've.

"Mr. Belhopsa, young Belhopsa, Ten, what a pleasant surprise. Father and son bonding experience?"

"Something like that." Zalez replied.

They saw Blap standing outside the conference room, waiting.

"I'm surprised your bloody wife let you bring the kid, Belhopsa."

"She didn't. I have to talk to her when I take Nate back. This is the last time you're using my family for anything, do you understand?"

Blap scoffed, "It's not your family I need, it's your son."

He led them into the conference and closed the door.

Nate smiled from ear to ear. "I'm so excited to be here."

"Good for you. You have the info-pad?"

Ten took it out of the messenger bag and put it down on the table, and Nate sat in Peezle's seat. He turned on the info-pad and typed in 'Blattodea.' All the accounting stuff came up, hovering above the info-pad.

"So, wot did you find out?"

"Not much. Galactic President Traf only funded the Cakerlak. I think these are all Cakerlak names, of their species. They all fall under the name Weta, whatever that's is. They are all part of something called the Order of Blattodea, so that's where the name came from. The password."

"I've heard of the Order." Zalez said, "Yerkal Peezle seems to know a lot about it."

"Good. Yerkal is on the way here. You did good, boy. Is there a way to copy everything onto a different info-pad? We need to get this one back to Traf's wife."

"I just need another info-pad. And I can do it." Nate smiled.

"Then I'll get one."

Peezle then walked into the room, and was surprised to see Nate, Ten and Zalez there.

"Oh, hello, friends. Didn't know you were all here. Ten, what happened to you? You're all colorful. We match."

"Care of the Belhopsa children, Mr. Peezle."

"Is your husband here yet?" Blap asked.

"He just arrived."

"Good. Boy, we are going to have grown up talk. Peezle, get him another info-pad and take him to your office."

Peezle nodded, "Nate, follow me."

Nate got up, picking up the info-pad. He followed Peezle out the room.

"I'll get you in a few minutes." Zalez said.

"Okay, father."

"Blaphaus, do you know what you're getting yourself into?"

"Yeah. Nothing. But Traf on the other hand... he doesn't seem quite so innocent now, does he?"

**CHAPTER 5**

Yerkal was led into the conference room by his husband. Zalez was already there, sitting at the table. Blap stood at the end of the table. Yerkal was dressed in a dark blue suit, with a tie and his hair looking immaculate once again. Ten stood in the corner, not saying a word.

"G.P. Maximus, it's good to see you again." Yerkal smiled.

"Did you enjoy going off AWOL?" Blap asked.

"No, I had things to find out. And I did find out a few things"

"Good for you."

"It concerns you, G.P. Maximus. Can I sit?"

"I don't care." Blap replied.

Yerkal sat in the seat that Southington usually sat in. Peezle sat in Dawber's seat, holding Yerkal's hand.

"I don't know where to start." Yerkal gulped.

"What is Blattodea?" Blaphaus asked.

"I'll start at the beginning." Yerkal said, "Too bad you can't sit, Blaphaus."

"I went to talk to Neop, the Cakerlak who threatened to assassinate you. He said he was sent to do that, and he mentioned the Order of the Blattodea, and said the Tooberosum and Cakerlak were enemies and fought a long time ago. Do you know about it?"

"No. Nothing."

"Well, as you know I went with Neop to Cakerlak..."

"Yes, you met with the enemy..."

"Turns out the planet has a Planet Mayor and he is part of the Order and was the one who sent Neop to assassinate you. Neop was taken away and I believed murdered for failing to kill you. I then came back here."

For the first time they heard Blap actually laugh, which wasn't the reaction they were expecting. Blap has a loud obnoxious sounding laugh.

"I haven't laughed in a long time." Blaphaus said, "I appreciate that, Peezle."

"What's so funny?" Yerkal asked.

"You met him, Blaphaus, the Planet Mayor. He was pleasant, right?" Peezle asked. "He didn't try to kill you there, right?"

"Nope. I think you're wrong, and Neop is a liar, as well as a lousy hit-Cakerlak."

"But Coleoptera, the Planet Mayor is..."

"Should not be Planet Mayor, and if he wanted me dead he had a chance."

Zalez said, "Didn't other Governors go with you?"

39

"Yep. Joorg, Haathee and the Smidge..."

"Maybe that's why he didn't do anything." Peezle said.

"Did he say anything about Traf?" Blaphaus asked.

"No, why would he?"

"It just so happens that the password to his personal info-pad is 'Blattodea.'"

Yerkal looked surprised, "What? How do you know?"

"Because we have it. Zalez's kid is working on it. Turns out Traf is not so innocent, wotever this Order is he was part of it."

"How did you find out the password?"

"I knew it." Ten replied.

"What do you think this means? This is deeper than I thought..."

"It means that it's a good thing Traf is not G.P. anymore." Blaphaus said. "Zalez, if the kid is done you can go. Yerkal, don't go talking to the Cakerlak anymore. Stay on this bloody planet." Blap went to the door.

Peezle asked, "Where are you going?"

"To find Joorg, Governor of the 'terrorist' planet."

Joorg sat in his office when Blap walked in.

"G.P. Maximus, everything okay?"

"Who is this Coleoptera?"

"He's the Planet Mayor... you met him..."

"Do you know he ordered the assassination on me?"

"No, why would he do that?"

"Do you know about the Order of Blattodea?"

"No, I don't know anything."

"You're useless, Cyrakuse. You're going to find out for me why the hell Traf had the word 'Blattodea' as a password. You're going to look at the information from Traf's info-pad, and you are going to give me answers. Understand?"

Joorg just nodded.

Blaphaus walked into Peezle's office where Nate sat in front of two info-pads on the desk.

"So? Done?"

Zalez stood behind Blaphaus, trying to get passed him.

"Yeah, it was easy."

"Good."

"What now, Blaphaus?" Zalez asked.

"I'm taking this back to Traf's family now I got everything copied."

"Anybody going with you?"

"Just Rubyspears..."

"We'll go with you." Zalez said, "Traf owned Dook Energy, if he was up to something that was illegal or secretive I want to talk to Mrs. Traf."

"You should speak to her boy. He's your boss now, Chordattian. Anyway, good for you, really piss off the old lady. You must really want to sleep on the couch tonight."

On Phytnes, a lot of species gathered in a park, eating and drinking and listening to music. A three piece Cyrakuse band the Stray Cyrakuse performed on stage. Everyone was having a good time... for now. A young man dressed in black, wearing a helmet cut a hole in a fence that surrounded the park. He slid in between the fence hole that he cut and walked in, blending in with the crowd. He then reached into his jacket and pulled out a blaster, then opened fire on a crowd. The people screamed, and ran for cover. Everything happened so quick, the band stopped playing and jumped off the stage and ran for cover themselves. After the blasterer was done, he put it into his jacket and ran back towards the fence, going through it. A black spotted tall necked orange Giraffeidae tried to capture him but no luck. The man ran through the woods, know one knowing who he was. He looked over his shoulder hearing the screams, and shouts. He thought he heard someone say three or four people were killed. Good enough, he just hoped the ones that sent him would think so as well.

Rubyspears drove his black limo-vehicle once again up the driveway of the Traf house. Nate's eyes opened wide at the sight and size of it.

"Father! This house is bigger than our house."

Zalez nodded, "It's bigger than THE House."

"Can I come in or do I have to wait here like before?" Rubyspears asked.

"Wot do you think?" Blap asked.

They got out the vehicle and went up to the door.

"You know this is your first official trip without other Governors." Zalez remarked.

"Yup. It should go smoothly then." he buzzed the door buzzer.

The door opened seconds later to reveal 1-4-3.

"Oh. Hello, Galactic President. You are here again." It wasn't a question.

"Yes, we have Traf's info-pad." Blap said, "We are bringing it back."

"Mrs. Traf is out back. Follow me."

They followed the robot through the house, Ten carrying the info-pad. Out back Mrs. Traf and her daughter Hoeka were swimming in the pool. Not another bloody swimming pool, Blap thought staying away from it.

"They have a pool." smiled Nate. "I'm jealous."

The robot stood at the pools edge and waited for Lilly Traf to swim close before she spoke.

"Mrs. Traf, you have visitors."

Mrs. Traf stopped swimming and looked up from the side of the pool. Hoeka already stopped swimming.

"Oh. Galactic President. What brought you back?"

"I have the info-pad we borrowed."

She spotted Nate and Zalez and frowned.

"Who are your friends?"

"I'm Zalez Belhopsa, ma'am, head of Dook Energy. This is my son Nate."

"Hello, Mrs. Traf. Sorry about your husband."

Lilly said, "oh, that's nice. Thank you. What a pleasant and charming young man."

She climbed up the ladder from the pool and the purple robot put a towel over her shoulders.

"My son is now head of Dook Energy, so he's your boss."

Zalez nodded, "Yeah, I guess so. Is he here? I don't think he's ever been to the space station and I'd love to give him a tour."

"He's not here. He went to Firvegas with some friends."

"Firvegas? The gambling station?" Zalez asked, "Isn't he a bit young?"

"Oh, he's not gambling. I don't think so. His father was a gambler sometimes though."

"That's not the only thing he was." Blap muttered, "And you don't know anything about Blattodea? Or an Order of some sort?" Blap asked.

She shook her head, "Nope."

"His password was Blattodea on this info-pad."

"I wouldn't know."

Blap sighed, "Well, this colorful robot here has the info-pad. We'll leave it in the office and be on our way."

"Okay. One will show you out. Thanks for coming."

Zalez said, "One more thing, when Narob comes back can you have him reach out to me?"

She nodded, "Of course. He's a good boy. His father would be proud of him."

She dropped her towel and dived into the pool.

A few minutes later the four walked outside the house, and went over to the limo-vehicle where Rubyspears waited.

"She's either lying or bloody useless." Blap remarked, "I'd go with the latter."

"I thought she was nice." Nate smiled.

"Ha! You think *I'm* nice." Blap remarked.

"So, where am I taking you?" Rubyspears asked, opening the beck door for them.

"The spaceport. We are all going back to Ceilingida." Blap said. "I'm done with this planet for the day."

They got in the vehicle and seconds after they drove off Haathee's 12 inch holo-call appeared before them, and he was crying.

"Wot is wrong with you?" Blap asked standing there.

"Thirty-three beings... thirty-three..."

"Thirty-three beings wot?"

"Dead. Murdered. On my planet."

Everyone in the vehicle looked shocked, except Ten.


The Leetric, wearing a black suit and tie sat at his desk in the studio and spoke.

"Breaking news: on Phytnes, one of the latest planets to join the Cabinet someone that is described as a human, has opened fire with a hand weapon, at a festival killing thirty-three innocent bystanders and injuring 117. The species that were injured were a few Giraffeidae, a Chordattian family, a Cyrakuse, a Bovi, and a number of Equidae. No word yet on why or who did this. This is the first time in this galaxy that anything like this has happened..."

The whole galaxy was in shock and flipped on its head. Peezle walked down the hallway at the House, Yerkal on his heels.

"This is it, Noj! This is the start of the invasion."

"One person is not an invasion, Yerkal."

"The blasterer could be part of the Order."

"Could. Maybe. Right now he got away so we don't know."

They walked into the conference room where the other Governors all started to file in. Haathee sat at the table already, crying as Gillian had her arms around him, comforting him.

Kaktovic, the tall white furred Bipolarab paced up and down, biting his black claws.

"Where's Maximus?" Zucaritas demanded.

"He's on his way back." Thaw said.

Southington said, "Haathee, Blaphaus will go with you to the planet first thing in the morning. Would you want any other Governor to go with you?"

"Yes, Joorg, will you go?"

Joorg nodded, "Yes, of course. A Cyrakuse was murdered there."

"But not a bloody Cakerlak." Blap remarked walking in. "If anyone from that planet is responsible..."

"Eye witnesses said the blasterer was human..."

"As far as they could tell." Zeb the brown bearded Chordattian Governor said, "Put a helmet on most of us we can look human."

"What kind of weapon did the bastard use?" Blap asked. "Was it one of your planets, Sugden?"

Sugden, the silver armored Illiger Governor from Xenartha replied, "It's possible. But I haven't seen the weapon. I will go to Phytnes as well and take a Brigidier from my army."

Southington said, "GNN will be there, but we better send a press statement real soon. Blaphaus, you should make a statement..."

"It's trunk boys' planet, he should..."

"You both should." Zeb said, "Everyone in the galaxy is going to be on edge."

"Fine." grunted Blaphaus.

Joorg went into his office while Blaphaus holo-recorded a response to the attack. A holo-call of Planet Mayor Coleoptera was before him on the desk.

"Are you responsible for the attack on Phytnes?"

"Me? Why would you ask that, Governor?"

"I don't know... Blaphaus is questioning you, wants me to investigate Traf and something called Order of Blattodea. Do you know what he's talking about?"

"No. No I don't. Tell him that we would help look for whoever did this and bring him to justice."

Joorg nodded, "I will."

The holo-call disappeared and Joorg sat back wondering if Coleoptera was lying.

Coleoptera walked into the Great Weta's chamber where the large Cakerlak sat.

"Great Weta, the Toob knows about the Order. He's not stupid, he could be more dangerous than we thought."

"I am not worried about him yet. This whole galaxy is going to be in for a shock..."

## CHAPTER 6

"We, in the Cabinet are devastated by the blastering of the 33 innocent beings, and the 117 that were injured. I will be going to Phytnes first thing in the morning with Governor Haathee. I promise we will get to the bottom of whoever did this. Hopefully something dramatic like this never happens again."

Blap turned away from the robot-cam that was hovering before him.

"Who writes this feces?"

Southington stood there with her arms crossed. "I did. Next time you have to say it again with more feeling."

"Wot next time?"

Dawber said, "That wasn't sent out live, Blaphaus."

Blap waved his arms, "Ugh! You lot get on my bloody nerves!"

Southington said, "Just read the teleprompter again, and be yourself."

"Myself? Are you sure about that?"

"Just do it." Southington said.

"Fine! Hello, beings in this galaxy, I am your Galactic President Blaphaus Maximus. We, members of the bloody Cabinet of idiots..."

Dawber looked at Southington and rolled her eyes.

Back on Ceilingida, Mal did not look happy. Both Zalez and Nate sat at the dining room table. Ten stood in the corner, Romana was up in her room. Mal stood over them, hands on her hips, face as red as her hair.

"You know this is the reason why I don't want Nate to go to anymore planets, 33 beings were killed for no reason."

"On Phytnes, Mal, not Launderington."

"If it could happen there it could happen on any other planet. Once again I don't want Blaphaus anywhere around the children... or here."

"Mother, what happened on Phytnes has nothing to do with Mr. Blaphaus." Nate said.

"How do we know that? This never happened when Traf was G.P. Do you see what's happening, Zalez?"

He shook his head, "I have no idea what you're talking about."

"Since Blaphaus came into our lives our lives have been disrupted, and I feel he's coming between us."

The next day, Space False One came down to land in the Phytnes spaceport. The ramp came down and Blaphaus, Sugden, Joorg and Haathee walked down the ramp to be met by a crowd and hovering robot-cams from GNN. Sugden, the most experienced Governor whispered to Blap.

"Wave and smile."

"I don't smile." Blap remarked, waving. "There's nothing to smile about."

Buterdau Kooper, the GNN Leetric reporter held a microphone as he stood to the side and spoke.

"G.P. Maximus has just landed at the Phytnes spaceport with Governors Sugden, Joorg and the Phytnes Governor Haathee. They are planning to take a ride over to the park where the devastating blastering happened yesterday. Buterdau Kooper, GNN."

The vehicles drove to the park, it was an entourage of the vehicles with the Cabinet members and then two military vehicles from Sugden's planet and then Buterdau and the GNN crew. A crowd was formed in front of the stage where the band played the day before. Microphones were set up on the stage but no teleprompter's. The vehicles stopped and Blap noticed there was a ramp and stairs up to the stage, but didn't say anything. They got out the vehicle to be met by an Iliiger Brigadier in uniform who saluted to them.

"After your speech I'll tell you what I found out." he told them.

"Speech? Wot speech?" Blap asked.

"We are supposed to do a speech." Haathee said.

"Where's the teleprompter's?"

"You have to wing it I think," Joorg remarked.

"I already did a speech. It's on GNN..."

"You have to do another one... here." Sugden said.

"Since I've become G.P. I have done more speeches than Traf did the whole time he was alive."

"They're waiting on us." Haathee said.

He walked up the steps to the stage and Blap shuffled up the ramp. Haathee let Blap get to the microphone first. Blap looked out at the crowd of different species, the GNN robot-cams hovered above. Blap saw not one bring in the audience was a Toob, a Gink or a Cakerlak. Apart from that it was a mixed lot.

"Hello. As G.P. I promise that we will find the bastard arsehole that did this." he said.

The beings just stared up at him. Then he started to get bombarded with questions and comments, and complaints.

"This never happened when Traf was alive!"

"We blame you!"

"What are you going to do about it, Toob?!"

"Are you going to give lucre to the victims' families?!"

"Go back where you came from!"

"What is the other galaxy like you went to?!"

"This is all your fault!"

Blap stepped back a few feet on the stage and motioned to Haathee.

"I'll let your Governor answer those questions." he whispered to Haathee, "Trunk nose, it's all yours."

He shuffled down the ramp to where the Sudgen was next to an Illiger Brigadier.

"Not much of a speaker, are you?" the Brig commented.

"Blaphaus, this is Brigadier Harkouk from the Xenartha Army. If the crowd  gets anymore rowdy the military will step in." told Sugden.

The crowd was getting a little more restless, but Haathee was doing his best to calm them down.

"I took care of you all as Planet Mayor, I will do more as Governor. There's the GBI here, and the military from Xenartha. I promise you, whoever did this will pay for the price. The Cabinet will pay for all medical expenses..."

"Wot is he telling them?" Blap asked.

"What he is supposed to." Joorg remarked.

In the House's conference room the other Governors were watching the holo-images of GNN's live footage.

Zeb shook his head, "Blap sure has no speaking skills."

"But Haathee is doing great. We'll send a press statement to say we'll pay for all the medical expenses." Southington remarked.

Jaboney remarked, "I kinda like the Toobs bluntness."

"So, the crowd on Phytnes did not like Galactic Blaphaus Maximus or his bluntness. They seemed to take to Haathee who most of them knew of when he was Planet Mayor. The GBI and Xenartha Army are going to start talking to the witnesses and try to figure out who did this horrible thing. It is true that nothing ever happened in this galaxy before. Buterdau Kooper, GNN."

Blap, Joorg and Haathee followed Harkouk to the side of the field where the blasterings started. The military was helping the GBI clear out the field area of the crowd. The GNN robot-cams were also gone, so it was just a quiet spot now.

"If you expect me to go through the woods, forget it." Blap remarked.

Harkouk looked Blap up and down, "Yeah, Galactic President Maximus, I can see. Having no legs must suck."

"What did you find out?" Haathee asked.

"Whoever did this, we know he was human, took off through these woods. A craft or vehicle probably was waiting on the other side."

"Wot about his weapon?" Blaphaus asked.

"Some of the crowd took holo-images and holo-scans, which would have to be examined." Harkouk said, "But we believe it was a Cakerlak weapon."

Blap glared at Joorg.

On Ceilingida, Fami Tapperdau walked up to the door of the pretty big house and buzzed the door buzzer. The front door opened to reveal Ten standing there, and he looked down at her.

"Hello, I am 10-E-C, can I help you?"

"Fancy." Fami smiled

""Excuse me, ma'am?"

"You're a very colorful robot."

"Yes, I know. And you are?"

"Oh, sorry. Yes, hello. My name is Fami Tapperdau, I'm looking for Mister or Mrs. Belhopsa. Are they home?"

"Mrs. Belhopsa is not here, neither is Mr. Belhopsa. Can I take a message, Ms. Tapperdau?"

"Umm... no, it's okay. I will check back later. Thank you."

"Of course, ma'am."

The door closed and Tapperdau headed back to her vehicle. She was getting no where fast, and it was bothering her.

Xenartha had a mix of species living on it, but the Illicit are the native species. A black and white six armed Cakerlak who seemed to wear a few necklaces and bracelets on his six arms walked into a Fencket department store, and looked around to see what he was up against. A short, squat gray haired male with tiny eyes and a snout walked up to the Cakerlak and smiled.

"Er, hello, sir. Welcome to Fencket, we don't see too many of your like here."

"What is that supposed to mean?" the Cakerlak looked at the name tag on the red vest of the store's employee. "Manager Palmer..."

Palmer, who was a Pekkary looked startled.

"I didn't mean nothing with it, sir."

"Good. I'll go do my shopping now."

Palmer watched the Cakerlak walk further into the store and felt in the pit of his fat stomach something was wrong. The Cakerlak walked around

the store, studying the species that were in there. He walked past a
Cycalopex that was like Governor Rüppell... for a minute he thought it was
the Governor. He spotted a Shypu, a Tayus, a species with big curved
horns that he didn't really know and a species with a large shell called a
Testundini. He approached the Testundini and talked him on the shoulder.

"Excuse me, how many planets in this galaxy?"

"Ur... excuse me?" the Testundini asked.

"I said how many planets... are in this... galaxy?" the Cakerlak asked
annoyed.

"Twenty-three I believe..."

"And in the Cabinet?"

"Cabinet? Well, twenty-two."

"Yes. And why is that?"

"Well, apparently the Tooberosum didn't want to be part of the
Cabinet..."

"And the G.P. is from what planet?"

The Testundini gulped, "A Tooberosum..."

"Have you ever seen one before? A Toob?"

"Well, I'm pretty old, so, yes I have. A long time ago though..."

"Well, you won't see one again."

The Cakerlak reached into his coat and pulled out two blasters and
opened fire. The Testundini put his head into his shell and gasped. He
heard screams, and shouts and weapon blasts. The Cakerkak ran around
the store, aiming fire at exactly 22 shoppers. The manager Palmer dived to
his info-pad to make a holo-call to the authorities. The Cakerlak left through
the back door of the store, got into a vehicle and drove off. Job done.

Back on Phytnes, Brigadier Harkouk approached Sugden and
whispered, "Governor, I have terrible news. There's been another
blastering..."

"Another? Where? On this planet?"

"No. On Xenartha... over 20 beings have been killed."

"What? This galaxy hasn't had anything ever like this and now twice?"

"There is a difference, this time it was definitely a Cakerlak."

"We know that for sure?"

The Illicit Brigadier nodded, "The manager of the store identified him."

"We need to tell Blaphaus... but on the shuttle. I need to tell Joorg first.
We'll go straight to Xenartha."

Sugden went over to where Blap stood, with Joorg and Haathee.

"Blaphaus, would you want to leave Phytnes?"

"Yes. I'm done here." Blap replied.

He and Haathee walked over, Joorg went to follow but Sugden grabbed him by the arm.

"Joorg, there's been another blastering."

"What? Where?"

"Xenartha..."

"Your home planet? Oh no. I'm so sorry. When did this happen?"

"While we were here."

"This is uncanny for this galaxy."

"Yes."

"Does the Toob know?"

"Not yet. I wanted you to know first."

"Why is that?"

"Because the blasterer was a Cakerlak."

Joorg gulped. What was going on with his planet?

A few minutes later the shuttle took off from Phytnes. Blap wanted to take off his Toob suit, but for some reason the Brigadier was with them.

"Why is he here?" Blap said, buckled to the bulkhead.

"Because we are going to Xenartha." Sugden replied.

"Really? And why is that?"

Haathee added, "Yes, why is that?"

"There's been another blastering there." Sugden replied.

"Another bloody one?" Blap asked actually surprised, "Wot the bloody hell?"

"Are they related?" Haathee asked, "The one on my planet and yours?"

"We don't know." Harkouk said, "But this time the blasterer was a Cakerlak."

Blap turned to Joorg, "This is my surprised face. I wouldn't be surprised if that six armed nasty species is responsible for the other one. So, wot are we going to do on Xenartha?"

"You're going to announce it to GNN. Good PR."

"Does the Cabinet know about it?" Joorg asked.

"No, not yet." Sugden said.

"Perfect." Blaphaus said, "Cyrakuse, you're going to tell the House and then you're going to tell the galaxy." Blap remarked.

Joorg just wanted to ask the Planet Mayor if he knew anything about it.

The Governors sat around the conference table at the House, as Joorg's holo-call was in the middle of the table.

"I have very dire news to tell you, there's been another blastering on Xenartha. We are heading there right now, to find out what happened."

"Another one?" Southington asked surprised.

"On Xenartha? The one planet with a military. That takes balls." Noam remarked.

"Is this connected to the other one? Can it be the same being?" Eastora asked.

Jaboney said, "They better not hit Old Eboracum."

Joorg said, "It was something different. We know it was a Cakerlak this time."

The Gink swallowed and leaned forward, "Are you sure?"

"Yes."

Peezle rubbed his temple, Yerkal is going to lose his mind, he thought.

Thaw said, "Let us talk to Maximus."

Blap's holo-call appeared, "I have nothing else to say."

Thaw said, "Maximus, when you come back here we need to talk about your social skills, and your couth."

"Ha! Wotever. You know wot you signed up for when I was chosen for this. You're lucky I care enough to go to Xenartha. Joorg will keep in touch with you. Contact GNN, Joorg is going to do the press conference. Over and out."

His holo-call ended. Joorg's one was still there and he shrugged.

"We will be in touch." Southington said.

Joorg nodded and his holo-call vanished.

"Why would the Cakerlak pull something like this?" the Gink asked.

"It's not the whole planet." Rüppell replied, "Just one rogue Cakerlak."

Dawber replied, "We don't know that. So far that planet has a reputation..."

Gillian said, "We don't know how many were murdered this time... or why these planets are being targeted. Do they have anything in common?"

"Phytnes and Xenartha... they are next to each other..." Southington said, then her eyes opened wide, "Oh no. Right next door is Mencken... my home planet."

Peezle looked across the table at her and started to tear up.

The GBI and Xenartha's military was already at the store on Xenartha that was all roped off, and cleared out. Space False One came down to land in the car park. The ramp descended and they all walked down the ramp, to be met by a human GBI agent.

"Galactic President, Governors." he saluted. "The GBI has never been so busy."

"How many were killed?" Sugden asked.

"Twenty-two, Governor." the agent replied. "Many more injures, just from running away. Unfortunately the Cakerkak got away, apparently out the back door."

"And it was definitely a Cakerkak?" Joorg asked.

"Yes, the manager of the store and a Testundini spoke to him. Both gave witness accounts. Both are here still if you want to talk to them."

"No." Blaphaus said, "Keep them away from GNN."

"Yes, G.P. Maximus, GNN is not here yet..."

A black GNN craft then started to come down on the other side of the car park.

"You spoke too soon." Blap said. "Cyrakuse, you better straighten your tie, you're on."

Joorg straightened his purple tie and looked worried.

Haathee said, "I pray for the victims from both planets."

The Brigadier said to Sugden, "This is our home planet, we should say something on GNN, right?"

Sugden nodded, "Yes. We will."


"We have robot-cams on Xenartha and Governor Joorg and Governor Sugden will give a press conference on what happened at the Fencket store on Xenartha..." Buterdau Kooper explained.


The robot-can hovered before Joorg who stood next to Sugden and the Brigadier with the roped off store in the background.

"Hello, I'm Governor Joorg, Governor of Cakerlak. Unfortunately on Xenartha at this store one of the Cakerlak species opened fire, killing twenty-two beings. I will go back to Cakerlak and help with the investigation. My heart goes out to what happened here, as well as Phytnes, which wasn't because of a Cakerkak. I'm here with Galactic President Blaphaus Maximus and Governor Sugden."

Sugden said, "Whoever did this will be found and held accountable. They won't get away. Myself, and all the Governors and the Galactic President won't let this happen again, as long as we can help it."

A robot-cam hovered in front of Blap and Kooper's voice came out of it.

"Galactic President, do you have anything to say?"

"Yes. Whoever did this and the blastering on Phytnes are bloody cowards. I dare you to attack another planet... whoever you are." Blap stepped forward and grabbed the camera, looking right into it. "I dare you."

"You heard it here, everybody, the Galactic President will not let this happen again, and he seems mad... and caring. Buterdau Kooper, GNN."

"I dare you to attack another planet... whoever you are." the yellow eye came close to the lens of the holo-image. The images went backwards and played again. "I dare you to attack another planet... whoever you are." And again. "I dare you to attack another planet... whoever you are."

Fami sat in a chair at a desk, studying the yellow eye. She smiled, taking a sip of the hot drink from the mug.

**CHAPTER 7**

The next day, Joorg was led into the dark chamber that had lit torches on the walls. He turned to Laterille and brushed his purple jackets sleeve.

"I'm Governor... you don't have to be so tough."

Coleoptera sat behind a stone desk and laughed.

"You're doing a terrible job keeping your planets species at bay. One of them attacked a store of beings on Xenartha, and you went and snitched to the whole galaxy."

"The Cakerkak wasn't in disguise. The human that attacked on Phytnes had the sense to be in disguise. No one knows for sure he was human, even. They do know the weapons came from this planet. Do you know anything about that?"

"Why would I? I'm just Planet Mayor..."

"The human Yerkal was here... he said you told him you were the one behind the plan to kill the Toob."

"The human lied." lied Coleoptera.

"Really... he also mentioned the Order of Blattodea. Do you know anything about that?"

"Only that they have existed for a very long time."

"So, they exist now?"

"Maybe. Right now I'd be more concerned about your home planet, Joorg."

"Cyrakuse? What about it?"

"Right about now someone is on that planet that is pretty close to you, someone that has been cheating on you with the Phytnes Governor. But that's the least of your worries now."

Joorg frowned, "What are you talking about?"

"You'll find out. You might want to warn a certain King though..." smiled Coleoptera evilly.

Joorg didn't know what to say.


On Cyrakuse, in a village called Cyrakuseskills, the Cyrakuse that were there were minding their own business. Inside a restaurant, Tostone sat with his wife at a table, having a nice lunch. Celley Tostone looked over her husbands shoulder as a female Cyrakuse walked in by herself, wearing all black. A brown little curly furred Cyrakuse greeted her at the door.

"Hello, welcome to Whiskers. Are you by yourself?"

The female Cyrakuse nodded, and was led to a table.

"That's is odd." Celley said.

Charcat frowned, "What do you mean, honey?"

"A really good looking and very skinny Cyrakuse walked in here by herself."

"So?" Charcat grinned, "We can't all be with our loved ones."

"Look around you, Charcat. All the other customers are couples or with a family."

Charcat looked around at everybody else in the restaurant.

"Yeah. And?"

"But she's by herself. Do you ever see anybody here in this planet by themselves? Ever? Even when we lived here growing up?"

Charcat shrugged, "I really never thought of it."

"Exactly." nodded Celley, watching the waitress take the one who was by herself order. "I notice these things. With what happened on Phytnes or Xenartha can happen here as well."

Tostone chuckled, "I notice things as well, darling. I noticed Blaphaus and thought he'd be a great G.P."

Celley wasn't amused, "Yeah, well, look how that is turning out to be."

"Well, I think you're getting para..."

Just then the female Cyrakuse who was alone shouted at the top of her lungs.

"By the Order of Blattodea... down with the Toob!"

She pulled two weapons from her jacket, leapt to the table and started blasting at everyone in the restaurant. Just then a spear flew through the window, hitting her in the chest and she blasted a few shots down at the table before she fell off it.


The holo-call of Joorg appeared before Zucaritas who was laying in his bed.

"Zucaritas, are you awake?"

Zucaritas sat up naked, and looked at the life-sized holo-call.

"I am now. What do you want?" he growled.

"It's Cyrakuse, I think that planet is going to have something happen to it like the others."

"Really now? And you think that is why?"


Southington walked through the spaceport on Mercken, with Dawber. A press area was set up with hovering robot-cams.

"I'm here if you need me to say anything." told Dawber.

"I'll be okay." Southington faced the robot-cams, "Hello, beings on Mercken, as your Governor I have ordered the GBI and Xenartha's military to be stationed all over this planet at any hotspots that a blastering can happen. If you witness anything suspicious, please let the authorities know."

Kooper's voice came out of the robot-cam that was in front of her.

"Governor Southington, we just got word that a restaurant on Cyrakuse was attacked by a blasterer, everyone inside it was killed, as well as the blasterer..."

Southington turned to Dawber in shock.

"NOOOOOJJJ!!!!" Yerkal cried out from the living room.

A shirtless Peezle walked from the bedroom in their flat over to Yerkal who was on the couch, watching GNN.

"Yerkal, what's going on?"

"Look..." Yerkal pointed to the holo-images of Buterdau Kooper who was speaking.

"The identity of the blasterer is unknown yet, but two of the victims of the attack at the restaurant on Cyrakuse was ex-Governor Charcat Tostone and his wife Celley Tostone."

Peezle immediately started to cry.

The King stood next to Lady Gerda in the throne room, the GNN robot-cam hovering before them.

"As King of this planet, I will do my best to find out why this happened. Why one of my own species did such a terrible thing. Charcat Tostone was a great Governor and great friend. Words cannot say enough. He and his wives funeral will take place at this palace. I will he reaching out to the Governors to make plans. I'm just glad one of my guards men was present and took out the one who did this, before she murdered anybody else."

At the House on Launderington, the Governors sat at the table as usual, minus Southington, Dawber, Joorg, Zucaritas, and Peezle.

"This is getting out of hand!" Noam cried out, standing on his chair. "Are all our damn planets going to go through this?!"

"I dare them to go to mine." muttered Bradypus.

"What are your species going to do?" Noam asked.

"We all need to calm down." Thaw remarked.

Peezle walked into the conference room and said liked at their horried faces.

"Where's Blaphaus?" Peezle asked.

The King's shuttle landed in front of the palace where he stood with his four guard Cyrakuse. The two Cyrakuse Governors walked down the ramp and approached him. The King hugged them both with one big group hug.

"I'm so sorry this had to happen." the King told them.

"What happened?" Zucaritas asked.

"You don't know? I thought that's why you sent for one of my shuttles."

"With the blasterings on the two planets I had a feeling Cyrakuse was next..." Joorg commented.

"Well, whatever gave you that feeling was correct, Governor." the King said sadly.

"So something happened here?"

"Not at the palace but in the town. A number of people were murdered in a restaurant, and Charcat and Celley were two of the victims. Luckily one of my guard killed the blasterer. It was a female Cyrakuse as well."

"Oh no." Zucaritas said, "We have to let the House know."

"GNN already reported it, I holo-recorded a statement. I'm surprised you two didn't know."

"We need a ride to the town." Zucaritas told the King.

He nodded, "I can arrange that."

Blaphaus shuffled out the lift and went down the hallway towards the conference room. He went inside it to see the Governors were all watching GNN which was playing the King's statement.

Blap said, "Wot the fornicate? Cyrakuse?"

Zeb nodded, "A female Cyrakuse opened fire at a restaurant on that planet, killing nine beings. Two of them was Charcat Tostone and Celley."

"Wot? Who did this?"

"We don't know yet. We think Joorg and Zucaritas headed to the planet."

"Tostone is dead?" Blap asked, "For real?" He sniffed.

"Are you crying inside there?" Zeb asked.

"Don't be bloody ridiculous, Chordattian."

"Cyrakuse doesn't have weapons..."

"We don't know where the weapon came from but one of the King's guard killed the blasterer with a spear."

"Then I'm going to that planet to find out."

Blap turned to leave the room, crying inside his suit. What has the galaxy come to?

At the Cyrakuseheter Hospital, a Cyrakuse with yellow fur and covered in rosettes, and wearing a lab coat approached the King, Zucaritas and Joorg in the waiting room.

"Hello, I'm Doctor Jackson, I did the autopsy on the blasterer. Would you want to see her?"

"Yes." Joorg said.

They followed Dr. Jackson into the autopsy room where the figure laid in the metal table, sheet over her. Jackson removed the top part of the sheet to reveal the face.

"No!" gasped Joorg, stepping back a few feet in shock.

Zucaritas frowned, "You know how who that is?"

"Yes. That was my wife..."


"AAARRRGGGHHH!" Blap kicked his Toob head and body, sending it flying across the office. He tore off the data-pad and threw that against the wall.

"Blap, what the hell are you doing?!" Governor Waydo stepped in, to see the angry human, who was clenching his fists.

"Oh, look who decided to speak up." Blap said angrily.

"Only because you're losing your mind, human."

Blap turned to face the Pilosa.

"You bet I'm losing my mind! Beings are dying because of me! Because of the bloody Toob! I'm sick of this, I'm sick of the politics and feces! I have a good mind to run outside, run down those bloody steps and yell this whole thing has been a lie! Maybe the killings would stop."

"Don't be absurd, man. You know as well as I do that would make things a whole lot worse. You've got to be strong, the galaxy needs you. We will get to the bottom of this."

"The galaxy doesn't need me, flat face. It needed Traf! The whole bloody galaxy was a lot better when he was G.P."

"Really? You think so? I don't. He did nothing, you're doing a lot..."

"Oh, yeah, the bloody crowd on Phytnes really saw that! They blamed me for what happened! That was two bloody blasterings ago! And now Tostone, the poor bastard who suggested I become G.P. is dead!"

Blap sat down on the floor, his back to the desk, and started crying again.

"Damn it, man! Get on your feet, put on that Toob suit and get to Cyrakuse now!" Waydo pounded his fist on the desk. "You're not doing anybody any good acting like a baby!"

Blap looked up, nodding, tears pouring out his eyes and snot pouring out his nose. Waydo thought to himself Blap looked better as a Toob.

The King walked into the courtyard of his palace, holding Lady Gerda's hand.

"I'm thinking of the reception for the funereal in this courtyard, my dear." he said, "What do you think?"

"We'll do whatever you think is good. Is it just for the Governors?"

The King shrugged, "That I don't know yet. But I'm sure they'll all be here."

Just then Blake walked Zucaritas and Joorg into the courtyard.

"Hello, you two. Any peasant news?"

Joorg said, "The blasterer was my wife. I don't know how or why but she had a weapon... from Cakerkak."

Blaphaus stood outside the front doors of the House, at the top of the stairs, with the Governors standing behind him, minus Southington and Dawber and the two Cyrakuse. the GNN robot-cam hovered before him.

"Well... you can't blame me on this... three planets in a row. Each time this was done by a different species, but with Cakerkak weaponry I'm guessing. Whoever is behind this, we will come for you. This will stop. So you might as well reveal yourself, because I'm not going to put up with it anymore. Thank you, have a nice life."

## CHAPTER 8

"Hello, I'm Buterdau Kooper, today in this galaxy there's over 30 funerals, on three different planets, with lots of broken hearts. The Galactic President and the Governors will be on Cyrakuse at a private funeral for ex-Governor of Cyrakuse Charcat Tostone and his wife Celley, who were victims in the latest blastering attack..."

It was the next day, at the funeral in the cemetery on Cyrakuse, the two coffins sat next to each other before the two holes. A bunch of chairs were set up for everybody to sit in. Blaphaus, followed by the Governors, the King and Lady Gerda, then Zalez all walked in down the aisle and took places in their seats, except for Blap who stood. Nitsiuj Rellim, head of the Faeligion Church stood next to a Cyrakuse in flowing red robes.

"Hello, all, we have all come together to pay respects to Charcat Tostone and Celley Tostone, as well as all the others that lost their lives the last few days with those senseless acts." the pastor said. "I am joined here with Bishop Holic from Cyrakuse. Bishop Holic..."

Bishop Holic faced everyone, "Fellow Cyrakuse, other species, if you can please lower your heads, and close your eyes in remembrance of Charcat and Celley, two wonderful beings."

Everyone lowered their heads, and closed their eyes except for Blap who thought this whole thing was stupid. Holic then started to making a meowing sound under his breath, and Zucaritas and Joorg and the King joined in. Blap wondered how long it was going to last. He looked at what the others were doing, and focused on the Gink, wondering why he never saw another Gink ever, and why no one questioned it. It was time someone to question it real soon. First he had to deal with the Cakerkak. The meowing stopped and Holic looked up.

"Thank you for the prayer. Now I'll turn your focus on our wonderful Galactic President. Blaphaus?"

"Me? Wonderful? You poor misguided soul. So, so much for Cyrakuse having more than one life."

Zucaritas and Joorg both looked at each other, wondering why the Bishop let Blap speak.

"That's all I'm saying. Let's get these two buried and move on."

An hour or so later they were all in the courtyard of the palace where tables were laid out full of food and drink. A holo-scan of the Tostone's was on the side, showing everybody how happy those two were. Blap stood there, not eating. The King walked up to him.

"You know, you can eat."

"Not hungry."

"I never saw you eat."

"How many times did we sit down to eat?" Blap asked.

"Not many. You're a very different type of being, aren't you, Galactic President?"

"If you say so."

"You don't hold back with your thoughts, my friend. Are you always like that?"

"Always. Life is too short not to."

"I wonder what your life was like before all this?" he motioned to the Governors who stood around.

"It was..." Blap watched the Gink closely. "Wot do you know about the Gink species?"

"The Gink? As much as I know about the Toobs."

"Have you ever seen another Gink?"

The King shrugged, "Good question. Nope. He's the only one. You should make a trip to his planet."

Blap pointed to the King, "That is the smartest idea I ever heard... you should be G.P."

"Ha! I'm a King... I cannot be anything else, but from you, my friend, that is a high compliment."

Blap stepped forward and waved his arm.

"You lot! I had a thought..."

Dawber whispered to Southington, "If he says he wants to step down let's not talk him out of it."

Southington chuckled.

"What is it?" Zucaritas asked.

"I think I need to go to every planet, and reaffirm that we are doing everything we can to find out why these killings are happening."

Zeb smiled, "I actually think that's a great idea. It'll help with the beings trusting you, Blaphaus. There's planets you haven't been to."

"Yes, like Gink for instance." Blap pointed to Guoz. "I've been to a number of planets but never seen another Gink. What do you say, Gink? How about a Cabinet summit to Gink?"

Guoz, the Gink nodded, "We will plan it. Yes."

"Good." Blap said.

Thaw remembered what Professor Phence said about the planet being a moon.

"Let's talk about it later, Blaphaus. Today we will celebrate the Tostone's life as well as everyone else's life that were murdered."

Haathee said to Joorg, "How are you doing? I am so sorry about your wife. I have no idea why she'd do this."

"Probably the same reason when you told her to push me into a bloody swimming pool."

Joorg said, "This is not the time, Toob. You don't know when to shut up, do you?" he marched off.

"So, trunky, how does it feel to know you boinked a mass killer?"

Haathee swung his trunk at Blap's face.

"I hate to say this, but you should've drowned."

Blap watched him storm off. Zalez walked over to him, wearing a black suit.

"Wot are you doing here? You're not Governor." Blap remarked.

"I was invited, Blaphaus, by Peezle. Nate wanted to come but I promised Mal I'd keep him away from all this."

"I don't blame her."

"Have you found out anything from Traf's info-pad, yet?"

"Nope. But I will. These blasterings are interrupting everything."

Zalez nodded, "Well, I hope you'll get to the bottom of it."

"I will. So, you have a lot of species on your Dook station, right?"

Zalez nodded, "I try to be diverse."

"So, any Ginks work there?"

"No, Blaphaus, and no Cakerkak or Toobs either." Zalez said seriously.

"Duh on the Toobs, no feces on the Cakerlak, I wouldn't want any of those working for me. Does Dook power their planet?"

Zalez shook his head, "No. There's not many planets we don't power..."

"In this galaxy. In my galaxy we just had one station that powered the planets."

Zalez frowned, "Really? You never talk about your galaxy."

"There's not much to say about it."

"Well, what was the company name of it?"

Blap said, "I have no bloody idea. Ever been to Gink?"

Zalez shook his head, "No, I was always told that they don't like other species going to it."

"Well, tough feces for them. I'm thinking of having summit on Gink, Belhopsa, you should go, bring Traf's kid as well, after all, he owns Dook Energy, right?"

Zalez nodded, "I'll see what I can do."

"Good. Bring your own kid as well, it'll be good for him."

"I don't think I'll bring Nate, I'm keeping him away from all this, remember?"

"Wotever, it's your kid."

The next day, Thaw took a shuttle first class to his rainy planet of Siahl, to meet with Professor Phence once again. Blaphaus mentioned at the reception about them all going to Gink, but he wanted advice. He NEEDED advice. No one knew Phence as much as he did, he got to know Phence when he was a student of his. He always wanted to be a professor, but chose the Governor life instead.

He walked into the grey brick building again and was approached by Phence himself. The human, spectacled man shook the Leetric's slimy hand.

"Governor Thaw, you know you can always holo-call me, save a flight across the galaxy."

"I know, Professor, but the rain does me good. I might need you to come to Launderington though."

Phence frowned, "You know I love going there. The House robots might be do for an upgrade."

"That might be good, can we talk in your office?"

"Of course, Governor."


A holo-call of the Gink appeared before the Great Weta in his chamber on Cakerkak.

"Great Weta, the Toob wants to have a summit with the Governors on Gink, what they all think is Gink. I think he suspects something."

"He doesn't suspect anything, trust me, Guoz." the Great Weta said.

"Well, 'Gink' is really a moon, none of the Governors, or anybody will survive on that. If they find out that's not where I come from..."

"Then, you know what to do."

"The fleet is at the edge of this galaxy, Great Weta, can we just order the invasion now?"

"No. When the time is ready. I have to make sure the galaxy is weaker."

"Are you behind these blasterings? They know the weapons are Cakerkak weapons..."

"Ha! They are so foolish, Guoz. They think they know where the weapons are from. You know what do for the Order, Gink. Do not fail me."

Guoz nodded and said, "And Joorg?"

"You know what to do with him. Go now back to your fake Governor life. And do. Not. Fail."

Guoz nodded again and left the chamber.

Coleoptera then stepped out the shadows where he was hiding.

"Great Weta, do you trust the Gink? We know nothing of them."

"No. I don't trust him, Coleoptera, and I know he will fail, which would only affect him, no one else. Everything is still coming into plan."

Thaw sat in front of Phence's desk, as Phence sat behind it speaking.

"Maximus seems to be not as popular with the galaxy citizens, Governor. Do you think these three blasterings are because if him?"

"I don't know, there's a lot of changes."

Phence pushed his spectacles up on his nose, "Yes, that is true. So, what did you come here to ask me?"

"You said you went to Toob, Professor, and there was nothing there, that it was a moon. What made you think it was Tooberosum?"

"Because that's the only planet that has to be it."

"So, you've never went to Gink?"

"No, or Cyrakuse, or Cakerlak, or Mesas. A lot of the planets I've never been too."

"Do you have a galaxy map?"

"Of course." Phence pushed something in his info-pad and a holo-map of the galaxy appeared between them. "This is Siahl, this is Launderington and here is the moon..." Phence pointed them all out.

"And this one?" Thaw pointed to the planet that was at the very top.

"That's Tooberosum."

Thaw frowned, "Are you sure?"

Phence chuckled, "No disrespect, Governor, my friend, but I am a Professor."

"This planet is what we *thought* was Tooberosum, Professor. We all went there."

"If that's not his planet, and this planet Tooberosum is not his planet, what planet did he come from? Or what galaxy?" Professor asked, staring at the holo-map.

On Launderington, all the Governors took their seats, but Thaw, who wasn't there yet. Blap shuffled in, looking at them.

"Where is the Leetric?" he asked.

"He's coming back from Siahl." Southington said, "He should be here soon."

"Well, I'm not starting without him. Gink, I want a summit and I want it on your planet."

"You said, but why Gink?"

"What's a summit?" Rüppell asked.

"You don't have summits here?" Blap asked.

"It's the highest point of a mountain." Kaktovic said, "We have lots of those on Ankerage.

"A summit is a meeting." Blap said.

Jaboney said, "This is a meeting."

"This is a joke." Blap said. "The summit will have everybody there, you lot, the Planet Mayor's, Belhopsa, the bloody pastor, head of Farvegas, everybody who is important..."

"Why are you taking an initiative all of a sudden?" Eastora asked.

Zeb said, "I would have thought you would have quit already."

"I don't quit, Chordattian, because if I'm going to be in this position I'm going to do it right. Apparently Traf kept a lot of feces from you, and it's boiling over. Cakerkak weapons are all over the galaxy it seems. Two blasterers are still out there and no one knows who they are, except one is human or so we think and the other is a Cakerlak, and there's still the Order of Blattodea to worry about. So, we need to all get together and sort this out, before we all end up in a morgue."

Thaw then walked into the conference room.

"Sorry I'm late."

"You didn't miss much, Governor, Blaphaus was saying he wants a summit on Gink." Zeb explained.

"I still don't know why Gink." Noam said, "No offence, Guoz."

"Blaphaus, after this meeting can I talk to you in private?" Thaw asked.

"If you're going to quit being Governor..."

"I'm not going to quit."

"Good." Blap turned to the others, "Figure our where on Gink to have the summit, you lot, who to invite and contact the GNN Leetric, I want everybody to know about this."

He followed Thaw out the room, and down the hallway.

"This better be good, Leetric."

"Why do you want the summit on Gink?"

"Ever meet another one? Ever been there? You know more about the Toobs than you do them I'm guessing."

He followed Thaw into his office where Phence waited.

"Who is this ponce of a human?"

"This is Professor Phence."

Phence shook Blap's hand, "It's a pleasure to meet you at last, Galactic President. I never met a Tooberosum before."

"Professor? I heard of you. You're a Professor of wot?"

"Well, my company built pretty much every robot you know, and I know a lot about maths, and..."

"You're not a Professor really, are you?"

"Well..."

Thaw said, "The Professor knows a lot about the galaxy, he's one of the smartest beings I know."

"Good for you. Have you been to all the planets, Phence? I bet you haven't been to Tooberosum."

"No, I haven't, have you?"

"Of course I have. I'm from there." he lied. "So, wot are you doing here? I have a summit to plan."

"Yes, I heard you want to have it on Gink."

Blap waved his arm, "Yep. Do you know anything about them, 'Professor'?"

"Not really, but let me show you something." he pulled out his small info-pad and a holo-map of the galaxy appeared, just like he showed Thaw.

"Point to your planet."

"Is this a joke?"

"Do it, Blaphaus. You know we've all been there." Thaw casually winked.

Blap looked at the map closely and pointed to the planet that they thought was Toob.

"Okay, see this planet?" Phence pointed to the moon.

"Wot do you think I am? That's not a planet, that's a bloody moon."

Thaw and Phence both looked at each other surprised.

"How... how do you know?" Thaw asked.

"Because my galaxy has one about the same size,..."

"Your galaxy?" Phence asked, "You're not from this galaxy?"

"You didn't know this was a moon?" Blaphaus asked, "Wot do they teach in schools? Every galaxy needs a moon, and a sun. You thought this moon was a planet?"

Phence shut down the map deflated, and sat on the desk.

"I thought it was your planet, Galactic President, I went there..."

"You went to the moon?"

"Yes, that's how I discovered what it was."

"You're a lousy Professor..."

"Be they as it may, the Gink said that moon is where he came from."

"He didn't come from the moon."

"We know." Thaw said, "Guoz lied."

"So, wot planet did he come from?"

"None from this galaxy..." Phence said.

Before he could finish Blap shuffled out of the office.

He went into the conference room where everyone still sat.

"Is everything okay?" Southington asked.

"Yep. So, the summit on Gink tomorrow?"

"That's what you want." Zucaritas said, "I'm inviting the King..."

Thaw walked in behind him, with Professor Phence.

"This is Professor Phence, his company Phencegate builds robots, and he knows a lot about galaxies, he's even been to Gink, so he'll be going to the summit as well."

Blap glared at the Gink who had no reaction whatsoever.

"Do you have a problem with that?"

Guoz said, "No, when is it?"

"The summit? Tomorrow. No time to waste." Blap said.

Guoz stood up and went to the door, "I'll go and let them know right away."

And he walked out the room.

Blap said, "See you here first thing in the morning, you lot. Can one of you arrange a room at that fancy hotel down the road?"

Thaw said, "I'll arrange a room for you and you, Professor."

The Professor nodded and smiled. He wondered how were they going to have the summit on the moon.


Zalez sat at his desk on the Dook Energy space station and said to the holo-call of Mal.

"Tomorrow I'm going to Gink for some kind of summit."

"Gink? Summit?" Mal asked, "What kind of summit?"

"That I don't know yet. A lot of beings are invited, it's this grand idea Blaphaus has. The King of Cyrakuse will be there, all the Governors, you make it. I know you won't want Nate there, but I just wanted to bring it up."

"What do you know about Gink?" Mal asked.

"Absolutely nothing. No one has been to the planet as far as I know, but the Gink Governor."

"With everything that's going on, Zalez, I say no, I don't want Nate to go."

Zalez nodded, "I totally understand. GNN will be there, so you can all watch. It should be interesting..."

"Or a feces show." she remarked.

Zalez scoffed, "Yeah, that's more like it."


Peezle's holo-recording appeared in the living room of the Traf's mansion. Mrs. Traf, Narob and Hoeka watched 1-4-3 play it.

"Hello, tomorrow Galactic President Blaphaus Maximus is holding a Galaxy Summit, the first of its kind. It'll be hosted by Gink. Narob, as current owner of Dook Energy, and as Zalez Belhopsa is going, you are invited. We are all meeting at 8 a.m. tomorrow morning. Hope to see you there."

The recording ended.

Mrs. Traf said to Narob, "That was sweet, honey. Your father would be proud."

"Why?"

"Because it's a big deal you're invited."

Hoeka said, "Maybe one day you'll be G.P., Narob. Blaphaus is not going to last forever."

Narob said, "Okay, I'll go. But I'm not looking forward to it."


Peezle actually sat on the couch, in his Launderington flat, next to Yerkal.

"Tomorrow Blaphaus wants to have a summit meeting with the Governors and everybody. I want you to come as well. Are you up for it?"

Yerkal looked into Peezle's eyes and nodded.

"Maybe we'll get answers..."

"Don't hold your breath."

They both laughed together.


Bodie's holo-call was on Planet Mayor Losergram's desk, that he sat behind, smoking a cigar.

"Hello, my friend, how are you doing?"

"Bodie... or should I say Governor? I'm sorry to hear about the blasterings, and the murder of Tostone. I'm glad no Canis were snuffed."

"Me too. So, tomorrow there's going to be a big summit on Gink, you're invited."

"Really? Well, that should be fun I say. Yes, tell the fat ugly bugger I'll be there."


The King sat on his throne as the life sized holo-call of Zucaritas appeared from the info-pad that Blake, the King's assistant was holding.

"Your majesty, Blaphaus is having some kind of summit on Gink tomorrow and he's inviting you. You just have to meet us at the House, on Launderington. Are you interested?"

"He's serious? Hmmm. I know he mentioned it, but didn't know he was serious. Sure, Lady Gerda and I will be there."

"Great. It should be interesting." Zucaritas commented.


Joorg's holo-call appeared before Coleoptera and said, "Cole, I don't know why this is happening but tomorrow there's going to be a summit on Gink, hosted by the Toob."

"On Gink? Joorg, do you know anything about that planet?"

Joorg said, "No, I know nothing."

"Well, let me fill you in, it's not a planet. It's a moon..."

"Guoz is from a moon? How is that possible?"

"No one will survive on that planet, so I will refrain myself from going."

"But everyone will be there... right now Cakerlak is public enemy number one, the Toob is blaming your planet for the blasterings. I think you should go..."

"Fine, Joorg, I will be there. Do not tell anyone the truth about Gink. Understood?"

"Yes, understood." Joorg's holo-call ended.

Coleoptera moved out his office to go tell the Great Weta right away. What was the Toob thinking? He went into the Great Weta's chamber but the Weta wasn't there. Coleoptera never knew the Weta not to be there. He had no idea what to do, or think.

"What are you doing?" a voice asked behind him.

Coleoptera spun around and gasped, "You! What are you doing here?"

"Starting what should be done." and the Gink blasted a weapon which evaporated Coleoptera to dust.

## CHAPTER 9

Summit day came, the day no one knew what to expect. Rubyspears stood at the bottom of the steps of the House, standing next to a long vehicle. He had no idea how he was going to fit all the Governors and Blaphaus, and the guests into it. Just then five Ultra driver pulled their vehicles up to the curb. Oh, that's how, he thought.

Inside the House, Joorg looked really worried. He sat in his office, trying to send a holo-call to Cole, but had no luck. He wanted to say something to one of the other Governors, but didn't know what to say. All the other guests had arrived, except for the Cakerkak Planet Mayor. He thought maybe no one would notice.

Zucaritas appeared in the doorway and said, "Your P.M. hasn't arrived? He's late."

Joorg said, "Maybe something happened to him."

"Maybe. You know you should pull away from that planet, my fellow Cyrakuse. I sure wouldn't want to be associated with them right now."

"I'm not stepping down as Governor, if that's what you're saying."

Zucaritas shrugged, "Shoot yourself. Anyway, Southington had an idea for a holo-scan to be taken with everybody at the top of the steps."

Joorg nodded and stood, "Well, I guess Coleoptera will be missed. Just don't tell Blaphaus..."

"Your ugly arse P.M. is late." Blap said as soon as Joorg stepped out the lift, into the foyer that was full with everybody.

"I know. I tried to holo..."

"Don't bother." Blap said, "This just proves my opinion on that species. I don't know how you got tangled up with them, I mean they turned your wife into..."

"Blaphaus, that's enough." Dawber said seriously, "Today is going to be a very historical and fun day."

"Wotever you say, woman."

"Blaphaus, this was your idea." Southington remarked.

"It's a marvelous idea if I don't say so myself." Bodie smiled.

Southington said, "Let's go outside for a holo-shoot."

Thaw went up to Blap as everyone started to go outside and said, "Blaphaus, we are not all seriously going to moon, are we?"

"Yup. But we are not stepping out."

Phence frowned, on the other side of Blaphaus.

"Then there's no summit?"

"Of course there's a summit, Professor. Just not on the moon. Trust me, this will be good."

They joined the others outside, all standing at the top of the steps. Blap stood in the middle of them thinking to himself if anyone wanted to wipe out every important being in this galaxy this was the time. A robot-can hovered in front of them, and took the holo-scan.

The entourage of vehicles, led by the long black limousine-vehicle that Rubyspears drove, with all the Governors and Blaphaus drove towards the spaceport.

"This is the first time I had all of you at one go." Rubyspears said, "I wish I was going with you all."

"No you don't." Zeb replied.

Jaboney said, ""How many of us are going on this trip? Space False One only carries forty people."

"There's 23 of us." said Peezle.

"Twenty-two and a half." Haathee joked, waving his trunk at Noam. They all laughed.

"Twenty-four with your big head, you big eared loaf." Noam retorted.

"I'm pretty tall." Kakertak said.

"Me too." Gillian added.

Jaboney said, "Twenty-three of us, but Blaphaus stands, so 22. So, how many more?"

Southington said, "Zalez and Ten, Yerkal, the King and Lady Gerda, P.M. Losergram  and Coleoptera..."

"Coleoptera is not coming." Joorg said, "He never showed up."

"Oh. That's too bad."

"Not really." Blap said.

"Today is a big day for the galaxy," Buterdau said sitting on the full Space False One, with the robot-cam hovering before him. "Everybody is here, the Governors and their guests and of course the Galactic President. Hopefully after this Galactic Summit his poll ratings will go up. They have been down more than ever since the first blastering on Phytnes. I'm sitting here next to Gunther Farvegas, the CEO and owner of the gambling/ entertainment space station Farvegas."

Farvegas was rich and looked the part. He wore an expensive dark gray suit. His fur was different shades of brown and orange and a bit of white. He looked like he was the most miserable Cyrakuse in the galaxy.

"Mister Farvegas, how do you feel about this summit?"

"Not happy. Wasting my time. Don't like the Toob. Don't trust the Gink."

"Really? Why is that?" Buterdau asked.

Farvegas glanced at the robot-cam, "We're live right now?"

"No, being holo-recorded. Feel free to say what you want."

"I don't like being away from my space station, I had to travel all the way from it to Launderington just to fly back to the other side of the galaxy. I don't trust a species I know a nothing about. Only one Toob and one Gink in this galaxy that I know of says a lot. Am I right, Kooper?"

Buterdau said, "Well, we're about to meet a lot more of the Gink on their planet."

"Maybe. Still don't trust them. Do you know what the betting odds on Farvegas that the Toob is not really a Toob."

Buterdau shook his head.

"A hundred to one."

Zalez sat next to Narob Traf, who looked as miserable as Farvegas was.

"Narob, what's wrong? You don't look happy."

"I'm not. I'm not like my father was... I'm not sociable."

Peezle sat across the aisle from him and leaned over, "Narob, your father was a real nice guy, but I wouldn't say he was sociable."

"Ever meet anyone who didn't like him? I mean, he was a lazy and useless G.P., but everyone liked him, right?"

Peezle nodded, "As his Assistant I have to say, yes, he was likable."

"Now we have the Toob who is not likable but gets feces done. This galaxy is messed up." Narob told them.

The Gink sat by a window, looking out at the stars whizzing by. He glanced over his shoulder to see Blap standing there, buckled in. His whole lie was about to be out in the open, and he had no idea what to do. Joorg sat next to him, in the window seat.

"Where is Coleoptera?" the Gink knew the answer, but didn't want Joorg to know obviously.

"I don't know. He never showed up. After we go to your planet for this summit I will go there and see what happened."

"I'll go with you if you want."

"That'll be great, Guoz. Thank you."

"I'm sorry about your wife, you must be sad."

"I'm still in the shocked faze." Joorg said.

The pilots voice spoke over the intercom, "We are approaching Gink... which my read-out here says... it's not a planet."

"What do you mean it's not a planet?" Noam asked.

Phence looked at Thaw who sat next to him. Thaw looked back at Blaphaus.

Jaboney asked, unbuckling himself, "The pilot must be malfunctioning. I'll find out." He went into the pilots area, snd looked over the pilots shoulder at the display panel and console.

"I have no idea what this mumbo-jumbo is. Can you explain?"

"Yes, Governor. There's no life on Gink, and it's a moon."

"What the feces is a moon?"

"A big green rock. There's really no atmosphere on it, none of you will survive if you step out into it if I land." the pilot explained.

Jaboney said, "Well, don't frigging land."

He went back to the passenger section and went over to Blap who already was unbuckled.

Buterdau also stood up and said to Farvegas, "Now we are live. I'm Buterdau Kooper and I'm on Space False One, where we were supposed to go to Gink but just found out it's not really a planet, but a moon."

He motioned the hovering robot-cam to follow him as he walked to the back or the shuttle.

"So, Gink, wot's the story?" Blap looked down at the Gink.

Everyone was looking at him, all confused.

"It is a planet, it's my planet." the Gink said.

"Really? Professor, tell us wot you know about it." Blap waved his arm at Phence.

"It's not a planet, it's a moon." Phence told them.

Gillian asked, "What's a moon?"

The King stood up, "Why are we all going there then?"

"If it's your planet, when we land you'll be the first to step out on it?" Thaw asked Guoz.

He nodded, "Yes. I will. I'll prove it to you"

Blap told Jaboney, "Let's land this baby then."

Yurkel stood up, "Guoz, do you know anything the Order of Blattodea?"

The Gink stood up and pointed his green finger at Blap's face, "Why don't you tell the truth about you, Maximus?"

Southington groaned, "This is not good."

Zucaritas said to Buterdau, "Turn off your robot-cam."

"But..."

"Now." Zeb said firmly.

Buterdau said to the robot-cam, "Turn off, please."

The robot-cam did so, settling down. By now everyone was pretty much standing.

Blap said, "Jaboney, have the pilot land this thing."

Jaboney nodded, "If you say so.."

"Can someone tell me what's going on?" Losergram asked.

Rüppell said, "I'm as confused as you are, mate."

Narob shook his head, "This is all a joke, right?"

Guoz pointed at Blaphaus, "It was your idea, Toob, to have the summit on Gink."

Yerkal said to Peezle, "Noj, this is crazy. We are all going to die."

Joorg said, "I think we are landing on Gink, whatever it is."

Guoz grinned and Blap held a fist up.

"I'll knock that grin off."

"Can you explain what the hell is going on?" Zucaritas asked, "I'm not into fun and games."

Noam stood on a seat and pointed to the Gink. "If this is not your planet I'll punch you in your Gink ass nads."

The Gink's antennas stuck straight up straight.

The pilot asked over the intercom, "Are we landing or not?"

Blap looked out the portal window to see the moon was green with craters and a lot of dust, and no buildings, water, civilization, nothing. It was a green and rocky barren landscape, where nothing could live on.

"Yes. Land." Blap said, "Leetric, turn on the robot-cam, go live on GNN."

Buterdau said, "We are on live as we just found out that the planet Gink is actually moon."

Space False One came down to land on the moon. Everybody tried to look out the windows, to see there was nothing out there.

Blap said, "I declare that Gink is no longer part of the Cabinet. I don't know where you came from, or who you are, but you're not welcome anymore."

"I don't think..." Zucaritas said.

"He lied. This is not a planet, is it?"

"You have too much power." spat the Gink. "I can ruin your whole life here if I want, but I'm not going to. This whole galaxy will soon be invaded, there's going to be millions of deaths and there's nothing you or any of you can do about it." Guoz spat.

"What's got into you?" Southington asked.

"You don't know what you're dealing with, any of you. I am just the beginning."

Narob glared at Guoz wanting him to shut up.

"Yeah, yeah, yeah... it's time you got off this shuttle, Gink." Blap pointed to the doorway.

"If the door opens, you will all die." the Gink said, "But I'll be glad to open the door."

He ran over to the door to open it, but Ten grabbed him by the throat and started to squeeze. The Gink gasped, trying to pry Ten off him, but Ten just squeezed tighter.

"Ten! What are you doing?!" Peezle cried out.

"Stopping all of you from dying."

"You can let him go." Dawber said, "I think you killed Guoz."

Ten turned his head to look at the Gink who was no longer struggling, but was limp in Ten's grip. Ten let go of the Gink who fell against the door, and started to laugh. He turned to them all and grinned an evil grin, which made him look ridiculous with his big round eyes.

"You thought you could stop me, robot? Haha."

The King, who was nearest to him grabbed him from behind quickly and broke his neck with a loud crack. The Gink collapsed to the floor, eyes still open because he had no eyelids. Everyone looked surprised.

"You killed him, my King." Lady Gerda said.

The King kicked the Gink in the side, with his sandaled foot just to make sure, but Guoz the Gink Governor did not move. Blap went over to him, with Phence at his side. Phence knelt down to examine him.

"He's dead, you broke his neck, your majesty." he said looking up at the King.

"There's thousands more of him out there." Yerkal told them.

"Sure." Blap said, turning to everybody. "I'm so sorry you all had to witness this, but obviously I did us all a favor." he turned to Buterdau, "Bet your ratings and my polls will go through the roof now."

Buterdau said, "No one saw this, Galactic President, we weren't holo-recording."

"The galaxy did not have to see this." Southington said, "Thank you, Buterdau."

"Ha! You lot sure know how to put on a show." smiled Losergram.

"This wasn't a show I don't think." Bodie told him.

"Of course it was, it was the best in show."

"We still don't know where the Gink came from." Zeb said.

"Not this galaxy, that's for sure." Phence said standing.

Jaboney asked, "What now?"

"Are we still having a summit?" Haathee asked.

"Look out the window, there's a summit. A big green dirt pile of one." Blap said. "Jaboney, tell your pilot to take us back to Launderington. You lot can all go home. Governors, tomorrow we are going to have a meeting." he turned to Joorg, "And we are going to figure out wot your planet is up to next."

They all took their seats, Joorg put his purple suit jacket over the dead Gink and Space False One lifted up from the moon.

Ninety minutes later, give or take a few minutes, Space False One was back in the spaceport on Launderington. Blap stood at the bottom of the ramp, as Peezle and Yerkal walked down it.

"Tomorrow morning, Peezle, we are having a meeting." Blap told him.

Peezle nodded, "Of course."

Yerkal grabbed Blap's skinny arm and said, "Galactic President, what are you going to do? Do you think we're going to be invaded?"

"First of, let go of my arm before you snap it off." Blap told him.

"Sorry." Yerkal let go of him.

"I'm not worried about an invasion yet." Blap said, "We have other feces to take care of first. I have a dead Governor on my shuttle."

Yerkal nodded and Peezle led him away. The King and Lady Gerda walked down the ramp next and stopped at Blaphaus.

"You know as King I can't be arrested for the Gink's murder..."

"It is wot it is, no one is going to be arrested."

The King said, "Well, I'm glad I'm not G.P., your life is too adventurous, my friend. I'm sure I'll be seeing you." he strolled off.

Lady Gerda whispered to Blap, "I don't know what's happening to this galaxy, but we support you, no matter what anybody says."

Blap said, "If you say so."

Planet Mayor Losergram and Bodie went down the ramp next.

"Good show, old boy." Losergram smiled.

Bodie said, "I'll see you in the morning."

Farvegas was next, "You need to start gambling. Come to Farvegas, I'll give you 1,000 dosh credits."

"Wotever."

Phence and Thaw were next, "Galactic President, if what Guoz said was true..."

"Leetric, I'm not worried about him. Or that."

Thaw led Phence away, "We need a historian. Do you know anyone?"

"Not that I can think of. But this proves there's other galaxies out there."

Zalez and Ten approached Blap.

"Good job, robot."

Zalez said, "I don't know what you're up to, Blaphaus, but I'm so glad I'm keeping my family away from you."

"Good. I don't need them anyway. I don't have to tell you that you're not to mention any of this to your uptight wife."

"I won't. It's just another one of your secrets I'll keep to myself." Zalez stormed off.

Narob marched down the ramp and said to Blap, "You are doing a good job, Toob, better than my father ever did. Don't let us down."

Blap watched the teenager marched off, catching up to Zalez.

"I have something to do in a few days, Mr. Belhopsa, but I'd like to see the Dook Energy space station sometime."

Zalez nodded, "I'd love to show it to you."

Blap watched as the other Governors walked down the ramp.

"So, what do we do with the dead Gink?" asked Noam.

Buterdau and the robot-cam joined them.

"I take it you'll do a press statement."

Southington said, "We'll let you know, Buterdau. In the meantime if you can keep this all hush hush, we'll appreciate it."

Buterdau nodded, "Of course."

He walked away with the robot-cam flying behind him.

Sugden said, "We'll keep the Gink's body on Xenartha if you want."

Blap said, "Keep him there for as long as you can. We might need it sometime."

Inside the shuttle the Gink still laid by the door, eyes wide open, with a smirk on his face.

Hours later, on Xenartha, the Gink laid in the black coffin, as he was wheeled into a room by the armed Vermilin, a species which had an elongated snout, and a tube shaped mouth, and short brown fur. He tapped the coffin twice, and from inside it there was three taps. The Vermilin nodded, smiled, and walked out the room, closing the door behind him.

He went down the hallway, and through a door that went outside.

An Illiger approached him and said, "Depatie, I thought you were supposed to guard the roo..."

Depatie the Vermilian blasted down the Illiger. He went to the street where the Ultra ride was waiting for him. A short, furry fat cheeked being with small black eyes stepped out the vehicle and opened the back door.

The Geomy said, "Hello, are you Depatie?"

"Yes." he replied before he blasted the Geomy down. He got into the vehicle behind the wheel, and drove off not realizing the Illiger he thought he killed was still alive.

On Launderingtom, Zalez and Ten walked into the Belhopsa house, where Mal sat on the couch, with the children.

"Father! You're home!" they cried with joy, running towards him, giving him a hug. Mal stood and saw he wasn't that happy looking.

"You look good in a suit and tie." she smiled.

He smiled, "Thank you."

"How was the big summit?" Nate said, "GNN's coverage was terrible."

Zalez said, "I'm glad. You didn't miss much, Nate."

Ten said, "Except for..."

"Except Blaphaus says hello." Zalez lied, cutting Ten off.

"I was going to say that." Ten remarked.

Mal said, "Children, time to go to bed. You have school tomorrow."

"Okay, mother." Romana said, going to the stairs. "Are you going to be here tomorrow, father?"

Zalez nodded, "Yes, I'll take you to school and pick you up."

"Yay!" smiled Nate. "Goodnight."

Nate hugged and kissed his kids on the top of their heads and they ran off up the stairs.

"Zalez, are you sure everything is okay?" Mal asked.

Zalez shook his head, "No, this whole galaxy is a mess. I wish I could take you and the kids and go off to another galaxy."

"And bring me too." Ten remarked.

"Sure, and you as well, Ten."

Mal chuckled, "You don't think there's other galaxies out there, do you?"

Zalez rubbed his forehead, "I have no idea what to think."

The gray haired man walked into a bar wearing a black jacket, purple shirt and black jeans. He sat at the bar where a woman with short blonde hair sat, three stools away. The robot bartender, with eight arms slid over to the man.

"Welcome to Hurry Canes, what can I get you?"

"I'll have a lurie... no ice."

Moments later one of the robots arms put a glass of lurie in front of the man. He drank the whole thing down in one go.

"Thirsty?" the woman asked him.

He turned to her and scoffed, "I don't think it's any of your bloody business."

"Bloody business? Hm. You don't sound like you're from Ceilingida." she said.

"Maybe I'm not."

"So, just passing through?"

"Lady, I'm just here to get a bloody drink, not to be questioned."

She nodded, "I get that. I'm sorry." she held out her hand, "Let's start again. Hello, sir, I'm Fami, next drink is on me."

"In that case... robot-bartender, there's too much air in this glass. Another lurie, please."

Seconds later he had a fresh glass in front of him, which he drank pretty quick again.

"So, you're not going to say your name?"

"Nope." he said.

"Fine. It's a free galaxy. Are you into politics?"

"I thought we were done with questions."

"Sorry. I'm just making conversation."

"I know. It's bloody annoying."

"You say that word a lot, sir..."

"Wot word?"

"You know... 'bloody.' I only know one other being that says that... do you know who?"

He shook his head, "Nope. And I don't care."

"The G.P., Blaphaus Maximus. Do you know who he is?"

Blap nodded, "Of course. That big fat ugly Toob."

She snickered, "That's one way to describe him. What do you think of him?"

"I think I just made it clear..."

"Political wise, sir. I think he's great. Better than the previous G.P., Traf. He was useless."

The man scoffed, "That's true. But since the last few weeks Blaphaus was G.P. there's been blasterings... an ex-Governor and his wife were even murdered."

"By another Governor's wife." Fami nodded, "Drama, right? The galaxy is a lot more exciting now than it was before."

"If innocent lives being wasted is exciting, then sure, lady. Robot-bartender, another lurie."

The robot gave him his third glass and he drank it down.

"Do you live around here?" Fami asked.

"That's my business. If you're think we are going to leave here together..."

"I was only asking because you're drinking and I..."

"Can take care of myself."

She nodded, "Very well. I'll let you be."

"Good." he said, "Robot-bartender, this woman.. what did you say your name was?"

"Fami..."

"Fami... I heard that name before. Fami here is paying for my drinks. I seemed to left my dosh at home."

"Of course, I'll pay..."

The man got off his stool and went to the door.

"Have a good night." she called out to him.

He nodded, not looking back, and just waved.

"Mr. Maximus..." she muttered under her breath, discreetly grabbing one of the glasses he drank from.

## CHAPTER 10

The next day, Blap went into the House conference room, where all the Governor's sat, except Guoz, for obvious reasons. No one sat in his chair at the table, or moved it. It was right there empty between Pinya's and Jaboney's.

"Why is that chair still there?" Blap asked, "He's not being replaced, so move it."

"Are we going to talk about the Pachyderm in the room?" Noam asked.

"Excuse me?" Haathee asked.

"No offense, it's a saying we have on Homunculus. It means..."

"I think we all know wot it means, shorty." Blap said.

"Did you know that Gink's planet was barren?" Southington asked.

"It's not a planet, it's a moon. And no, not until that Professor bloke told me. I wondered why we haven't seen any Gink's before, with all the planets we've been too. I thought maybe he was a human pretending to be a different species as well."

"So, you think he was from a different galaxy like you?" Kakertak asked.

"Yes, but here's the kicker... he's not from my galaxy."

"How can you be sure?" Zeb asked.

"Because there's only a handful of planets in my galaxy, and with the look of him he'd stick out."

Thaw said, "Professor Phence told me of other galaxies and now we have two different proofs."

Peezle added, "Could the Order of Blattodea be from this other galaxy? Yerkal said that the Cakerlak assassin mentioned one of the Governors being a member of the Order..."

"Why didn't we know this?" Kakertak asked.

"Guess he was right, if it's true." Dawber said.

Joorg leaned forward, "It's taken care of now anyway. The Gink is dead and..."

"He was a Governor for a long time, a member of the Cabinet even before me." Southington said, "Even before most of you. It makes me ill that he wasn't really from a planet in this galaxy, and was lying all this time. He knows what you're really are, Blaphaus, if he was some sort of spy he could've told whoever."

"I'm not worried about that." Blaphaus said.

Just then a holo-call of Brigadier Harkouk appeared in the middle of the table, facing Sugden.

"Governor Sugden, I hope I'm not interrupting anything but there's been another blastering on Xenartha, at one of our military bases."

"By whom?" Sugden asked.

"A Vermilian named Depatie. He was a guard here on the base. He stole an Ultra vehicle, killed the driver and drove off killing 22 beings. We are on the search for the vehicle and Depatie now, and the GBI are here helping."

"How do you know all this?" Zeb asked.

"He blasted an Illiger soldier, who survived and the watched him take the Ultra vehicle. Twenty-three beings were killed altogether."

"Has GNN been contacted?" Southington asked.

"No, not as far as I know." the 12 inch holo-call replied.

"Good." Blaphaus said, "I don't want them to know."

"They'll find out sooner or later." Zucaritas remarked.

"Has this Vermilin mentioned the Order of Blattodea?" Noam asked.

"Do not know." the Brigadier replied.

"Wot weapon did he use?" Blap asked.

"His own." the Brigadier replied, "There's one other thing I have to mention. Depatie's job was to guard the room where Gink's coffin was held."

"And?" Dawber asked.

"Just thought you should know."

Sugden said, "I'll head to Xenartha right away, before GNN gets there." He stood up and said, "I'll go by myself. I'll let you know if I need you there, Blaphaus."

"Wotever." Blaphaus said, "If you lot find this Vermilin ask him he's part of this Order."

Sugden nodded and left the room and the holo-call ended.

Rüppell said, "This is kind of getting out of hand, don't you think?"

Gillian said, "It's hard to trust anyone. Not that I don't trust any of you."

"I don't trust anyone." Blaphaus said, "Which brings me to you, Cyrakuse." he pointed to Joorg.

Joorg look startled, "Me? Why me? I didn't do anything..."

"No, but your wife did, and I'm not talking about when she shoved me into a swimming pool at the Pachyderm mansion..."

"Can we not talk about that?" Haathee asked.

"Your wife got herself killed because she killed a bunch of beings on Cyrakuse. We still don't know why, but she used Cakerlak weapons. Which brings us to a few questions... where and how did she get the weapons? How come you didn't know, Joorg, and more importantly where was the Planet Mayor when we had the summit? He never showed, and you never heard from him."

Joorg shook his head, "I don't know why. I tried to contact him."

"I don't trust the Cakerlak, and you being their Governor makes me trust you even less than I trust anyone."

Zucaritas said, "Governor Joorg is innocent..."

"Not yet he isn't. He's going to Cakerlak and I'm going with him." Blap pointed out.

"Do you think that's safe?" Southington asked.

"No, but we don't have a choice. I want to ask him directly about this feces Order. I'm going to get to the bottom of it, as none of you have yet."

Joorg nodded, "I'll go of course."

Blaphaus said, "That's good, Cyrakuse, because you don't really have a choice."

"Hello, I'm Buterdau Kooper, we just got word that a number of beings have been blasted killed on Xenartha outside an Illiger military base. It's believed to be done by a Vermilian guard. We do know an Ultra driver was killed and his vehicle stolen by the blasterer. I have Vistrat Calasteel, head of Ultra on Ceilingida, who used to be Galactic Blaphaus' boss coming up in a little bit."

Fami stepped through the double doors, into the dark office where the shortish being sat being his desk. She sat in front of it and watched him lean forward.

"You have good news for me I take it, my dear?" he asked.

"I do, sir. I know Maximus is definitely not a Toob."

"Really? How do you know this for sure?"

"I met him at a pub on Ceilingida. He was..."

"Yes?"

"Human. I think."

"Did you get close to the Belhopsa family?" he asked.

"No, I haven't had the chance, but look what I got..."

She pulled from the inside of her jacket pocket the glass wrapped up in a napkin. She unwrapped it and held the glass up.

"An empty glass?" he asked.

"Not just *any* empty glass, but one Blaphaus drank from."

"I don't see the relevance..." he said.

"We could do some kind of test on it and it might be able to tell us who he really is."

He looked at her, not saying a word, and glanced down at the glass.

"Doctor, you can do that, am I right?"

Doctor Sahii leaned forward, into the light so she could see him and nodded.

"Yes, my dear, I'm sure I can. Good work."
She nodded, smiling and relieved.

A little while later on Xenartha, Brigadier Harkouk led Sugden down the hallway to the door that was to the room the coffin was in. He unlocked it and they both went inside.
"We need a doctor or someone with some kind of medical experience to check on Guoz's body." Sugden commented.
Harkouk nodded, "I'll find one."
Sugden nodded, "Well, I guess I have to face the press about the blasterings in the meantime."

On Space Force One, Blaphaus took off his Toob suit and sat in a seat, opposite side of the cabin that Joorg sat.
"You don't want to sit next to me?"
"Uhhhhh... no. There's only the two of us, Cyrakuse, so why sit next to each other? Besides, you smell."
"Why did you take off the Toob suit?"
"Three reasons. One: I can bloody sit, and two: it's a flight across the whole galaxy and I didn't feel like standing if I didn't have to..."
"That's only two reasons, Galactic President."
"Oh, I also have a headache from downing three lurie in a matter of minutes."
"You drank? Where?"
"At this pub on Ceilingida... near where I live."
"In 'costume'?"
"No, idiot, I went as this..." he motioned to his human body.
"Oh, that's brave."
"Rubbish. There was only one woman there, and the robot-bartender. It was all right."
"If you say so, Blaphaus."
Blap nodded.
"You don't like me, do you?" Joorg asked.
"Cyrakuse, I don't like a lot of beings."
"Why is that?"
"Wot? Is this turning into some kind of therapy session?"
"No, it's just none of us really know anything about you, and that scares us."
"Yet, I was chosen for this gig. And I still haven't been paid."
"Well, you need to let us in."
"You're lucky you know I'm really human."

"Well, we didn't know anything about the Gink and look how he turned out to be, Blaphaus."

"Ha! You were married to an assassin, you striped idiot. So you can talk. And she was sitting on the Pachyderm's lap doing Creator knows what to him."

"Do you have a loved one you left back home?" Joorg asked, "On your planet you left?"

"I'm not telling you anything about my personal life. Ever."

Joorg just nodded, staring at the human version of Blaphaus.

"Hello, I'm Buterdau Kooper, joined here with Vistrat Calasteel, owner of Ultra on Ceilingida."

Calasteel sat next to Buterdau at the desk in the studio. He had full facial hair now, looking like the Chordattian that he was.

"Glad to be here, Buterdau."

"So, Mr. Calasteel, the G.P. used to be a driver for Ultra, he was one of your employees, how was he then?"

"The same he is now. Arrogant, rude, blunt, but for some reason he often received five stars."

"Really? And why do you think that was?"

"Probably because he didn't really chat, like he was supposed to, and he was never late."

"Do you think that's why when he picked up the Governor Tostone he got where he is today?"

"Well..." thought Calasteel, "He became very sought after. I think if he wasn't a Toob it would be a whole different story."

"Is that why you hired Blaphaus Maximus, sir? Because he was a Tooberosum."

"No, I offered him the job when he applied because he had a vehicle and I needed another driver."

"You fired him though, right?"

"Yeah, because he was running his mouth."

"Do you regret that?" Buterdau asked.

"Yes. And no. I have a sign on my building that says the Galactic President worked there. You know, beings still ask for him as their driver..."

"Hang on, Mr. Calasteel, Governor Sugden is going to do a speech on Xenartha about the latest blasterings."

Sugden stood before the GNN robot-cam outside the main military base building on Xenartha.

"On behalf of all the Governors in the House, and the Galactic President our hearts go out to the families of the victims. We don't know who is behind this, if all the blasterings are related but we will get to the bottom of it. The Xenartha Army and the GBI are working side by side. Thank you."

Calasteel turned to Buterdau and scoffed, "That was the lamest speech ever. Where is the Toob? Shouldn't he have been there?"
"I'm sure there's a good reason, Mr. Calasteel. Thanks for your time."


Space False One landed on the side of the cliff like before. Joorg stood as Blaphaus pulled on his purple jacket over the Toob suit. Blap turned to see Joorg staring at him.
"Wot are you looking at?"
"Uh... nothing." Joorg replied.
The ramp descended and they went down it to be met by Laterille just like before, Blap now looking like a Toob again.
"Oh, Governor Joorg, what a big surprise! And Galactic President Maximus... this is a real surprise. I hope you are having a wonderful day..."
"Blah blah blah... where is the Planet Mayor?" demanded Blaphaus.
"Coleoptera is not here. No one has seen him."
"He didn't go to the summit." told Joorg, "Where do you think he went?"
"I don't know." Laterille said.
"Terrific." Blaphaus complained, "This trip was for nothing."
Another Cakerkak approached them from within the mountain and told them, "The Great Weta requests your company."
"Who is the Great Weta, Cyrakuse?" Blap asked.
Joorg shrugged, "I have no idea."
"Then we'll find out together wot's so great."
Laterille whispered to the other Cakerlak, "Are you sure this is the right thing to do?"
The taller Cakerlak nodded, "Trust me."
He led them off to the castle.
"Still smells as bad as it did before." Blap remarked.
Inside the castle, they walked into the chamber where the taller and bigger Great Weta was.
"I thought I was big and ugly." Blaphaus muttered.
"The great Tooberosum Galactic President at last." the Great Weta remarked, "You are a legend, do you know that?"
"Wotever. Wot are you? Some kind of King? Ruler?"
"I am neither, Blaphaus Maximus, I'm an old relic from the days of the war between your kind and the Cakerlak."
"But you call yourself 'great.' Ego maybe?"

"I was around before there was a Galactic President, before the Governors, before the House, before any of it."

"And you're still alive?" Blap asked. "Joorg, how come you didn't know about this Great Weta?"

Joorg bowed for some reason before Weta.

"I am Governor Joorg, governor of this planet."

The Great Weta laughed, "Only by name, Cyrakuse. You do not govern us. We are not part of the House."

"Wot are you talking about?" Blap asked.

"You didn't tell your Toob leader how you've become Governor? Tsk, tsk."

"No, but I am Governor..."

"You kept telling yourself that." the Great Weta said. "So, when I was told your shuttle was coming here I didn't believe it. Why are you here again, Toob? Planning an invasion of your kind?"

Blap said, "I had a summit, the Planet Mayor was supposed to be there but never showed up. I suppose you're going to say there is no Planet Mayor..."

"There was. Coleoptera. Unfortunately he is missing."

"Really?" Blaphaus asked, "Lost in the cliffs maybe?"

"I think he's dead." the Great Weta replied.

"Terrific. So, you've been around a long time, Cakerlak. Do you know anything about the Order of Blattodea?"

"Ooohhh... I was wondering when you were going to bring that up, Toob. Didn't your ancestors ever teach you that? Or are the Toobs ashamed?"

"I have no bloody idea wot you're talking about. But I believe the Gink Governor was a member and the Cakerlak that tried to assassinate me was a member. So, wot do you know about it?"

"You need to do some research, Toob, know what you're getting into. If I were you I'd resign from your Galactic President position before anybody else ends up dead."

"Really? That a threat?"

"It's a promise."

Joorg got scared and stood behind Blaphaus.

"Coleoptera said that Traf, the previous G.P. funded this feces hole of a planet, and I agreed it'll continue as it was now part of the House. But you're telling me the Cyrakuse here in his fancy purple suit is not Governor, and you're not part of the House. I'm withdrawing funding. Your weapons, or this planet's weapons have caused too much damage, so that will end as well."

"Do you know why we have weapons, Toob?" the Great Weta asked. "To keep the Toob at bay."

"Considering I'm the only one that's been seen in a long time, and I'm here facing you, it's not doing very good."

"Just you right now, Blaphaus, but once your other species come out of hiding to invade the galaxy, everyone will be begging us for help."

"My kind are not hiding and will not invade the galaxy..."

"Really? Where are they then if they're not hiding? Do you know a secret about the weapons we have on this planet? The weapons that were used in the blasterings, that killed all those innocent people? The weapon your wife used, Joorg... those weapons are not built by Cakerlak, they are Toob weapons. Once word gets out that the Toobs funded and are behind this, how do you think the galaxy and your Governors will feel? They probably don't trust you as it is."

"The Toob don't have weapons..."

"And you know that how? Traf knew about it, too bad you can't ask him about it, he's dead. Traf approves lethal weapon sales to us Cyrakuse, from the Toobs."

"Traf never met a Toob... he hardly met me."

"You think you are so special. You should ask Tostone about it... oh wait, he's dead too. What a shame."

Blaphaus said, "So, you sit on your throne, thinking you are controlling everything?"

"That's the way, Toob. The Cakerlak are not the enemy. You thought the Gink was the enemy. You should look at your circle a little more closely, once word gets out the Toob are a threat you're not going to be liked very much. Like I said, step down from the role."

"Never. You don't know me very well, Weta, but I'm not a quitter. I will find out what this Order is about, and why these blasterings are happening. You're cut off. No more funding, no more weapons. Nothing."

"Threat all you want, Toob, this galaxy will be torn apart, and you will be the one to blame. I would seriously talk to the human Yerkal though. He knows about the Order, he visited the Cakerlak who attempted to kill you in jail, and came here with him."

Blap walked to the chamber entrance.

"Have a nice life, Cakerkak."

Joorg followed him quickly, not believing what he just witnessed.

"You're going to let him go just like that?" the Cakerkak asked the Great Weta.

"Of course I am. It's no good to kill him here, when no one will know what happened. Besides, I want to see his face when the invasion happens. Get in touch with Guoz, he and I need to chat."

In the shuttle, Joorg slumped in a seat, running his head.

"Can you tell me what just happened?"

"Yeah." Blap said, "You are no longer Governor, this planet is no longer part of the House. The Great Weta, wotever he is thinks he can bully me, and do wot he wants. Wrong."

"Please buckle in." the pilot said over the intercom,"We'll be taking off in 20 seconds."

"If I'm no longer Governor what do I do?"

"Have no idea." Blap said, "Yet."

"So, what now?"

"Now I have a chat with Yerkal."

***CHAPTER 11***

Blaphaus stepped out the limousine-vehicle outside the House.

Rubyspears smiled at him, "Have a good day."

Blap didn't reply, just made his way to the lift on the left side of the steps, the lift that was put there for him. He rounded the corner to see a tall, dark haired man in a black suit leaning on it, wearing dark sun-spectacles.

"Well, you are as ugly that they said." he said, taking his sun-spectacles off.

"Yeah, but I'm gorgeous inside." Blap smirked. "You're in my way."

"That's your lift?" the man asked, looking it over.

"Yup."

"Why don't you just take the steps?"

"Does it look like I can go up steps?" Blap asked annoyed.

"You know you could if you reeeeaaaalllly wanted, Galactic President."

"Sure." he scooted the man aside and stepped into the lift.

"You know, you shouldn't brush me off like that, I could be your best friend and your best ally."

"And I could disappear and you lot won't have a G.P. But that's not going to happen. Maybe."

He pressed a red button and the lift went up. The man watched him go up.

"Well, that's very impressive." he said sarcastically. "My name is Allard Felipe! Look me up!"

Blap put up his middle finger, looking down at the man he wanted to punch in the face.

Blap walked into the conference room where the Governors sat. He saw Joorg was siting at the table in his seat.

"Wot are you doing here?" he asked.

"He's supposed to be here. He's a Governor." Zucaritas replied.

"You didn't tell them?" Blap asked.

Joorg shook his head, "I thought you would and we'd work it out."

"What is he talking about?" Zeb asked.

"So, turns out that the Cakerlak P.M. is missing, which I reckon he's dead. There's this pretty big Cakerlak that lives there and seems to be an arsehole and running everything."

"Why shouldn't Joorg be here?" Zucaritas asked again.

"Because this Cakerlak who calls himself the Great Weta seems to be in charge and said Joorg is not Governor and that nasty planet is not part of the Cabinet anymore." Blap brushed his hands together. "I'm like good. I'm done with that lot. I wish there was a huge machine we could point at that planet and blow it up. That'll teach them."

"Stop! You can't say stuff like that." Southington said seriously.

"Why not? It's just you lot here."

"Because you can't." Southington said.

"It's not like he really wants to blow the planet up." Kakertak said.

"Yes I do." Blap said.

"Well, you can't." Zeb told him.

"Did you ask about the Order of Blattodea?" Thaw asked.

"Yes. He never said he was a part of it but never denied it either."

"So, back to Joorg." Zucaritas said. "Joorg, what are you going to do now you're not Governor?"

"I don't know. Maybe I can be a security advisor..."

"Maybe you can mourn your wife." Blap said, "But then again she was a killer."

Southington said, "Joorg, we'd love you to be a security advisor..."

"No we don't." Blaphaus remarked.

"Friend, I'm sorry you're not Governor anymore." Haathee said.

"This is frigging ridiculous." Jaboney said, "The Gink planet wasn't a planet and now the Cakerlak have pulled out. We're dropping planets quicker than we gained them."

"We can't tell the press. Not yet anyway." Southington said, "We need to work on your poll ratings, Blaphaus. If the public finds out we lost two planets..."

"More bloody secrets then." Blaphaus said, "By the way, the Weta being said that the weapons the Cakerlak have are Toob weapons."

"Can that be true?" Thaw asked.

"How am I expect to know? I know nothing about the Toob, except they were ugly and had no legs." Blaphaus replied.

"Doesn't matter where the weapons came from, we need to make sure there's no more killings. Two of the blasterers are still out there." Sugden said.

"Silver face, how many ships does your Army have?"

"Ships? We don't have any ships."

"What's a ship?" Eastora asked.

"Space ship. Shuttle. Craft. Flying vehicle." Blap waved his arms. "You have nothing?"

"We have ground vehicles and a few shuttles."

"So, if there was an invasion there's nothing to protect the space ways?" Blap asked.

They all shook their heads, muttering.

Peezle asked, "Did your galaxy have a space fleet?"

"Yes. All the planets did. So, you lot hardly have any protection. Nothing to protect the planets?"

"The planets don't need protecting." Dawber said, "The beings on the planets are what needs protecting."

"How did you lot manage all these years?" Blap asked, "The Cyrakuse and Canis fought a war, wot did you two use?"

Zucaritas said, "That was way before our time but I believe the fighting was on both planets."

"That's true. Shuttles don't have weapons. The fighting wasn't with weapons, it was hand to hand combat."

"This is the worst galaxy." Blap groaned.

"We need something in between the planets to keep watch..."

"Watch for what?" Noam asked.

"The Cakerlak, invasion..."

"I don't think there's going to be an invasion to this galaxy." Gillian said, "It'll be hard to come here unnoticed."

"Really? Picture the galaxy in your heads..."

"We can't." Zeb said, "There's a lot of planets and stuff."

Thaw replied, "I can. I saw a holo-map of it, Phence showed it to me."

"Good. Then you lot picture me standing here. I'm the galaxy... my head is where you thought Tooberosum was, my right side is where we are and Ceilingida, and those planets, under my feet would be some other planets and to my left is Phytnes, Mesas and Cakerlak just to name a few. So, how many sides can I be attacked?"

"Four." Bodie said, "Actually three as you're standing."

"Four is right." Blap said, "We'd be screwed if an invasion would arrive."

"Which side did you come from?" Peezle asked.

"Good question. The right side. This planet's side."

"So, what do you suggest we do?" Jaboney asked, "I don't think there's going to be an invasion."

"Really?" Blap asked, "Where the bloody hell are the Gink, then? You know at least one of them 'invaded' and I'm here from another galaxy undetected when I arrived. We need some type of space Army."

"How are we going to keep anything like that in space?" Zeb asked, "Between the planets?"

"Yeah, and we have the space stations." Rüppell said.

"You're a genius." Blap said, "Three stations... the gambling one, the church one and Dook Energy. Those three we will use."

"I can tell you Farvegas is not going to like that." Haathee said.

"Or the church." Dawber said.

"Well, guess wot? We're the Cabinet, they have no choice. They will be the space army bases, keeping an eye out for possible invasions."

"And you're going to convince them how?" Zucaritas asked.

"You will go to each one and tell them. As far as the public will know you're visiting them." Southington smiled, "That should be good PR."

"We already have a good relationship with Zalez and Narob Traf." Thaw said.

"Good. I'll go to Dook Energy first." Blap told them, "Peezle, you're coming with me."

Peezle nodded, "If you say so."

"I do." Blaphaus said, "I definitely do."

On Ceilingda, Fami sat at the restaurant table waiting for Doctor Sahii to arrive with the news. The gray faced little Rodentia with white hair and gray suit walked into the room and sat at the table facing her. He was glad to see there was a glass of red mone waiting for him. He picked up the glass and sipped from it.

"Well, Doctor?" Fami asked. "Did you find out anything?"

"I sure did, my dear. The DNA I took from the glass that you gave me is human. Pure 100% human."

"Ha! I knew it! Why do you think he's disguising himself as a Tooberosum of all species?"

"Ms. Tapperdau, I don't know. But that's the results."

"Most beings won't even know what DNA means, Doctor."

"We have to tell them another way." Sahii said, "But this is the first step to prove that Blaphaus Maximus is not really Tooberosum... but human." he smiled.

"So, what now?"

He smiled at her and sipped some more mone.

At the Belhopsa house, once again Fami Tapperdau buzzed the door buzzer and stood waiting. The door opened to reveal Ten standing there.

"Hello, Ms. Tapperdau. How are you today?"

"You remember my name?" she asked.

"Yes, ma'am, I'm a robot and I remember names. You are here looking for the Belhopsa's."

"Yes, I want any of them. Even the children. Are any of them home?"

"No, Ms. Tapperdau. No one is here but me."

"Do you know when they will be back? It's important I talk to them."

"I cannot tell you that, Ms. Tapperdau. I am sorry."

Fami sighed and nodded, "I understand. I'll be back."

Ten nodded, "I will see you again then."

Before Fami could do what she wanted to do, which was to shut the robot down, Ten closed the door on her. Fami swore under her breath. She turned to leave when a blue car parked in front of the house. Mal stepped outside of it and saw Fami who casually waved at her.

"Mrs. Belhopsa?"

"Yes, that's me. Can I help you?"

"Yes, you can. My name is Fami Tupperdau and I'm here to help you."

"Help me? Help me how?" Mal frowned.

"To get rid of the Galactic President for good." smiled Fami.


Rubyspears drove the limousine-vehicle with Blap standing in the back of it and Peezle sat next to him.

"We're going to the Traf house?" Peezle asked.

"No. First we are going to visit your husband." Blaphaus explained.

"Yerkal? Why is that?"

"Because the Cakerlak consider him on their side, and I tend to believe them."

"What? How? Why?" Peezle asked surprised.

Rubyspears couldn't believe what he was listening to.

"First of he went missing, and didn't tell you wot was going on."

"After he learnt of the Order by that one Cakerlak..."

"Yup. Then wot did he do? Go to Cakerlak with that same assassin who wanted to kill me. I'm thinking he knows more about the Order than wot he's saying."

Peezle said, "He thought he was doing the right thing trying to get answers."

"Really? Was he doing the right thing when he killed all those beings on Phytnes?"

"Blaphaus! You can't possibly think that was Yerkal doing that."

"Can't I? Why not?"

"Blaphaus, he was on Launderington at the House when that first blastering happened."

"That means nothing. He could still be behind it. Face it, Yerkal might not be so innocent."

Peezle just shook his head and looked outside the window.

***************************************************************************************

Inside the Belhopsa house, Yami sat on the couch drinking a glass of dark fizzy drink. Mal sat in the love seat across from her. Ten stood quiet in the corner, listening to the women talk very closely.

"Thank you for the fizzy, Mrs. Belhopsa..."

"Call me Mal. So, you were saying you can get rid of the Galactic President? Is that a good thing?"

"Well, since New Galaxy Day there's been a number of blasterings, so many beings have been killed, his ratings are lower than any G.P. in the past."

"I understand, but why are you here telling *me*?"

"The being I work for has been watching the Toob. We know he's close to your family, even making your young son Governor..."

"Just real briefly..."

"But he still did, Mal. Your husband Zalez is also close to the G.P. I need to know everything you can tell me about him."

"Like what?"

"Like you had him over for dinner, right?"

"Yeah, before he was G.P."

"What did he eat, Mal?"

"Ummm... he didn't."

"You had him over for dinner and he didn't eat? Didn't you think that was odd?"

Mal shrugged, "I thought maybe he didn't like the food I served but was polite to say anything."

"Did you ever think it's weird he was a Toob, when no one has seen that species in a long time?"

"No, it never occurred to me. But I will say I don't want him around my family, at least my children and myself."

"Why is that?"

"Because political life and this galaxy is dangerous all of a sudden."

"Did Zalez ever express his feelings about Blaphaus?"

Mal nodded, "Yes, but he has to 'work' with him unfortunately."

"Is Zalez on his Dook Energy space station?"

Mal nodded, "Yes, I believe so."

"And your children are at school?"

Mal nodded, "Yes, they are."

"I'd like to talk to your son Nate today if that's okay."

Mal nodded, "I guess so."

Fami finished her fizzy, put the glass on the table and stood up.

"Terrific. Let's go then."

Mal frowned, "Go? Go where?"

"To the school, so I can talk to Nate."

"Oh."

There was a knock on the door of the flat. Yerkal got off the couch and went to open it. When he did he saw the Cakerlak who did the blastering in the store on Xenartha standing there.

"Oh! Can I help you?" Yerkal asked stunned.

The Cakerlak pulled a weapon out from inside his jacket and pointed it at Yerkal's chest.

"Yup, human, you sure can."

Yerkal felt a lump in his throat.

Outside the flat Rubyspears parked the vehicle and Peezle and Blaphaus got out of it.

"Want me to wait here?" Rubyspears asked.

"Yes, please." Peezle nodded.

"I hope you don't have steps." Blap remarked.

"No, there's a lift." Peezle replied.

They went inside the building and over to the lift.

Yerkal sat on the couch as the Cakerlak stood over him.

"Look, I really don't know what you..."

Just then they heard keys unlock the door. The Cakerlak threw his weapon at Yerkal who caught it just as the door opened and Peezle and Blaphaus walked in.

"Yerkal!" gasped Peezle.

"It's not what this looks like." Yerkal said.

"It is exactly what you think." the Cakerlak said, walking to the door.

"Governor, Galactic President Toob. See you around." he smiled and left.

"Wot the bloody hell was that about?" Blap asked.

"Why are you holding a blaster?" Peezle asked.

Yerkal looked down at it in his hands and dropped it on the couch in shock.

Mal parked her vehicle at the school and the two women made their way to front office.

"Hello, Mrs. Belhopsa, you're here early to pick up your children." the receptionist said.

"Is Principal Garcey here?" Mal asked.

"Yes, he's in his office. I'll go get him."

She stood up and headed to the office.

"Can't we just go to the classroom?" Yami asked.

"Ms. Tapperdau, do you have children?"

"Well, no, I'm too busy."

"Well, there's certain things we have to do. I'm not just going to walk to the classroom."

Principal Garcey, the chubby human walked out from his office.

"Hello, Mrs. Belhopsa. It's been over a week, since New Galaxy Day. How have you been? I'm so glad that things have gotten back to normal for the children."

"Principal Garcey, this is Fami Tapperdau, she'd like to chat to Nate if possible."

"Sure." Garcey said, "Are you a reporter?"

Fami shook her head, "No, I'm just a friend."

Mal gave her a puzzled look.

A holo-call of Garcey appeared in the classroom next to Ms. Beezlee's desk.

"Sorry to interrupt the class, Nate, can you come to the office please?"

"Are you going to miss another school day?" Nog asked, sitting behind Nate.

"I don't think so." Nate stood and headed to the door.

Romana said, "Let me know if everything is okay, Nate."

He nodded, "Of course."

He left the classroom and Nog crossed his arms.

"Hmph! Nate is still the luckiest child I know!"

Mrs. Beezlee clapped her hands three times, "Focus, children, back to learning."

Nate walked into the office to see his mother standing next to a shorter woman with short blonde hair and spectacles, and Principal Garcey.

"Hello, mother. Is everything okay?"

"Yes, Nate. This is Ms. Fami Tapperdau, she would like to ask you a few questions."

He frowned, "Am I in trouble?"

Fami shook her head, "No, you're good. Can we talk in a private room?"

"Sure." Garcey nodded, "You can have my office."

Fami led Nate back there, and Garcey turned to Mal.

"Who is she really?"

Mal shook her head, "I have no idea."

Fami and Nate sat in the two chairs in front of Garcey's desk.

"So, who are you?" Nate asked, "Do you work for the Cabinet?"

Fami chuckled, "No, Nate. I'll tell you who I work for but you can't tell anybody."

Nate looked worried, "Not even my parents?"

"No, not your parents. No one. Can I trust you?"

Nate nodded, "Yes. I can keep a secret."

"I work with a being named…"

"Blattodea?" Nate asked almost excited.

"No. Who's that?" Fami asked.

"I don't know. Just something I heard about, ma'am. Sorry to interrupt."

"It's okay. I work for a very important being named Doctor Sahii. He's interested in learning about the Galactic President and the Tooberosum."

"And you need my help?" Nate asked.

"You were Governor for this planet for a short while, do you think the Cabinet knows a lot about G.P. Maximus?"

"I think they know some."

"What do you think of the Galactic President, Nate?"

"He seems to be okay. I met him when he was just a driver."

"What do you think about him being a Toob?"

"Well, I'm not sure. You see, when I first met him I knew he was a Tooberosum and myself and my sister Romana tried to research his race, but found out nothing. Maybe he's the last one."

"Nate, is you had to put lucre and bet on what he is, what would you think?"

Nate hesitated for a minute before he replied, "If I tell you you promise not to say anything to anybody. Not even the Doctor."

"I promise, Nate."

"I don't think he's really a Tooberosum, but I don't know what he is really."


Yerkal sat on the couch, running his fingers through his normally perfect hair.

"I'm telling you this is not what it seems like."

"Hmmm. Let me see... you are suspected to be working with the Cakerlak, a member of the bloody Order and now there's one of that nasty species in your flat, and you have a weapon. A weapon! This is good! That idiot left his weapon here!" Blap almost smiled.

"Why is that good, Blaphaus?" Peezle asked.

"Because it's one less they have and we can take it to some weapon expert to see if it's a Cakerlak weapon or a Toob weapon."

Yerkal looked up at his husband, "I swear I'm not working with them. I'm just trying to get answers... as a Solicitor."

Noj nodded, "I know. I believe you."

"I don't." Blap replied.

"You don't?" asked Yerkal.

"Guilty until proven innocent." Blaphaus remarked.

"Shouldn't that be the opposite?" Yerkal asked.

"No." Blap replied.

Just then a holo-call of Southington appeared over the desk across the living room.

"Yerkal, Noj, hello!" she waved.

Yerkal stood up as Peezle ran over to her.

"Southington, what's wrong?"

"GNN just reported that Yerkal is working with the Cakerlak. That's not good."

"I'm not working with them." moaned Yerkal.

"Well, you need to fix this. This is the last thing we need. If that damn Blaphaus finds out..."

Blap stepped forward in her view.

"Trust me, the 'damn Blaphaus' knows." Blap remarked. "It'll be taken care of."

"Keep me posted. I'll talk to Jaboney, his brother works for GNN and might have an idea."

"Good." Blap said.

"I thought you were going to Dook Energy." Southington said.

"We are." Peezle said. "Thank the Creator we came here first."

Back at the school, Fami and Nate walked out the office where Mal and Garcey waited.

"Thank you very much." Fami told them, "This young man is going to go far in the future. He was a big help."

"I'm glad." the Principal smiled, "Nate is the smartest child we have in the school."

"You can go back to class now." Mal told Nate, "I will see you later."

"Thanks, mother, thanks Ms. Fami. You're very nice."

"Thank you. Remember not to talk about we we discussed."

"I promise."

He walked off, heading down the hallway.

Fami said, "I can't thank you enough, Mrs. Belhopsa. I need to talk to your husband as well. So, please, when you see him let him know. I'll be in touch."

She walked off, heading outside.

"What is this all about if you don't mind me asking?" Garcey asked.

Mal shook her head, "I wish I knew. But if it's about Blaphaus it can't be good. I need to let Zalez know."

**************************************************************************

Nekkod and Zalez stood in the shuttle hangar on the Dook Energy space station as the blue Dook shuttle flew in and landed. A few moments later Narob Traf, wearing a black suit and tie walked down the ramp and over to them, shaking their hands.

"Welcome to Dook's space station." Zalez said. "I was surprised when you said you were coming today. I thought you had plans."

"I did, but someone else took care of it."

"I'm so sorry about your father." Nekkod said, "He was a good man."

"No he wasn't. He was a loser that did nothing for this galaxy." Narob replied.

"Oh." Nekkod didn't know what to say.

"Let me give you a tour." Zalez told Narob.

They walked out the hangar and down a corridor.

"Do you know why Dook Energy is named that?" Zalez asked.

"Yes. It was founded by two brothers... Bigrocin and Oldpound Dook. My dad purchased the company from them before he was G.P."

"Correct. It was Bigrocin that hired me."

"Well, those two were losers." Narob said seriously. "I'm changing the name from Dook Energy to Narob Energy."

"I don't think you can just change the name, Narob."

"I can do what I want."

Zalez decided to change the subject, "So, Dook gives power and energy and lights to all the planets in this galaxy..."

"All but Cakerlak and Old Eboracum, and we know not Gink. And Tooberosum if I'm right."

"Cakerlak doesn't have any electricity and Old Eberocum have their own."

"Not for long." Narob said, "I want to take over the company that is on Old Eboracum."

Zalez chuckled, "I don't know if that's possible..."

"We are going to have Narob Energy on every planet."

"Let me give you the tour, then we can talk in my office."

In Space False One, Blaphaus really wanted to rip off his Toob outfit but with Yerkal on the flight he decided it's best not to. He stood in the back, glaring at the back of Yerkal's head. The Peezle's sat next to each other, holding hands.

"Noj, I'm so sorry. This is all a big mess."

Noj Peezle nodded, "It'll work out."

100

"We are approaching the Dook Energy space station." the pilot said over the intercom, "We have permission to dock."

Nekkod stepped into Zalez's office where Zalez sat behind his desk, Narob the other side of it. Nekkod thought to himself that Narob is a miserable teenager, which was surprising considering his father was so polite and nice.

"I don't think Governor Jaboney would approve us taking over powering Old Eborocum..."

"He has no choice." Narob said firmly.

Nekkod thought it'll be a good time to interrupt.

"Zalez, the G.P.'s Space False One is docking here. I gave the go ahead and let them, I hope it's okay."

"Wow, lots of visitors today." Zalez said. "Escort the G.P. here to the office."

"Sure." the bald assistant nodded and left.

"Why is the Toob here?" Narob asked.

"I have no idea." Zalez replied, "With him there's no telling."

The yellow shuttle landed in the hangar, Nekkod stood waiting for the ramp to come down.

Inside the shuttle Blaphaus said to Yerkal, "You're waiting right here."

Yerkal nodded, not getting out of his seat. Peezle followed Blap down the ramp, and Nekkod walked over to them.

"This is a surprise, Galactic President."

"Is Belhopsa here?" Blaphaus demanded.

"Mr. Belhopsa is in his office." Nekkod said.

"Good." Blaphaus remarked.

A few minutes later Nekkod led Blaphaus and Peezle into the office. Zalez stood up but Narob didn't even move.

"G.P. Blaphaus, Governor Peezle. Welcome, what can I do for you? This is a surprise."

"This space station is going to be one of the three watching for an invasion." Blaphaus told him.

Narob now stood you, "No, it's not. As owner of Dook Energy we are not going to be involved with whatever you have going on. There's going to be no invasion."

"Blaphaus, Narob here is the new owner of Dook Energy, soon to be Narob Energy."

"You're changing the name?" Peezle asked.

"Yes. And Narob Energy is going to power Old Eborocum and Tooberosum."

"Ha!" Blaphaus said.

Just then Mal's holo-call appeared on Zalez's desk.

"Zalez, thank the Creator you're there. I tried to contact you earlier."

"Sorry, I was giving Narob Traf a tour of the station. This is not a good time, so if this isn't urgent..."

"It kind of is. Nate had a visitor at the school today, a woman named Fami Tapperdau, she had a bunch of questions. It's something about Blaphaus..."

Zalez glanced at Blap and said, "This is not a good time. I will come home later."

"But..."

He made the holo-call disappear.

"You have some balls." Blap told Zalez.

"Fami Tapperdau?" asked Peezle, "I met her!"

"You did?" Zalez asked.

"Yes, she was at the House a few days ago. She was asking me a bunch of questions, and wanted to meet with you, Blaphaus."

"I knew I heard that bloody name before." Blap pointed out.

Peezle shrugged, "I don't know where she went, she never showed back up."

Blaphaus smirked, thinking of the woman he met at the pub. He knew exactly who she was... and she met him when he was himself.

## CHAPTER 12

Allard Felipe, the tall dark haired handsome man walked up the steps of the House. He took off his sun-spectacles before he went inside to the foyer. The House robot approached him and scanned him from head to toe.

"Welcome to the House. Who are you?" the House asked in its female voice.

"Allard Felipe." he said with a smile.

The robot shook its head and replied, "That name does not compute."

"Is Governor Dawber here? She'll know who I am."

"As far as I know Governor Dawber is here."

"Then do me a favor and fetch her."

"I will be back soon."

Allard smiled, "Good robot." He patted it on the silver head.


Zalez and Narob stood in the hangar watching Space Force One lift up, turn around and fly out of the space station.

"Good, they are gone." Narob smirked, "I want to go to Tooberosum. Take me there, Belhopsa."

Zalez said, "I really don't think that's a good idea."

"Why not?" Narob said, "You've been there, right?"

"Look, I need to go home, take care of some family stuff. Then we'll discuss it."

Narob nodded, "Fine. Set up a meeting with Governor Jaboney. I am going to buy him out."

Zalez nodded, thinking he did not like Narob. Maybe he should just send him to "Tooberosum"... so he can learn the truth about that planet.

On Space False One, Blap stood in the back once again while Peezle and Yerkal sat next to each other, holding hands.

"Where do we go from here?" Yerkal asked.

"We are going to Church." Blap grumbled from behind them.


Dawber stepped out her office to meet Allard, who stood with the robot. He smiled at Dawber, making her blush.

"Hello, Cris, you look good as ever."

"Still the charmer." she replied, "Come on in."

She led him into the nondescript office, closing the door.

"What brings you to the House, Allard? You lost your chance years ago being Governor. You would've made a great G.P. as well."

He sat on the edge of the desk, "But you guys had to go with the fake Tooberosum..."

"It wasn't my idea, trust me. Wait. What do you mean 'fake' Tooberosum?" she felt a lump in her throat.

"You really don't know?" Allard asked, "You *have* to know."

"What do *you* know?" Dawber asked back.

Allard sighed, "You really want me to tell you?"

She crossed her arms, "Yes. Do tell."

"Okay, I know that Blaphaus is not really a Tooberosum, and there's this organization that also knows that. They are trying to find a way to prove it."

Dawber said, "How do you know he's not a Toob? What species would he be?"

"That I don't know, Cris. But rumor is he's a human... and not even from his galaxy."

She just stared at him, a million thoughts going through her head.

"Judging by the look on your face I'm right. Right?" he smiled.

She nodded, "Yes, Allard, but if word gets out, it's not going to be good."

He stood up straight, "That's where I come in. I am going to make sure no one finds out. But it's going to be tricky, they are on to him."

"How do you know any of this?"

He chuckled as he walked to the door.

"Oh, silly Cris, I can't reveal all my secrets. I also know the Gink Governor is not a part of the Cabinet anymore."

She said, "How do you know that?"

He tapped the side of his nose as he opened the office door.

"Not saying. By the way, I met Blaphaus briefly, outside. I was going to tell him what I know but didn't get a chance to. I'll be in touch."

He walked out whistling, leaving a stunned Dawber to stand there looking perplexed.


The Faeligion Church space station was pretty big, bigger than Dook Energy's space station. It had to be big enough for anybody in the galaxy that wanted to go to it. Some species has their own religions and churches, such as the Cyrakuse and the Canisma church on Canis, but most species and beings would travel to the Faeligion Church. It had fake stained glass windows around it and a tall glowing cross above it, that on a clear day could be seen by the few planets around it.

Nitsiuj Rellim, head of the Faeligion Church stood in his red and black robes as the yellow shuttle approached. When it landed in the hangar, he held his arms wide open. The ramp descended and Blaphaus, Peezle and Yerkal came down from it.

"Praise the Creator, you are here, Galactic President Maximus."

"Don't get too excited, I'm not here to pray." Blap replied.

"Oh, but there's other ways to worship the Creator."

"Is there somewhere we can talk?" Peezle asked, "Instead of the hangar?"

"Of course. Follow me." Pastor Rellim said.

He led them out the hangar and they passed a coffee bar which Blaphaus thought was kind of odd. Where he came from churches were so much smaller and intimate, but this was a completely different galaxy. They went into a large office, which had a pretty big desk and fancy furniture.

"So, what brings you three here?" the Pastor asked.

"There's a bloody chance there's going to be an invasion." Blaphaus said, "To this galaxy. Three space stations are going to be the look out military bases."

"Military base? Invasion? Invasion from where?" the Pastor asked.

"Another galaxy." Peezle replied.

"The Creator only created this galaxy." the Pastor told them.

"The Gink is from another galaxy." Blap told him.

"I pray for you every day, Galactic President."

"There's probably more of him coming." explained Peezle.

"I don't believe there's another galaxy."

"*I'm* from another galaxy." Blaphaus said aggravated.

"Have you heard of the Order of Blattodea?" Yerkal asked.

"My elderly Chaplain's might have heard of that, but I have not."

"Then I want to talk to the Chaplain then." Blaphaus said.

Yerkal asked, "Is he here now?"

The Pastor nodded, "Yes, he is. I'll take you to him."

Yerkal and Noj both looked at each other and smiled.

Dawber took her place at the table in the conference room, where the other Governors were also taking their places.

"Where's Joorg?" she asked.

"Being Governor no longer he just left." Eastora replied.

Rüppell said, "I feel bad for him. What's left for him to do?"

"Peezle is still with Blaphaus so he won't be here." Zeb told them.

"Why this emergency meeting, Cris?" asked Southington.

"I had a visitor a little bit ago, a friend from Canola. I don't know what he's doing now but he knows that Blaphaus is not really a Toob."

"How?" asked Noam.

"He wouldn't say. But he also said there's this organization that also knows and wants to prove it, and reveal to the galaxy the truth."

"Organization? Like the Order of Blattodea?" Thaw asked.

"No, I think it's something different altogether."

"Well, how do they know?" Southington asked. "Unless Blaphaus was foolish enough to say something or go out as his human self..."

"We need to ask him about it." Kakertak said.

"Not until he gets back here." Dawber said. "We still have three blasterers out there as well as the invasion that could happen."

"Do you think this is all connected?" Gillian asked.

"Somehow, yes." Dawber said. "And the two that we can blame for Blaphaus being G.P. are dead."

"We need to bring your friend here to ask him what he knows." Noam said.

"Who is it?" Zucaritas asked.

"Allard Filipe." she said.

"That swarmy bastard?" Noam asked. "I hate that tall freaking human."


Back on the Church space station, the Pastor knocked on a wooden door.

"Chaplain Aweley, you have some very important visitors."

"Come in then." the voice called out from inside.

The Pastor opened the door and led the three inside. Sitting behind a desk in black and white robes was a wrinkly faced Canis with a short muzzled face.

"Oh, wow, the Toob Galaxy President." Aweley said.

He rushed around the desk and shook Blaphaus' hand, squeezing it hard.

"It's a pleasure."

The Pastor sat in a chair at the back of the office.

"Who are your friends, G.P.?"

"I'm Governor Peezle and this is my husband Yerkal."

"Husband? We at the Church don't believe in same sex marriages, or different species getting married."

"And I don't believe in your Creator." Blap retorted. "If he was real he sure had a sense of humor creating this screwed up planet."

"What do you believe in, G.P. Maximus?" the Chaplain asked.

"You don't want to know."

The Pastor thought it was time for him to step in. He stood and walked over to them.

"Chaplain Aweley, they are here on official business. The Church is going to house some military personnel, looking out to protect the galaxy from an invasion."

"An invasion? What kind of invasion?" Aweley asked.

"Probably Gink." Blaphaus said. "If I had to guess."

"Gink? Don't you have a Gink Governor?"

"Not anymore." Peezle replied.

"They have a question for you, Chaplain."

"Question? Good. I love questions."

"Have you heard of the Order of Blattodea?"

"Ooohhh... that *is* a question." Aweley's eyes almost popped out of his head. He sat down in a chair next to the desk.

"G.P. Maximus, you're a Tooberosum, you should know ALL about the Order."

"Humor me. Wot do you know about it?"

"Many, many years ago the Cakerlak and your species, the Tooberosum fought in a Great War. It wasn't like my species' war with the Cyrakuse, that was more like a tiff. The war between the Cakerlak and the Toob was brutal, thousands and thousands were killed on each side."

"What was the war about?" Peezle asked.

"No one knows. It's believed though that it was to rule the galaxy, to take over."

"Did other species take part in this?" Yerkal asked.

"The other species on the other planets did not interfere at all, as both planets had manufactured weapons. The longer the war went on the more weapons were made, and the more weapons that were made the more powerful they got."

"How long did this last and who won?" Blap asked.

"Well, this is one answer you should already know." Aweley sat up, "It lasted for many, many years. As for who won? The Cakerlak won. Their planet is still striving and the Toobs disappeared... until you showed up of course."

"Why would the previous Traf have the word 'Blattodea' as his password on his personal info-pad?" Blap asked.

"Maybe he was a history buff, it's hard to say. Maybe it was a coincidence."

"I don't think so." Blap asked, "It's too obscure of a word. Have you heard of the Great Weta?"

Aweley shook his head, "No, can't say I have."

"Do you think the blasterings have anything to do with the Order?"

"No, I don't think so. Other species were killed, the Order was just between the Cakerlak and the Toobs."

"I heard the Order being named on Cakerlak, they are the ones who sent the Cakerlak to assassinate Blaphaus. Do you think the Order is coming back again?" Yerkal asked.

"Coming back? They probably never left. There was no one to fight... until Blaphaus became famous and became Galactic President."

"They had numerous chances to kill me but didn't." Blap said.

"Perhaps they know the truth." Aweley said standing up.

"Wot's that?" Blap asked.

"That you're not really a Toob..."


Zalez drove his car toward his house on Ceilingida. He parked and got out, walking up to the front door. He unlocked it, walking in to see Allard sitting at the dining room table, eating a sandwich, with a headless Ten laying on the floor. The head of Ten was now a centerpiece on the table.

"What the hell happened to Ten? Who are you?" Zalez asked through gritted teeth.

"Your fancy looking robot here wouldn't let me in and wait for you like I kindly asked, so I threatened to take off his head. He didn't believe me..." Allard stood up and patted the top of Ten's head. "So I proved it to him. You might be able to attach it again, but he's just a robot. They can be replaced..."

Zalez walked quickly over to Allard, grabbing him by his jackets lapels.

"Who are you and what do you want?"

Allard moved Zalez's hands from his jacket.

"Careful, a respected Chordattian like you attacking a human like me is not good. What would your Dook Energy friends think?"

"I don't get angry often, but you're making me very angry. Why are you in my house? My family could've been here."

"Ahhh. Your children are at school and your lovely, gorgeous wife Mal is at her dance school. I planned this well, my friend." Allard grinned. "I've been in this business a long time."

"What business?" Zalez asked.

"Well, that's hard to say. Anyway, I have to ask you, Blaphaus Maximus, our present Galactic President is not really a Tooberosum, is he?"

Zalez frowned, "What makes you ask that? Is that what you think?"

"It's not what *I* think, it's what the Committee thinks."

"The what?"

"Committee. It's made up on a bunch of different species who kind of watch over the Cabinet from the shadows. For a long, long time they didn't have to do anything, but now with the series of blasterings and the 'Toob' being Galactic President..." he used air quotes when he said "Toob."

"What are they going to do about it?" Zalez asked.

"Try to prove that the Toob is not what he says he is... or what the Cabinet says."

"And what is your position with this?" Zalez asked, "Are you part of the Committee?"

"I used to be. I broke free. I am part of a group who watch over the Committee." he chuckled.

"How do you know that the Committee is doing anything or knows about Blaphaus?"

"One of them secretly contacts me and informs me what's going on... which has been nothing. Until recently that is. I believe one of their agents, Fami Tapperdau is looking for the Toob... and your family."

Zalez nodded, "That's why I'm here. My wife informed me that a Fami Tapperdau stopped by my children's school to talk to my son."

"She went to the school? Creator knows what she told him. We need to find her, Zalez. Are you with me?"

Zalez looked at his headless robot's body and the head on the table.

"How can I trust you, Allard? How do I know you're not lying?"

Allard shrugged, "You don't. But what other choice do you have?"

"Do they have proof on what they think about Blaphaus?"

"No, not yet as far as I know. That'll be their next step."

"Then I need to warn him."

"Good luck with that, Belhopsa. I tried to warn him in person but he didn't listen."

"He'll listen to someone I know for sure."

"Who is that?"

"Nate, my son." sighed Zalez.

On Space False One, Yerkal sat next to Peezle again, as Blaphaus stood in the back in his normal spot.

"What did that Chaplain mean about Blaphaus not being a Toob?" Yerkal whispered to Noj.

"I wouldn't worry about that right now."

"There's a lot to worry about all of a sudden, Noj."

"I know. But that's not one of them."

Yerkal unbuckled his seatbelt and stood, turning towards Blaphaus.

"Where are we going now?" Yerkal asked.

"Farvegas." Blaphaus replied.

"Of course." mumbled Yerkal, sitting back down.

Mal drove her vehicle with the two children in the backseat.

"Mother, Nate won't tell me why he had to go to the office." Romana whined.

"He's not entitled to, Romana."

"I promised Ms. Tapperdau I wouldn't say anything." Nate remarked.

"Why not?" Romana asked, "What's the big secret?"

"I can't say" Nate said firmly again.

"You think your feces doesn't stink because Mr. Blaphaus thinks you're so great!"

"Romana!" Mal cried out, "We don't use that kind of language!"

"I'm just saying that since Nate has been all over the place, and was Governor and spent time with them all he thinks he's so great!"

"No I don't and those days are over. Right, mother?"

"Correct, Nate."

They approached their house and the children spotted their father's vehicle parked in front of it.

"Father is here!" they both exclaimed.

"Thank the Creator." Mal said under her breath.

They got out the vehicle and ran over to the front door. Mal followed them up the pathway and unlocked the front door. They walked inside to see Zalez sitting in the living room with a tall man in a dark suit.

"Father!" they ran over to him, jumping on him, giving him a hug.

"Hello, children!"

"Glad you're here, Zalez."

"Who is that?" Romana pointed around the man on the couch.

"Romana, that's not polite." Mal said.

"It's good. I'm Allard Filipe, a friend of your father." Allard smiled and chuckled.

"Do you work for Dook Energy as well?" Romana asked.

"No, but that would be fun. I'm actually here to talk to your brother."

"Of course you are!" Romana cried out, jumping to her feet and ran up the stairs.

Mal gave Allard and Zalez a dirty look and walked up the stairs to comfort Romana.

"Me?" Nate asked, "Are you friends with Ms. Tapperdau?"

"No, but I know who she is." smiled Allard, "You need to keep away from her if she comes around..."

"Where's Ten?" Nate asked.

"Son, we are talking about Miss..."

Nate stood up and looked around the living room.

"Where is he?"

"I took his head off." Allard told him, "Your father put him in the closet."

"You took his head off?!" Nate cried out mad, "Why would you do that? Ten was our friend!"

"He was a bad robot..."

"That's enough." Zalez snapped.

"That's two robot's that we had that had their heads taken off." Nate sobbed, "First Ten took off O-U's head and now you took off Ten's head. I hope no one takes off *your* head, Mr. Allard!"

"Me too." smiled Allard, "So, Ms. Fami... what did she talk about?"

"I promised her I wouldn't tell anybody." Nate said.

"I understand, Nate, but she's on the bad being side. She might seem nice but really she's evil."

Nate shook his head, "I'm good at reading beings and I don't think so."

"Why is that?"

"She didn't take the head off our robot."

"Touché, Nate." chuckled Allard. "But she is part of a group of beings that want to stop Mr. Blaphaus from being Galactic President."

"Good." Nate said.

"What do you mean good?" Zalez asked.

"Father, do you remember what I said about Mr. Blaphaus on New Galaxy Day!"

Zalez nodded, "Yes..."

"Well, I was right. Mr. Blaphaus is not really a Tooberosum. Told you I was good reading beings."

Zalez and Allard both glanced at each other.


Space False One landed inside the neon lit, multi-colored glowing space station Farvegas.

Inside, a short gray furred species in a white suit walked into the office really quick. He had a long pointed snout and small beady eyes. His long pink tail came out of the hole in the back of his pants, dragging on the floor. Gunther Farvegas sat behind his desk, counting huge piles of lucre.

"Mr. Farvegas, sir, a shuttle is approaching the space station." the Shroo said quickly, out of breath.

Farvegas looked up, and grunted. He was a fat, gray Cyrakuse who was the richest being in the galaxy.

"Virago, can't you see I'm busy counting? Shuttles come here all the time, from all over the galaxy."

"True, true, but this one is different. It's bright yellow."

"Yellow did you say? There's only one yellow shuttle I'm aware of. Last time I was on it I witnessed a murder."

"What?" Virago asked, "Murder? When was this?"

Farvegas waved his hand, "It doesn't matter. Did they say who was on this shuttle?"

"The pilot, when he asked for permission to land, said he was with the G.P. and a Governor. I don't know which one though."

Farvegas stood up, "It doesn't matter which one. The G.P. Toob is finally coming here." the normally miserable looking Farvegas smiled, "This is the greatest! Come on, Virago, let's greet the crazy Toob!"

The shuttle landed in the docking bay, which had slot machines all over the place, and gamble-robots which were small brown robots where you pulled down one arm and it'll randomly told you if you won, how much you won and then spat out lucre from their mouths. The ramp descended, and Blap and Peezle walked down it. Yerkal went to follow when Blap motioned for him to go back into the shuttle.

"You're staying here."

"Why?" Yerkal asked.

"Because I said so." Blaphaus replied.

"It'll be okay, Yerkal, just stay here. We won't be long."

"Nobody goes to Farvegas and says 'they won't be long.'" Yerkal grumbled, going back inside, and sitting down.

When the two reached the docking bay, and went though the huge glass doors decorated with a lights and paint, fanfare played, confetti shot from tiny cabins and a voice spoke over the P.A.

"Ladies and gentlebeings, please welcome to Farvegas... Galactic President Blaphaus Maximus!"

"Wot the bloody hell?" Blap asked.

Before he and Peezle knew it they were the center of attention. Every being close enough watched them walk through the casino, some handing them lucre, some even putting gold necklaces over their heads. A Jiraffe who was tall enough, helped pull the necklaces down over Blap's big head. He tried to brush them off, not wanting the Toob suit to get damaged. Peezle couldn't help to smile, thinking Yerkal would love this.

"They like you here for some reason." Peezle said to Blaphaus.

"Yeah, because they're all pissed drunk." Blap replied.

Two almost naked Cyrakuse walked up to them and did a short sexual dance in front of Blap. He secretly wished they were human females, but he still half smiled. He was led over to a table by a pointed eared, black species in a gray shirt and matching pants. It had some kind of cape over his shoulders, making it look like wings. Blaphaus saw it was a game of dice, where players were shouting out numbers before the dice was rolled.

"Play a game of shits with us, Galactic President." the caped being told him.

"I don't think so." Blaphaus said, "I've got feces to do."

"Just one game."

"Wow, what a small galaxy. Hello, Toobie." someone said behind Blaphaus.

He recognized that annoying voice right away. He turned to see a Leetric standing there smiling.

"Do you remember me? You were our driver a few times... a few weeks ago."

"Yes, I remember you." Blaphaus replied, "Are the twins here with you?"

"No, Toobie, I'm by myself. Doing a bit of gambling. What brings you here?"

"Official business." Blap replied.

"Playing shits is official business? Golly, I want to be G.P.! Congrats by the way. I was on Launderington for New Galaxy Day. You've come a long way in such a short time."

"If you say so..."

"Galactic President Maximus!" someone else cried out.

Everyone turned to see Farvegas stroll across the casino floor, holding his arms out wide. He made his way to Blaphaus giving him a huge hug. Blap pushed him away quickly.

"Don't hug me."

"Welcome to Farvegas!" Farvegas smiled, "I knew you'd come here eventually."

Peezle said to Farvegas, "We are not here to play or gamble, Mister Farvegas, we are here on official business."

"Of course! You can have all the chips you want when you're done." he noticed the lucre in Blap's hands. "But looks like you're ready to play."

Blap shoved the dosh into Erick the Leetric's hands.

"This for me, Toobie?"

"Yep. Don't blow it all at once."

"Come to my office, or do you want to hang out by one of the pools?" Farvegas asked.

"Office." Blap and Peezle said the same time.

They went to the office, followed by Virago, who looked nervous.

"We're going to keep this simple and quick." Blaphaus told Farvegas, "I'm having Governor Sugden put some of his military on this space station, along with the Church station and Dook's station."

"Military? That would scare away some of my clientele..."

"I don't give a feces. There's a possible chance there's going to be an invasion and with the blasterings happening..."

"An invasion? You mean like the Gink? You took care of him, I witnessed that myself."

"There's more than him." Blaphaus said.

"It's to be safe. That's all." Peezle added. "They will be discreet."

"I'm G.P., anyway, so you don't have a choice."

"The last G.P. used to spend quite some time here. You need to, G.P. Maximus, it's good for business."

"It's possible." Blaphaus said.

"At least play a few games, take some holo-scans, please. Then you can have all the military you want here... as long as it's discreet."

"Deal." Peezle smiled.

Blap just grunted a reply.


"Nate is not going anywhere!" Mal yelled at Peezle and Allard.

"It's hard to get Blaphaus to come here." Zalez said.

"I don't know if Mr. Blaphaus will listen to me." Nate said, "If he's not who he says he is."

"It'll be just to Launderington." Allard said, "Blaphaus trusts Nate, so if Nate warns him about the Committee..."

"I don't trust Mr. Blaphaus." Nate said, "If he's not really a Tooberosum I don't like him."

Mal sat on the couch, next to Nate.

"Is that was Ms. Tapperdau said? That Blaphaus isn't a Tooberosum?"

"I can't say anything else." Nate said, "I wish you would all leave me alone."

"Well, maybe it'll be a good idea for Blaphaus to come here." Allard said, "After all, he supposedly lives on this planet."

Mal said, "He's not coming to our house again."

Romana came down the stairs and looked around.

"Where is Ten?" she asked.

"Yeah, where is that robot?" Mal stood, looking around for him.

"Mr. Felipe killed him." Nate said, "Everything is bad."


Blaphaus and Peezle were led back through the casino by Virago, and everyone still stared at them.

Erick rushed back up to Blap and asked, "Are you leaving, Toobie?"

"Yup."

"Oh, that's too bad. I was hoping you'd stick around. I have a lot to tell you."

"Nothing you can tell me I'll be interested with." Blap told him.

"This might..."

"The Galactic President said he's not interested..." Virago snapped.

"I can fend for myself, twitchy." Blap said, "Why don't you go roll some shits or something? Didn't I give you enough dosh?"

"Yes, but you might need to know this. It's important. It's to do with all the crazy feces that's been happening in the galaxy."

Blap and Peezle stopped walking, and Virago bumped into them.

"Wot?"

"Remember when you dropped me and the girls off that one time and I met this shadowy figure?"

"Yes. So?"

"It was a Cakerlak, we were doing business with. I told you that I was in the trade business, right?"

"I had hundreds of passengers, I didn't pay attention to half the feces they all said."

"But you remember the figure, right?"

"I said yes."

"Well, he did this trade with me and asked me if I'd be interested in joining the Order of Blat something or other. I said no, it seemed odd. Then I thought of you.. your name being Blap and thought maybe it was the Order of Blaphaus. Then not long after you became G.P., and I thought that was odd. Now with all these killings and everything, and then you're here on Farvegas..."

"That's enough." Blap said, "You're giving me a bloody headache."

"Well, I just thought you should know."

Peezle said, "Do you have the name of this Cakerlak you were doing business with?"

"Yeah. Neop." Erick replied.

"Of course he was." Blaphaus muttered.

"Did I do the right thing?" Erick asked.

"Yes, Leetric, you did the right thing. Have a nice life... again." Blap hurried off.

Peezle and Virago followed again. They walked through the glass doors, and went through the docking bay.

Just then a GNN robot-can appeared in front of them and a voice said from it.

"Hello, G.P. Maximus, I'm Crisp Jaboney, from GNN. Are you having fun on Farvegas when the galaxy is an turmoil?"

"I'm here on official business, and the galaxy is hardly in turmoil." Blaphaus replied.

"Then what's with the gold necklaces you're wearing, G.P.? That your new style now?"

Virago pushed his way in front of Blaphaus and said to the robot-cam.

"He was here on official business.  You can ask Gunther Farvegas about it."

"Oh, I will." Jaboney's voice said, "I will."

Blaphaus pushed past the robot-cam and made his way to the Space False One as Peezle followed.

"I'll just ask my brother, the Governor. This is Crisp Jaboney, GNN, watching Galactic President Maximus' every move."

***CHAPTER 13***

Joorg had no idea what to do. He stood in the spaceport looking at the huge display of which shuttles were coming and going. He wanted to get to Cakerlak and find out more on who this Great Weta was. He had no idea how to get back to the planet he used to be Governor on. He should've been surprised that not one flight was to or from Cakerlak. Then he saw at the bottom of the screen one flight was going there. He smirked, and rushed off to buy a ticket.

Thaw sat at his desk in the House, as Phence's 12 inch holo-call appeared on top of it.
"Hello, Governor, what can I do for you?"
"I have a question... Blaphaus wants to put military on the three space stations in case there's an invasion. What is your opinion?"
"Well, I wouldn't have thought of doing that, but that kind of makes sense. Did he say why?"
"Apparently the stations can look out for any invasion. He thinks the Gink are going to invade."
"I've been trying to do some research on them, after the whole summit business and they are definitely not from this galaxy. It's so odd that a species like that, or any species not from this galaxy could be here, and no one bats an eyelid. I think no matter how prepared we are for an invasion it's not going to be enough. You might want to let the Governors and Blaphaus know. The invasion has already happened, just not on a grand scale... yet."
"What do you know about the Cakerlak?"
Phence rubbed his chin, and adjusted his spectacles.
"A nasty old war species, not to be trusted. If I was a betting man I'd say they were behind the blasterings."
"But other species were involved..."
"I didn't say they did it, I said they were behind it."
"Good point. Professor, I always appreciate your knowledge."
"I'm always glad to be of help."

On Space False One, Blap stood in the back, not saying a word. The necklaces he was given were laying over the back of the seat in front of him. Peezle and Yerkal sat in the front, whispering to each other. Blap didn't care what they were talking about, except for if Yerkal really couldn't be trusted could Peezle? He wasn't about to fire the Ceilingida Governor yet... he knew that two Governors down already did not look good. Just then

117

Rüppell's holo-call appeared in front of the shuttle, in full size. Blaphaus thought now wot?

"Hello, G.P., Governor Peezle... hope you're having success with your trips to the space stations."

Blap unbuckled himself and stepped forward, down the aisle towards the holo-call.

"Get to the point, Lycalopex."

The Lycalopex said, "A friend of mine on Mesas thinks he knows who the blasterer was on Xenartha."

"Wot makes your friend thinks it's him?"

"He was approached by a Vermilian named Depatie and asked if he'd want to be a member of the Order. My friend said yes, and is hanging out with him now."

"The Order..." gulped Yerkal.

"Did you tell the GBI? Or Sugden?" Blap asked, "To send his military there?"

"No, you're the first one I told. Thought you should know."

"Thank you." Peezle said, "We will head right there." he got up and made his way to the pilot's cabin.

"Where are you going?" Blap asked.

"To tell the pilot to turn around, we are going to Mesas, not Launderington."

"Why are we going there?" Blaphaus asked.

"To confront this blasterer..."

"And do wot? The GBI are the ones to confront him."

"But, Blaphaus, you if anybody should make an appearance once he's caught."

"If you're going to Mesas then so am I." Rüppell replied.

"Bloody hell." grumbled Blap. "I hate that planet. It's too bloody hot. Okay, we will go there... real quickly." he turned to Rüppell, "Tell Sugden, contact the GBI."

"And GNN." Peezle said, "This should get the ratings up."

Rüppell said, "My friend will meet you at the spaceport on Mesas."

"This day will never bloody end." muttered Blaphaus.


The Belhopsa door buzzer buzzed and Nate stood up from the couch. "I'll get it."

Allard, who was still there looked out the front window.

"Stop, Nate, don't open the door." he said.

"Why not?" Zalez asked, "If you didn't behead our robot..."

The buzzer buzzed again. Mal walked over to it impatiently.

"Someone has to get it."

"It's Tapperdau." Allard said firmly, "We need to get going. Mr. Belhopsa, I'm taking Nate with me, you should come as well."

"Nate is not going anywhere." Mal pointed out.

The buzzer buzzed again. Fami tried to look through the front window, when she saw the tall man in the black suit pull the curtains closed. She swore under her breath, she knew exactly who he was. She did not like it he beat her to the Belhopsa's. She thought she should've "kidnapped" Nate at the school when she had the chance. She buzzed the door buzzer once again. She wasn't going anywhere. Inside the house Allard turned to Zalez.

"I take it you have a back door here."

Zalez motioned to the kitchen. "Yeah, back there."

"My vehicle is parked a few streets away. We should be able to get there without being seen going out the back door."

"Where am I going?" Nate asked.

"To find Maximus." Allard said, "We have to warn him, and tell him what's going on."

"I don't know what he is really. I don't want to see or talk to him."

The buzzer buzzed again.

"I know what he is." Zalez said quickly, "I'll explain on the way. Come on."

"He's not going anywhere." Mal said firmly. "He has school tomorrow. This whole thing is crazy."

Romana sat quietly the whole time listening and watching. She had enough and stood up.

"Stop it! Father, take Nate quickly. Mother, stay here. I'll answer the door and tell this lady no one is home." she walked over to Nate and gave him a big hug.

"Do what you have to do, little brother."

Allard shooed them out through the kitchen, Mal hid in the living room and for one of the first times ever Romana opened the front door herself.

"Hello." she smiled up at Fami.

"Aren't you the cutest?" Fami asked, "Are your parents here?"

"No."

"Is your brother here?"

"No."

"What about the colorful robot you have?"

"He's broken."

Fami frowned, something didn't seem right.

"So, you're by yourself? Aren't you a little young to be left home by yourself?"

Romana shrugged, "I'm mature, lady."

"I see. Well, tell your parents that Fami Tapperdau stopped by."

Romans nodded, "I will. Bye."

She closed the door on Fami's face. Fami wanted to be mad, but couldn't. This family was getting on her nerves though.

Allard led Zalez and Nate down the street to his expensive black vehicle. Nate got in the backseat and Zalez and Allard got in a front. A few moments later it turned the corner going past Fami who was crossing the street. She spotted the vehicle drive down the road, and she knew exactly who was driving and who was in the vehicle.

Nate looked out the back window at Fami, who stood there with her hands on her hips.

"So, is Ms. Fami in the bad beings side?" Nate asked.

"Yes, Nate, but it's more the people she works for."


Blaphaus has been to quite a few planets since he was given the position of G.P. Most planets he did not like Cakerlak for obvious reasons. Another planet he *really* didn't like was Mesas. That planet was too hot, and the reason was it was because of Farvegas which was close by. Blaphaus didn't believe that one bit. But to him it didn't make any difference why it was hot, it was just hot. And his Toob suit had no air conditioning inside of it. Ceilingida was a warm planet, but not hot like Mesas. Another thing he didn't like about Mesas was the shuttle shook when it entered the atmosphere and it did the same this time. Blap stood at the back of the cabin, holding on tight. Yerkal who went through this before looked scared out of his mind again, hugging Noj's arm. Noj just gripped the arm of his seat, wondering what was going on. The shuttle settled and flew calmly over the planet.

"Of all the bloody planets for the Vermilian to go to..." Blap muttered.

"Attention, we are going to be landing in a few minutes." the pilot said over the intercom. "Sorry I didn't warn you about the turbulence."

Space False One came down to land on the hot, tan planet. A long faced and gray haired species wearing a purple tank top watched the shuttle land and the ramp descend. He smiled brightly as Blap came down the ramp.

"I stayed behind last time I was here." Yerkal said, "Think I'll do the same."

"No, you're coming with us." ordered Blaphaus.

"Come on." Peezle walked down the ramp, unbuttoning his pink shirt. Yerkal took off his jacket and tie, rolled up his sleeves and followed.

"Hello, Galactic President Maximus, the greatest G.P. ever to live. I'm Dibo, do you want a guided tour?"

This was the same annoying tour guide he met before, at the same spot. "I'm a huge fan and it's great to meet you."

"We met before..." Blaphaus muttered.

"Who are we supposed to meet here?" Peezle asked sweating, wondering how Blap felt inside the Toob suit.

"A friend of Rüppell's." Blap replied.

"Do you need a tour? A friend? Anything?" the annoying Dibo asked.

Just then a roofless vehicle drive up, with a black and red species, with long antennae's.

"Hey there! Again!" the six armed Cakerlak got out his vehicle and approached them.

"No..." Yerkal looked horrified at the Cakerlak, hiding behind Peezle.

"What's your problem, human?" the Cakerlak asked.

"He doesn't like your kind. Feces, I don't like your kind either." Blap told him.

"And I don't like Toobs, but here we are." the Cakerlak chuckled, "Kidding! We met before... a few weeks ago. I'm Bock, remember?"

Blap replied, "How could I forget? So, you're Rüppell's friend we are supposed to meet?"

"Yep. You're looking for a Vermilian named Depatie... I know where he is staying. The Planet Mayor... or Governor I should say said he's the one the GBI are looking for who killed innocent beings on Xenartha."

"Yep, the GBI should be here to arrest him."

"He's staying at the Nightsout motel a few towns away. He was hanging out at the bar, playing stabber. Guess he thought no one would know him here."

"And you met him?" Peezle asked, sweating.

"Yeah, he opened up to me... asked if I belonged to some kind of Order. I told him, yup, which is a lie."

"Well, I want to meet this bastard." Blap said, "After the GBI arrests his arse."

"Get in my vehicle, you can stand in the back, G.P., he should be arrested by time we get there."

"I'll wait behind here." Yerkal said.

"No, you're coming with us." Blap told him.


Depatie laid in bed in his motel room when the door was busted open and four GBI Agents barged in, all armed, and surrounded the Vermilian.

"Depatie, you are under arrest." one human Agent told him.

Depatie just smiled, raising his arms above his head.
"You got me."

Allard, Zalez and Nate sat in the Dook Energy shuttle, which was flying to Launderington.
"Father, you still didn't tell me what Mr. Blaphaus really is."
Allard glanced at Zalez and smirked, "You said you would, Belhopsa."
"I know, but I think Blaphaus himself should say something."
"What about if he doesn't?" Nate asked.
"Then he doesn't." Allard told Nate, "The main thing is though you have to convince Blaphaus that the Committee coming for him."
Nate crossed his arms, "I'll try but I'm just a child."
"A child the Toob trusts." Allard replied.

Fami's holo-call appeared in the canter of the circle where the figures sat in their seats in the Committee Council room.
"Does the Doctor know you are working with us?" a white Cyrakuse asked, wearing a black suit.
"No, he has no idea. He'd be heart broken." she said.
"Good. So, you let Filipe leave with the Belhopsa's?" the Cyrakuse asked.
"He beat me to the house. Trust me, I will get to them..." she said.
"We'll send Phedorra instead." a female pointed out.
"No offense but Phedorra is an old man, he's about to retire." Fami pointed out.
"Phedorra is the best we have. He might be able to get to Blaphaus before anyone else."
"I will go and try to get Blaphaus." Fami told them, "I am so close."
Her holo-call nodded and disappeared.

Depatie sat in the stone interrogation cell, wrists cuffed in front of him. His ears perked up as he heard the voices outside the room. He recognized one of the voices and smirked to himself.
In the corridor outside the room, Bock, Blaphaus, and the Peezle's stood before the prison guard, who was a Squamata, a  horned species with scales instead of fur or hair. GBI agents stood to the side, just to make sure nothing crazy would happen.
"He's in there. I have to tell you I wanted to rip his friggin' throat open." the Squamata remarked.
"Not until we talk to him." Blaphaus remarked. "Or the Solicitor here does."

"I'm not going in there and talk to him." Yerkal said scared.

"Why not? You talked to the arsehole who wanted to assassinate me."

"That was different! Neop didn't do anything, this one actually killed a bunch of innocent beings."

"Same difference. You can find out who sent him."

Bock said, "I'll go in there with you."

"No... it's okay. I'm not going in there."

"Open the door." Blaphaus ordered the guard.

The guard did so and Blap shoved Yerkal in and the door closed.

"Blaphaus, you can't do that." Peezle complained.

"I just did."

In the interrogation room, a nervous Yerkal stood in front of the table Depatie sat behind. He had his arms on the table, wrists cuffed. He looked up at the shaking human before him.

"Whoa, you're the most nervous looking being I ever saw. What's your deal?"

Yerkal sat across the table as the others looked through the one sided window into the room.

"M-my deal? My deal is I was shoved in here... by... by..."

"The Galactic President... the Toob. I saw. I also have good ears and heard his annoying voice. So, you're not a Governor I'm guessing... you don't look like a GBI type... too neat and handsome. And you're practically crapping in your pants so I'll say you're some kind of Solicitor."

Yerkal nodded, "Well done. And you?"

"Me? I work for one of the military bases on Xenartha. Fort Cowl. You heard of it?"

Yerkal nodded, "Yes, I heard of it. That's the base where you killed a bunch of innocent beings."

"Actually, most of the beings were killed when I left the base. Do you know who I was supposed to be guarding?"

"The Gink Governor Guoz. But he is dead."

Depatie sat back in his chair, "What makes you say that?"

"I saw him die." Yerkal glared across the table.

"You *think* you saw him die." Depatie laughed, "You all have no idea."

"I'm not here to talk about the Gink. I'm here to talk about you. Why did you murder all those innocent beings and why stop at twenty-two?"

"That was the number I was told."

"Told? So, you work for someone?"

"We all work for someone, human. No matter how high up on the pole you are there's someone above you."

"So, are you a member of the Order of Blattodea?"

“You could say that.”

“But you’re not a Cakerlak...”

“Do you think only Cakerlak belong to the Order?”

“No.. but…“

“Apparently a long time ago the Cakerlak started the Order, but that was then. You name a species, human, they are in the Order. There’s thousands and thousands of us.”

Yerkal gulped, “Where are the Gink from? Not from this galaxy we know, so how did they get involved?”

“Why don’t you ask your Toob G.P.?” Depatie asked. “He probably has more answers than he says.”

Yerkal stood up and Depatie almost looked surprised.

“That’s it? No more questions?”

“Nope. I heard enough.”

“Really? Did I hit a nerve? I have so many more answers.”

“That’s okay, I’m good. You’re going to spend a long time in prison, Depatie. I hope you think you made the right decision.”

“It doesn’t matter what my decision was... it was for the Order. I hope you survive all this when this is over.”

“When what is over?” Yerkal asked.

“You said you had no more questions, human. Nice talking to you.”

Yerkal went to the door that the Squamata opened. Yerkal stepped out the room and the door was closed. Rüppell and Sugden were standing there with the others.

“Governor Sugden… Governor Rüppell…” Yerkal nodded to them.

“Wot did he say?” Blap asked.

“He admitted to the blasterings which he couldn’t really deny. He said a lot of different species are part of the Order and that you have more answers than he has.”

“I have no answers.” Blaphaus said, “Did he mention the Great Weta?”

Yerkal shook his head, “No, no mention of anything in particular. Except the Gink...”

Sugden said, “He was supposed to be guarding the room the coffin was in. What did he say?”

“He didn’t really say, but hinted the Gink is still alive.”

“The King killed him, we saw it.” Peezle remarked.

“Did we?” Yerkal asked.

Sugden said, “I’ll get a medical robot to examine him.”

Allard, Zalez and Nate walked through the vehicle park area at the spaceport on Launderington. They reached a black sleek looking vehicle, that looked just like the one Allard had on Ceilingida.

"You have two vehicles?" Nate asked.

"I have more than that, my friend. I have vehicles on most planets. In my business you never know which planet you'd end up on." Allard smiled, opening the back door for them.

Joorg stepped outside the small craft, which was on the side of the cliff, which a species that Blaphaus met in the casino, black with pointed ears and a flat face piloted.

"That's 1.000 lucre, Cyrakuse."

"That's too expensive." complained Joorg, reaching inside his purple jacket, handing the Bach some paper dosh.

"I flew your ass across the galaxy, to this creepy planet. I should charge you more."

Joorg said, "I'll pay you another thousand to fly me back in a bit."

Laterille stepped out the door of the castle, with two Cakerlak guards holding six swords each, one in each hand.

"What are you doing here, Cyrakuse? You are not welcome."

"I'm here to see the Great Weta, Laterille. Move out of the way."

"As I said, you are not welcome here." she said.

The Bach looked through the windshield of his craft at the situation that was going outside. He knew of the Cakerlak's reputation and didn't want to be involved, or dragged into any nonsense. He also didn't want to watch the Cakerlak get murdered. Behind Joorg the craft lifted up, spun around and flew up to the sky. So much for waiting, Joorg thought. He swallowed hard, clenching his fists.

"Let me see the Great Weta." he pleaded once more.

Laterille thought for a moment, then stepped aside. Joorg puffed out his chest and strolled into the castle. Laterille motioned for the guards to follow her, and they followed Joorg.

The Great Weta sat in his chamber on one throne when Joorg marched into the chamber.

"Great Weta!"

The Great Weta looked down at the Cyrakuse in the purple suit.

"How dare you come into this chamber!" the Weta cried out.

"You had my wife murdered!"

"Your wife let herself get murdered. At least she did what she was supposed to do."

"This all stops now. I don't know what the end game is, but whatever your Order of Blattodea is doing it needs to stop."

"It's not going to stop until the time is ready. And that's not going to happen until I say it's ready."

"No, it's ending now." Joorg stupidly ran and leapt at the Great Weta who flung him back, with all six arms. Joorg rolled on the chamber floor, before he sat up. He huffed and puffed as he climbed to his feet.

"If you kill me, Cyrakuse, which won't happen, but if you do then everything will happen to this galaxy a lot quicker. You don't want that."

Joorg said, "You took everything I had away from me. I will kill you."

Laterille and the guards watched from the shadows as Joorg attempted the second time to run and leap at the Great Weta, who this time grabbed the Cyrakuse with his three left arms. Joorg struggled to break free but the Great Weta just squeezed harder. Joorg reached out, grabbing either side of the Cakerlak's black head. The guards quickly pulled Joorg off the Great Weta and went to stab him to death with their spears.

"Stop!" shouted the Weta.

They did so, steeping back from Joorg who laid there on the ground.

"Cyrakuse, you are now part of the Order and will do exactly what I ask of you, or you will be reunited with your wife before you know it."

It was at that moment Laterille realized she didn't want to be a part of this any longer.

## CHAPTER 14

Allard, Zalez and Nate walked up the steps of the House and through the front glass doors into the foyer where the House robot greeted them.

"Hello, Mr. Belhopsa, Young Nate Belhopsa, Allard Felipe. How can I help you?"

"We are here to see the G.P., or if he isn't here any Governor. Presumably Dawber. But at this point we'll take anyone." Allard told the robot.

"I will take you upstairs." the robot replied.

Nate said, "Last time I was here was when I was going through Mr. Traf's info-pad files."

Allard frowned and looked down at Nate.

"Traf's info-pad? Do tell."

Dawber looked up from her desk when the robot appeared in the doorway.

"Governor Dawber, you have some friends visiting."

Allard and the other two stepped into the office as Dawber stood up quickly.

"Allard, what is the meaning of this?"

"Hello, Governor Dawber." smiled Nate.

"It's a long story, you and the other Governors are going to want to hear. Especially the Toob. First thing first though, where is Traf's info-pad?" Allard asked.

"It was taken back to his house. Why?"

"Because I want to see the files young Nate looked at."

"They were copied into Governor Peezle's info-pad." Nate said.

"Peezle is not here. He should be heading back though soon, with Blaphaus." Dawber told them.

Allard sat down in a chair and out his feet up on the desk, and hands behind the back of his head.

"Then you might want to order dinner for everyone, it's going to be a long night."

Blaphaus and the Peezle's went through the Launderington spaceport with the GNN robot-cams following their moves.

"I wish those bloody things would go away." Blap muttered.

They passed the Sunquid shop as the woman with the short blonde hair turned her head. Fami almost spat out her drink, the timing couldn't be more perfect. She slowly followed them, not getting too close. Phedorra could suck it, she thought to herself.

Narob Traf walked down the stairs in the Traf house on Launderington. His hair was all slicked back, and he wore a black and gray suit and tie. He walked into the living room where 1-4-3 stood. His mother sat on the couch, eyes closed. Narob touched her on the shoulder and she woke with a stir.

"Honey! Sorry! I was sleeping!"

"You look nice, Master Narob." One told him.

"Buterdau Kooper from GNN is stopping by, mother."

"Buterdau? I like him." she smiled, "Is it a date?"

Narob made a disgusted look, "Nooo! He's going to be interviewing me about Narob Energy."

"Narob Energy? What's that?"

Narob rolled his eyes, "I told you I'm changing the name of Dook Energy to Narob Energy."

"Ooohhh. I thought you were kidding."

The door buzzer then buzzed. One went to the front door and opened it up to see Buterdau standing there, with a robot-cam hovering next to him.

"Hello, Mr. Kooper, come on in. Master Narob is expecting you."

The news Leetric nodded and smiled, "Thank you."

He stepped inside and Narob approached him, handing his hand out.

"Welcome, thanks for coming by."

They shook hands.

"Of course."

The Peezle's walked through the doors of the House moments before Blaphaus who had to use the lift. The House robot approached them.

"Hello, Galactic President, Governor Peezle, Mister Yerkal Peezle. You have visitors upstairs waiting on you. They have been here for hours."

"I don't want visitors." Blap said, "I had a long day."

Buterdau and Narob sat outside by the swimming pool. The robot-cam hovered before them, looking from side to side.

"Hello, I'm Buterdau Kooper, live on Launderington at the late Galactic President Traf's house, meeting with Narob Thaw, Algar's son. Hello, Narob, how are you?"

"I'm doing okay, Buterdau."

"So, how have you been doing since your father passed away?"

"I'm not doing too bad."

"Can you explain to everyone why you invited me here today?"

"Yes, I invited you here so I can tell the galaxy that as owner of Dook Energy I am changing the name to Narob Energy."

"Why is that?" Buterdau asked.

"The Dook Brothers have been dead for years. I never knew why my father didn't change the name to Traf Energy."

"So, it's not an ego thing?"

"It's new times, Mr. Kooper. A new galaxy as the Toob G.P. said."

"True. So, what do you think of how G.P. Maximus is doing as Galactic President?"

"Honestly, my father was a useless G.P., but at least the galaxy was at peace. Now the Cakerlak are aggregated, there's blasterings happening..."

Blaphaus and the Peezle's walked into the conference room where the Governor's sat watching the holo-images of GNN, watching the interview. All were there but Peezle, Sugden and Allard, Zalez and Nate walked up the steps of the House and through the front glass doors into the foyer where the House robot greeted them.

"Hello, Mr. Belhopsa, Young Nate Belhopsa, Allard Felipe. How can I help you?"

"We are here to see the G.P., or if he isn't here any Governor. Presumably Dawber. But at this point we'll take anyone." Allard told the robot.

"I will take you upstairs." the robot replied.

Nate said,"Last time I was here was when I was going through Mr. Traf's info-pad files."

Allard frowned and looked down at Nate.

"Traf's info-pad? Do tell."

Dawber looked up from her desk when the robot appeared in the doorway.

"Governor Dawber, you have some friends visiting."

Allard and the other two stepped into the office. Dawber stood up quickly.

"Allard, whst is the meaning of this?"

"Hello, Governor Dawber." smiled Nate.

"It's a long story, you and the other Governors are going to want to hear. Especially the Toob. First thing first though, where is Traf's info-pad?"

"It was taken back to his house. Why?"

"Because I want to see the files young Nate looked at."

"They were copied into Governor Peezle's info-pad." Nate said.

"Peezle is not here. He should be heading back though soon, with Blaphaus." Dawber told them.

Allard sat down in a chair and out his feet up on the desk, and hands behind the back of his head.

"Then you might want to order dinner for everyone, it's going to be a long night."

Blaphaus, Rüppell and the Peezle's went through the Launderington spaceport with the GNN robot-cams following their moves.

"I wish those bloody things would go away." Blap muttered.

They passed the Sunquid shop as the woman with the short blonde hair turned her head. Fami almost spat out her drink, the timing couldn't be more perfect. She slowly followed them, not getting too close. Phedorra could suck it, she thought to herself.

Narob Traf walked down the stairs in the Traf house on Launderington. His hair was all slicked back, and he wore a black and gray suit and tie. He walked into the living room where 1-4-3 stood. His mother sat on the couch, eyes closed. Narob touched her on the shoulder and she woke with a stir.

"Honey! Sorry! I was sleeping!"

"You look nice, Master Narob." One told him.

"Buterdau Kooper from GNN is stopping by, mother."

"Buterdau? I like him." she smiled, "Is it a date?"

Narob made a disgusted look, "Nooo! He's going to be interviewing me about Narob Energy."

"Narob Energy? What's that?"

Narob rolled his eyes, "I told you I'm changing the name of Dook Energy to Narob Energy."

"Ooohhh. I thought you were kidding."

The door buzzer just buzzed. One went to the front door and opened it up to see Buterdau standing there, with a robot-cam hovering next to him.

"Hello, Mr. Kooper, come on in. Master Narob is expecting you."

The news Leetric nodded and smiled, "Thank you."

He stepped inside and Narob approached him, handing his hand out.

"Welcome, thanks for coming by."

They shook hands.

"Of course."

The Peezle's and Rüppell walked through the doors of the House moments before Blaphaus who had to use the lift. The House robot approached them.

"Hello, Galactic President, Governor Peezle, Governor Rüppell, Mister Yerkal Peezle. You have visitors upstairs waiting on you. They have been here for hours."

"I don't want visitors." Blap said, "I had a long day."

Buterdau and Narob sat outside by the swimming pool. The robot-cam hovered before them, looking from side to side.

"Hello, I'm Buterdau Kooper, live on Launderington at the late Galactic President Traf's house, meeting with Narob Thaw, Algar's son. Hello, Narob, how are you?"

"I'm doing okay, Buterdau."

"So, how have you been doing since your father passed away?"

"I'm not doing too bad. I invited you here so I can tell the galaxy that as owner of Dook Energy I am changing the name to Narob Energy."

"Why is that?" Buterdau asked.

"The Dook Brothers have been dead for years. I never knew why my father didn't change the name to Traf Energy."

"So, it's not an ego thing?"

"It's new times, Mr. Kooper. A new galaxy as the Toob G.P. said."

"True. So, what do you think of how G.P. Maximus is doing as Galactic President?"

"Honestly, my father was a useless G.P., but at least the galaxy was at peace. Now the Cakerlak are aggregated, there's blasterings happening…"

Blaphaus, Rüppell and the Peezle's walked into the conference room where the Governor's sat watching the holo-images of GNN, watching the interview. All were there Sugden, but Allard was sitting there as well.

"You know that's not good he's talking about the Order." Thaw commented.

"Who are you? Wot's going on here?" Blap asked.

"Welcome back." Southington said.

Dawber motioned to Allard who sat next to her.

"This is Allard Filipe, Blaphaus. He's a friend."

"You're the swarmy, good looking idiot who was hanging out here the other day." Blap pointed out.

"Yeah, I tried to talk to you, but you are as stubborn in real life as you seem on GNN." Allard said, standing up.

"I was told there's visitors here. Is that you?"

"Me and two friends of yours, yes."

"Where are they?"

"I'll show you."

Narob said on GNN, "I will be telling Governor Jaboney that Narob Energy will be taking over powering Old Eborocum."

"What?! Who does he think he is?" Jaboney asked.

"Peezle, I heard you have Traf's files on your info-pad." Allard said to Peezle.

"Uhhhhh... yeah."

"I need to see it."

"What do you think Governor Jaboney will say about that, Narob?" Buterdau asked.

"I don't care, he's not going to have a choice."

"What about the other planets that Dook... I mean Narob Energy doesn't give power and electricity to?"

"Those will be dealt with afterwards."

"Dealt with?"

"Yes, I plan to meet with representatives from all the planets."

Peezle led Allard and Yerkal into his office, as Blaphaus watched.

"Who are you before we show you anything?" Blaphaus asked.

"Let's just day I'm your security advisor, G.P. Maximus." Allard smiled, "I could be your and the Cabinet's greatest ally. You have enemies out there."

"Everyone has enemies." Blap replied.

"Not everyone is as important as you are though. Go to Dawber's office, you have friends waiting for you there. We also have dinner waiting."

Yerkal said, "I'll walk with you, Blaphaus."

Allard sat behind Peezle's desk and rubbed his hands together.

"Okay, Governor Peezle, let's see what is on Traf's files."

Yerkal led Blaphaus to Dawber's office where Nate and Zalez were sitting, having dinner.

"Mister Blaphaus!" Nate jumped to his feet wanting to hug the G.P., but then studiod him closely.

"Kid? Wot are you doing here? Belhopsa, I don't like surprises." he told Zalez.

"I know. But Mr. Filipe suggested that we come here, to talk to you. Nate has a lot to tell you."

"I like this kid, so I'll listen. Wot is it, kid?"

Nate swallowed, trying to figure out how to start.

"This lady came by the school, asking to talk to me. She said her name was Fami Tapperdau..."

"Tapperdau?" Blap asked, "Yeah, I heard. Wot did she say?"

"She asked me lots of questions about you, Me. Blaphaus. She said you are not who you say you are."

"Oh, really? Who did she say I was?"

"She didn't."

"Young Nate here doesn't think you are who you say you are either." told Allard, walking into the office.

Zalez stood up, "That's enough. You can't put words in my son's mouth."

"No, let the kid tell me." Blap looked down at Nate. "Who am I?"

"I don't know who you are, but I don't think you're really a Tooberosum." Nate said seriously.

"Really? Have you ever met a Tooberosum before, kid?"

"No. Have you?" Nate frowned.

"Wot do you think?"

"I think no one in this office has met a real a Tooberosum."

Yerkal said, "That's what makes Blaphaus unique."

Blap turned to Zalez and Peezle, they knew the truth.

"You are a stubborn bastard, Blaphaus." chuckled Allard.

"What's going on?" Yerkal's eyes were wide open. "I feel like I'm missing an inside joke. Noj, what's going on?"

Peezle rubbed his head, "Mr. Felipe, did you discover anything with Algar's files?"

"Yeah, I need to look more though, but I know what the words are with the numbers."

"Are they planets?" Nate asked, "From a different galaxy?"

All of a sudden they forgot about the conversation about what Blaphaus was.

"No, not planets. Beings." Allard pointed out. "We'll talk about that later. Right now, Blaphaus you need to listen to the boy here."

"The kid who doesn't think I'm real?" Blaphaus asked.

"I don't know what you are, Mr. Blaphaus, but there's a group of beings, who Mr. Allard says are the Committee and they want to reveal who or what you're really are."

Blaphaus said, "Let them. I don't care wot they think. Or wot you think, kid. You wasted a perfectly good day of school for this?"

Jaboney then appeared in the doorway, and went over at Zalez.

"Sorry to interrupt, Mr. Belhopsa, but Traf's son said he wants to meet with me on Old Eborocum. He wants his company to take over powering the planet. I don't know what to say to the kid. Want to come with me?"

Zalez said, "I'd love to, but I have Nate here..."

"I'm not meeting Narob by myself. I don't trust him."

Nate said, "I want to go, father, and I think Mr. Blaphaus should go as well."

"Blaphaus?" asked Zalez.

"Fine. I'll go." Blaphaus said.

Allard said, "Before you go, I have to tell you that those names from Traf's computer are members of the Committee's names... and some others I don't know."

"You're coming to Old Eborocum as well, Filipe."

"You want *me* to go?"

"You're my security advisor, right?"

Allard winked.


Sugden walked into the building on the base, greeted by Brigadier Harkouk.

"Governor, I have two soldiers guarding the room the coffin is in."

They went down the hallway towards the room which was guarded by two Illicit guards. One of them unlocked the door, and they went inside to see the Illicit doctor standing there in his white lab coat next to the black shiny coffin.

"Governor." the doctor shook Sugden's hand.

"Doctor Dasy, good to see you. Did you open the coffin?"

"Not yet, I was told to wait for you, Governor."

"Fair enough, doctor. I'm here now. Open the coffin."

The Brigadier and the guards pointed their blasters at the cabin just in case something went crazy. Doctor Dasy unlocked the coffin, and slowly lifted the top part up. They peered into it to see the Gink laying there, eyes wide open. They could see he wasn't breathing though, and even with his large eyes open he still looked like he was dead. The doctor pulled out a small electronic device from his pocket and ran it over the Gink's body.

"I'm going to get medic-robots to examine him in the morgue, Governor Sugden, but according to this device he is dead, with a broken neck."

Sugden nodded and said, "Close the lid."

The doctor closed up the coffin.

"I'll let the Cabinet know right away before I go to Launderington. Thank you, doctor."

"You're welcome, Governor."

The doctor watched the Governor and the soldiers including the Brigadier walk out the room. Discreetly Dasy tapped into the coffin lid three times.


Fami waited outside the House, at the bottom of the steps. At the top inside the foyer, Allard looked through the glass doors to see Fami at the bottom of the steps.

"She won't quit."

"Who?" Jaboney asked.

Jaboney stood with Zalez, Nate and Blaphaus in the House foyer.

"Fami Tapperdau." Allard said, "She's outside, at the bottom of the steps."

"Who is she?" Jaboney asked.

"I'll go out there and give her a piece of my mind." Blap went to the glass doors and looked out. As soon as he saw her he knew exactly who she was. It was her, the one he met at the pub. He knew it.

"Feces! I know who she is."

"You met her?" Allard asked.

"Yeah, long story."

"You can tell us on the way to my planet." Jaboney said, "We need to get going."

"Is there an exit other than these front doors?" Allard asked.

No one said a word, they all looked blank.

The turned to the House robot who stood watching them all.

"Well?" Allard asked the robot.

"No, this is the only entrance and exit." the robot replied.

"Well, we are not leaving." Allard said. "She knows you Nate. Does she know you, Belhopsa?"

Zalez shook his head, "No, I don't know who she is."

Outside a few robot-cams from GNN arrived, and hovered outside the House. Fami spotted them and hastily went across the street to where the long reflecting pool was. She did not want to be seen on GNN. Allard spotted this and chuckled.

"Love the media. Blaphaus, you're not going to fit in my car."

"Rubyspears will take me."

"Where is this Rubyspears?"

The robot said, "I'll contact him."

Allard smiled, "Perfect. I'm going to go and say hello to my friend. As soon as your vehicle shows up hop into it."

Allard went outside and down the steps, and across the street whistling. Fami spotted him and did not look happy.

"What are you doing here, Felipe?"

"You know, trying to be Governor." Allard joked, "What about you?"

"I am not telling you what I'm doing." she said.

Behind Allard Rubyspears drove his limousine-vehicle up in front of the House. He stepped out and Blaphaus walked out the building with the other three. He went to his lift, the others went down the steps. Fami's eyes opened wide, spotting them all. She went to go across the street but Allard grabbed her by the arm, holding her.

"Allard! Let go!" she struggled, trying to get free.

The others got into the long black vehicle which moments later drove off. It was then that Allard let go of Fami's arm.

"You're not getting to the Toob that easy, Fami."

"You know he's not a Toob, right?"

"Yep. But for the sake of the galaxy you're not going to expose him."

"I might not, but one of the Committee members will. They are sending Phedorra."

For once Allard did not look happy.

"Phedorra? That old man didn't retire yet?"

She smirked, "Not yet. I do not know what your deal is in this whole thing, Allard, but you better be careful. Feces is going to hit the fan."


"This is Crisp Jaboney, it looks like my brother the Governor of Old Eborocum and Zalez Belhopsa and his son Nate as well as the Galactic President is leaving the House. It looks like they are going to head to Old Eborocum to meet with Narob Traf. We will keep you posted."


The holo-call of Narob stood in the dark chamber.

"Governor Jaboney is on the way to Old Eborocum to meet with myself. Is there anything I could do?"

The Great Weta shook his head, "Keep doing what you're doing, Narob. I am very proud of you. You did a good job on Phytnes. The Order of Blattodea is proud to have you as one of our own."

"My father could not hack it, so I'm proud to be a member. I just want to know when the final and major attack will happen."

"Soon, young Narob, you have to be patient."

Narob nodded, thinking he wasn't going to wait forever.


Allard was the last to board Space False One, the others were already on board.

"Space False One? That's pretty clever." chuckled Allard, taking a seat.

"Thank you, I came up with it myself." Jaboney replied, sitting in his seat.

Across the aisle Nate sat next to his father. Blaphaus was strapped in in the back as normal. Allard looked over his shoulder at him.

"You know you can make things a lot easier for yourself, Blaphaus."

"And you can shut your bloody gob." Blap remarked.

The pilot said over the intercom, "Please sit back, buckle in. We'll be taking off to Old Eborocum in a minute."

"I have no idea why Narob couldn't just meet at the House or his house on Launderington." Jaboney said.

"He's a teenager, you know how teenagers are." Allard said.

"So, Allard, what are the names?" Zalez asked, "That are on his father's info-pad?"

"Like I said, members of the Committee and a bunch of other names. Lots of them."

"The password on the info-pad was 'Blattodea,' Mr. Allard." Nate told the tall man. "Was the Galactic President a goodie or a baddie?"

"That I don't know. Unfortunately he's dead, so we can't ask. But I'll be glad to ask his kid today." he looked back at Blaphaus, "As for you, Blaphaus, your species has a reputation."

"Humans have a reputation as well."

"Yeah, but at least we weren't in a war with the Cakerlak."

"Yet." Blaphaus muttered.

Just then the yellow shuttle lifted and flew up to the sky and to space.

A little while later the black vehicle drove up to the old Planet Mayor's building in the city of Old Eborocum. Bella, Jaboney's Cyrakuse Assistant stood outside the building as the vehicle passengers got out.

"Governor Jaboney! Welcome back, sir!" Bella gave Jaboney a big hug. It was the first time she saw him in over a week.

"Your guest is inside. It's Narob Traf."

"Thank you, Bella." Jaboney said. "How is he?"

"Weeeelll... he's a piece... no, I don't want to be disrespectful, sir."

"He's a punk arse teenager." Blaphaus remarked.

"A rich punk ass teenager." Allard smirked.

Nate chuckled a bit and Zalez gave a disapproving look.

"He's just... standoffish." Bella remarked. "He also seems impatient."

"If he would have met us Launderington." Jaboney replied, "We were all there. But it's good to be here back home. Let's get this over with."

He made his way to go inside, followed by Blap and Allard.

Zalez whispered to Nate, "I don't know if this is appropriate for you, son. Just stay quiet and blend in."

"Sure, father." Nate looked up at the tall buildings of the city in the near distance.

"I want to see the city."

"Not this trip. Maybe we'll come back as a family." Zalez told Nate, leading him inside.

Inside, Narob sat in the waiting area, the same as the two Governors sat in when Blaphaus first came to the planet to talk Jaboney into becoming Governor. He stood up, straightening his jacket when he saw Jaboney walk in with Bella. He shook Jaboney's hand tightly.

"Thank you for meeting with me, Governor." Narob then spotted the others and was taken back. "Why are they here?"

"If it's a meeting to do with anything in the galaxy then the Galaxy President should be involved." Jaboney replied, "And Zalez Belhopsa is the head of Dook Energy so he should be involved."

Narob frowned at Nate, "Shouldn't you be in school?"

"I'm on a 'business' trip." Nate grinned.

"And who are you?" Narob asked Allard rudely.

"Allard Felipe, the G.P.'s Security Advisor. Nice to meet you, Master Traf."

"Since when does the G.P. need a Security Advisor? My father never had one..."

"He had Peezle." Blap said, "And no disrespect, kid, but no one ever threatened to kill your father."

Narob frowned, "Because he wasn't a member of an ultra-rare species that in the past wiped out millions of beings."

"Let's not argue here." Jaboney told them, "Let's go to my meeting room and we can discuss business."

They all made their way to the meeting room. Jaboney sat at the end of the table. Narob sat to his right, Allard to his left. Blaphaus stood at the opposite end of the wooden table. Zalez sat next to Allard, with Nate sitting next to him, studying everyone's body language.. especially Blaphaus' who pretty much just blinked now and then and moved his arms and hands quite a bit. Especially when he spoke.

"So, you want Dook Energy to take over powering this planet." Jaboney commented. "Am I right?"

Narob replied, "Well, it's not Dook Energy anymore, Governor, it's Narob Energy now."

"If it says 'Dook' on the side of the space station it's still Dook." Jaboney said. "You can't just change the name. I mean, Zalez is wearing a blue Dook uniform with the Dook Energy logo."

"That will change. Since my father passed away and I became the owner of the space station I have the right to change the name."

"Who will own it when you pass away?" Allard asked, staring across the table at the teenager.

"Are you threatening me, Security Advisor?" Narob asked bravely.

"No, but with all the blasterings that happened, no one is really safe." Allard commented.

"Who knows if there's going to be another blastering?" Narob asked.

"I don't know." Allard remarked.

"My sister takes over. But I am going to have that changed. She's not suitable to run a business."

"And you are?" Allard asked.

"Yes. This meeting is supposed to be with Governor Jaboney, not you."

Allard nodded, "I agree. Sorry to interrupt."

Jaboney gave a slight smile to Allard. He liked him, he was cool and suave and smart like Jaboney was, so he thought.

"Mister Traf, I own Consolidated, it's a company that my father owned and my grandfather before him. One day I hope to have a son and pass it down to him, like your father passed down Dook to you."

"Consolidated is a small company, Governor, powering one planet. Narob Energy powers all the other planets..."

"Actually, Narob, Dook... or Narob Energy doesn't power *all* the planets. Tooberosum is not powered by us."

Narob turned to look at Zalez, "I'm here to talk to Jaboney about taking over Consolidated. That's it." Narob was getting irritated, he was not happy they were all there.

"You won't be able to afford to buy my company, young man. And you're not going to put my employees out of work."

"Give me a number." Narob looked Jaboney in the eyes.

"500,000 lucre."

"Five hundred thousand?" Narob asked surprised, "This whole planet is not worth 500,000!"

"Can I ask you a question?" Allard asked Narob.

"If you must, Mr. Felipe."

"Have you heard of the Order of Blattodea?"

Narob tried to hide his anger and surprise, "Excuse me?"

"The Order. Of. Blattodea." Allard said slowly.

Inside Blaphaus was actually smiling.

"What does that have to do with this business deal?"

"It's a major part." Allard said, standing up. "Do you know who they are?"

"No. And I don't care." he lied.

"Okay, have you heard of the Committee?"

"I heard of a few different committee's."

"What about *the* Committee?"

"No, should I?" Narob asked.

Allard shrugged, "Depends. Do you know that the House borrowed your father's info-pad?"

"Yes, the G.P. and some of his Governor's showed up at my house to borrow it."

"Really? And you let them?"

"Sure. It wasn't mine."

"Blaphaus, what did you want the info-pad for?" Allard turned to Blaphaus surprisingly.

"To research Traf funding Cakerlak and to see wot else Traf was up to."

"And what did you find out?"

Nate spoke up, "I looked through the files! It was a bunch of numbers and names."

Zalez gave Nate a dirty look to shush him.

"What names?" Allard asked, knowing the answer.

"I don't know... " Nate looked at his father for some advice.

"I don't know where you're going with this." Zalez told the man standing next to him.

"This has nothing to do with this business deal." Narob said, "I don't know why you're talking about this. What my father did has nothing to do with me."

"The password on the info-pad was what, Nate?" Allard asked.

Nate looked at his father again, not sure what he should say.

"The word was 'Blattodea.'" Blaphaus remarked.

"So, your father knew of the Order." Allard said.

"So?"

"Some of the names are members of the Committee." Allard told him.

"Like I said, I don't know. You know it all it seems though, Mr. Felipe."

Allard smiled, "I know a lot, but I wouldn't say I know it all. Why do you think your father had Blattodea as a password?"

"I don't know. Maybe he was part of the Order..."

"I don't think so, Narob. I don't think that was his info-pad."

"It was taken from his office..."

"That means nothing." Allard said.

"Then whose info-pad was it?"

"Was it yours?" Jaboney asked Narob.

Allard smiled at the Governor, glad he was catching on.

"No, it wasn't mine." Narob said.

"I believe that." Allard said sitting back down. "You may continue your business deal now."

"Thank the Creator." sighed Jaboney. "Kid, for 500,000 you can't have Consolidated."

"Three hundred thousand." Narob counter offered.

"How about 450,000 and you don't lay off any of my employees. And the company stays in the building on this planet."

Narob said, "How about 400,000 and I won't let anybody off?"

"Deal." Jaboney shook Narob's hand, looking across the long table at Blaphaus. "You agree, G.P. Maximus?"

Blap snorted, "Your company, not mine."

Narob smiled and stood up, "I'll have my Solicitor draw up the contract and I'll get you the dosh."

Jaboney stood as well, "We'll make the announcement together."

"Sure."

"My Assistant Bella will see you out, Narob."

Narob went to the doors, which opened to reveal Bella.

Narob turned to the others, "Whatever my father was doing it has nothing to do with me. We are two different people."

"Wotever." Blap told him.

Narob left with Bella who closed the doors. Jaboney sighed and sat down.

"I hope I made the right decision."

"You didn't, but that's not a big deal." Allard remarked.

Zalez said, "I definitely don't like his business skills... he's a teenager with too much power."

"Forget him." Blap waved a hand, "So, whose info-pad was it?"

"His father's." Allard told them, "But Narob's name was on it..."

***CHAPTER 15***

Narob sat in the backseat of the vehicle that was ordered for him to go back to the spaceport. His mind was reeling about what that smug tall Security Advisor talked about. That computer wasn't his, but if it was his father's why was "Blattodea" the password? Was his father a member of the Order? When Narob was approached by a member of the Order when he was at school he did not take it seriously. He was told that it'll be good for the galaxy. Then his father had to die from a stupid heart attack and the Toob was chosen as Galaxy President. It was explained to him that the blasterings had to happen, it was the only way to "save" the galaxy. Now the Toob hired some kind of Security Advisor who seems to know more than Narob liked. Who was this Committee, what were their names? Did the Order or the Great Weta know about it? Narob decided he wasn't going to go to Launderington right away, he was going to go to Cakerlak and speak to Great Weta in person.

"Narob's name?" Jaboney asked Allard.

"Traf's father?" Blaphaus asked.

Allard nodded, "Yes, I believe so. Somehow I think Traf knew about the Order, he definitely knew about the Committee. Anyway, I think that kid knows more than he's letting on. That damn kid was lying."

"Lying is not good." Nate pointed out.

"Everyone lies." Blap told the boy.

"Not everyone." Zalez gave Blap a dirty look.

"Oh, really, Chordattian? Tell me... when your kid asks you about me, wot I am, you don't say anything?"

"That's not lying, that's keeping the truth."

"Which is lying where I come from."

"Which is where?" Allard asked.

Jaboney stood up, "I'd love to sit here and hear you argue but I have to go to my Consolidated building and tell them I'm not their boss anymore. What did I just do?"

"Got a little bit richer." Allard winked.

"Dosh is not everything." Jaboney remarked.

"It is where I come from." Blaphaus muttered.

"Zalez, can you come with me to help talk to my employees? You're head of Doo... Narob Energy, you can help me explain to them."

Zalez nodded, "Sure I can."

"And Blaphaus, you as well?"

"Me as well wot?"

"Come to the Consolidated building? Hopefully if you're there it might help as well."

"I doubt it, Jaboney. I'm not liked."

"You are on this planet. Trust me."

"As Security Advisor I recommend you go." Allard told Blaphaus, "I'll be there with you."

"Wotever."

"Well, it looks like we are all taking the train then." Jaboney smiled.

Nate grinned, "Yay! I've never been on a train before."

Yerkal walked down the House steps, looking perplexed as normal. Fami walked across the street hastily, and headed right to him.

"Mr. Peezle? Mr. Peezle, right?"

He stopped and turned to face her.

"Ummm... yeah, can I help you?"

"My name is Fami Tapperdau and I need to speak to the G.P., or any of the Governors. Can you help me with that?"

"Well, my husband is inside, and some other Governors. As far as the G.P. goes, I don't know when he'll be back."

"I met your husband before. I don't know if he mentioned to the G.P. I was here."

Yerkal just shrugged, "I can't help you."

"That's understandable, sir. If you see the G.P. mention to him I was asking about him."

Yerkal gave a slight smile, "I sure will."

She then took his arm and brought his ear close to her mouth.

"I know what Blaphaus really is. I think your husband and the Governors also know. You might want to ask them if you don't."

She stepped back, smiled and adjusted her spectacles before she walked off leaving him standing there dumbfounded.

Blaphaus, Zalez, Nate, Jaboney and Allard rode on the train going through the city. They were the only ones in what was labeled "The Planet Mayor Compartment." Not being a P.M. anymore Jaboney made a mental note that needed to be changed. Nate was in awe, looking out the windows at the big buildings going by. To him this was the coolest looking planet he's been on, which wasn't that many. His father used the compartment info-pad to contact Mal. Her twelve inch holo-call appeared in front of him.

"Hello, darling." he smiled, nervous of what she'll say.

"How's every going on Launderington, Zalez?"

"It was okay. Nate is doing good. We are now in a train on..."

"A train? There's no trains on Launderington..."

"We are not on Launderington anymore, Mal. We had to go to Old Eborocum."

"Old Eborocum! That's far away."

"Not too far. We had to come here as Narob Traf just purchased Consolidated, Governor Jaboney's power company."

"Zalez! You have to let me know when you take Nate to other planets! I do not believe you did this again!"

"I'm sorry, but I didn't have a choice..."

Nate piped in, "It's okay, mother! I'm on a train and it's so much fun!"

"I'm sure you're having a good time, Nate, but it's still not good that you're on a planet that I didn't know you were on."

Jaboney told Zalez, "Tell her nothing can go wrong on Old Eborocum."

"Tell the Governor I bet the other planets where the blasterings took place thought the same thing."

"I know your concern, Mal, and I agree. After this we'll come right back home. I promise."

The train pulled into the station outside the tall black Consolidated building. Allard stood and stretched.

"Looks like we are here."

They all stepped off the train to be confronted with two GNN robot-cams.

Crisp Jaboney's voice came out of one of them.

"We are here on Old Eborocum where my brother the Governor got off a train with the G.P. and a few friends. Hello, brother."

"Crisp, I don't have time for this." Jaboney scowled.

"I just have a few questions for the G.P."

"I don't have answers. I wish someone would buy GNN and shut these bloody robots down."

"That's a shame. GNN has been contacted by an anonymous being saying that you, Galactic President Maximus are working hand in hand with the Cakerlak and is planning an invasion of Toobs to this galaxy. What do you think of that claim?"

"I don't know wot the bloody hell you are talking about."

"You have been to Cakerlak a few times and even recently sent the Cakerlak Governor Joorg there, am I right?" the voice from the robot-cam said.

Jaboney pointed you it and remarked, "Brother, this is not the time."

"Whoever said this is full of feces. I'm not working with the bloody Cakerlak on anything and as far as the Governor for that bloody planet goes Cakerlak is not part of the Cabinet anymore and Joorg is not Governor."

Allard smiled charmingly at the robot's lens and said, "As the G.P.'s Security Advisor I say this conversation is over, we have business to attend to."

Zalez pulled Nate discreetly away so his son wouldn't he caught in the images and broadcast.

"If Cakerlak is not part of the Cabinet when were you going to announce this to the public?" the "robot" asked.

"When I bloody felt like it." Blap turned to walk off, getting irritated.

One of the robot-cams followed him.

"Do you know where the Cakerlak Governor is, Galactic President?"

Blap turned to face the hovering robot, "Nope. And I really don't care."

"Do you know anything about the ex-G.P. Traf giving lucre to fund the weapons on Cakerlak, and he might've funded the blasterings on the planets?"

"The Galaxy President has no comment." Allard replied.

"Do you know that Narob Traf is heading to Cakerlak as we speak?" the "robot" asked again.

"He just left Old Eborocum to go back to Launderington." Jaboney said, "Brother, we'll be making a press statement soon to the business that we have with Mr. Narob."

"Well, word is he's on a flight to Cakerlak now."

"That will be enough." Allard quickly led Blaphaus away and Jaboney gave the robot-cam a dirty look.

Mal's holo-call crossed her arms and said, "I heard all that, and I am not happy."

In the GNN studio Crisp Jaboney smiled smugly.

"Well, my friends, it looks like Blaphaus Maximus doesn't like confrontation. It also looks like whoever that tall man is with him is his spokes-being or something. I will try and get an interview with my brother, the Governor of Old Eborocum soon. As I said before, we are watching the Galaxy President's every move."

"What the hell is he up to?" Zeb asked the other Governors in the House conference room.

Southington shrugged, "I don't know. I don't even know where they are."

Dawber said, "It looks like it was on Old Eborocum. With Allard with him, as well as Jaboney and Zalez I think they'll watch over him."

Noam sat on the table, and crossed his arms.

"I don't. His poll ratings are not good. I don't know about any of you but I think we made a big mistake in agreeing to pick him as G.P. If he *is* involved with the Cakerlak that's going to make us all look bad."

Gillian said, "We can't give up on him now, Noam. We worked really hard on this."

Governor Ace held up his hand, "Can I say something?"

They all turned to look at the skinny human Governor who never said a word.

"You're alive?" Rüppell chuckled, "Yikes, I never heard you speak."

Ace turned to face the red furred Governor.

"Maybe I had nothing to say before, Rüppell. You all sit here, working out the problems that you created. When Traf was alive and was G.P. everything was hunky dory, absolute peaceful, no drama. Definitely there wasn't anybody getting massacred. Testone thought it was a great idea to have a Toob become G.P., the galaxy will love him. We should've pulled the curtain on that when he revealed he's just another human. Now we are stuck with him, like it or not."

Thaw nodded, "I agree with Ace. We have to deal with our choices like it or not."

"I say we get rid of him and chose another G.P." Noam said.

"No." Southington remarked, "We have to keep putting on a brave face, and dealing with what we all agreed on. I say we call it a night, all head home and see what tomorrow brings. We'll get him in here and discuss it with him."

Bodie tapped on the table and nodded, "I'm surprised he didn't just resign."

"He's too damn stubborn." Zucaritas said.

Blap and his group walked into the lobby of Consolidated to be met by a Sciur, a gray furred species with a bushy tail. This one had a bald head like he was scalped and wore the Consolidated black overalls. When he saw who entered the building he threw down his cig he was smoking and picked up his data-pad. The lobby of Consolidated looked all black and dark, and everything seemed to be made of metal and industrial looking. He approached Jaboney who held out his arms to hug him. Once they got closer they did hug, generally glad to see each other.

"Governor Jaboney! Man, Gov... that's crazy, you're Gov! How the hell are you?"

The Sciur was very boisterous, which made Blap cringe inside.

"Good to see you, Rooboydau!"

Rooboydau went to hug Blap who held up his hand.

"Don't touch new."

Rooboydau chuckled, "Of course, G.P., it's a pleasure to meet you at last. I wondered if you were gonna come here."

Jaboney explained to the others, "Rooboydau, or Roob as he likes to be called is head of Consolidated."

"Roob! Rhymes with Toob!" Roob laughed, "I met a Toob a long time ago! That is I think I did! Maybe I was just high on Canis-weed. You look like a gerquin vegetable, you know that?"

"Tell him the news so we can go." Blap told Jaboney.

"First of, this is Zalez Belhopsa, he's the head of Dook Energy."

"Narob Energy now." smiled Nate, "Remember?"

Roob looked at the Dook logo on Zalez's blue overalls.

"It says 'Dook.'"

Zalez shook Roob's hand. "Narob Traf owns Dook now and is changing the name."

"Narob Traf? That's the old G.P's boy, right? Isn't he a little young to run a business? How do you feel that he's your boss, Belhopsa?"

Zalez said, "I'm not sure yet."

"You're about to find out yourself." Blap pointed out.

"What do you mean?"

"Ummm... can we talk in your office, Roob?" asked Jaboney.


"What the fornication do you mean that young man is my new boss?!" Roob gelled angrily, spitting saliva as he yelled.

Zalez said to Nate, "I think you should wait outside the office, son."

"Why? I'll still be able to hear him. The whole building could hear him."

"Gov! You sold this company?! How could you?!" Roob yelled at Jaboney.

"It seemed like a good idea. No one is going to lose their jobs..."

"Do we have to go work on that space station? I don't want to be floating around in space!"

"That's to be determined." Jaboney said.

Zalez said, "It'll be too hard and too expensive for the station to start powering this planet. You will still be here on this planet, in this building, and I'm sure things will pretty much stay the same."

"Nothing is the same!" yelled Roob.

"Tell me about it." Blap said, "Are we done here yet?"

Jaboney said, "I'm going to stay here and talk to the employees. Zalez, can you stay and help?"

"I have to get Nate back home." Zakez said. "You heard his mother is not happy with him being here."

"Zalez will work with you, Roob, you'll be a good team." Jaboney told Roob. "Everything will be fine."

"Can we stay over night?" Nate asked, "I'll talk to mother and explain. She listens to me."

"I don't know." Zalez remarked.

"Well, you lot figure this out." Blap remarked. "I'm heading back to Ceilingida."

Allard said, "I'll come with you. Zalez, we can take Nate back home if you'd like."

"I want to stay here." Nate said.

"You're not missing anymore school, Nate. Let me contact your mother and see what she says."

"No! He's not traveling with Blaphaus and someone I don't even know that well! Allard killed Ten, remember?" Mal's holo-call complained a few minutes later.

"Then I can spend the night?!" Nate grinned. "I'm so happy!"

"Are you sure?" Zalez asked.

"Yes. But I'm not happy with this, Zalez. When is this going to end? Our son shouldn't be dragged around like this."

"He's not being dragged around."

"Tell your old lady he's getting a better education than his bloody school is giving him." Blap remarked.

"I heard you, Blaphaus, and that's not true." Mal said. "Nate, have a good night. Are you staying in a nice hotel?"

Jaboney told her, "The Inn Aptitude is the fanciest hotel we have here on Old Eborocum. They'll be in the suite."

"We are not paying for it." Mal pointed out.

"Of course not. It's on me." smiled Jaboney.

Mal said, "I want you two back here tomorrow morning. Understand?"

Zalez nodded, "Good night, my dear."

"Night, mother." Nate waved.

She blew a kiss before her holo-call ended.

"In that case, Governor, I'm not in a hurry to leave. Blaphaus, let's get a room together." Allard said.

"I'm not that kind of..."

"No, I mean let's stay here for the night. Tomorrow we'll go back."

Jaboney smiled, "We'll do the press announcement together then."

"Fine. I'll stay the night." Blap said, "But in the morning I'm gone."

"Back to Launderington... yes." Allard said.

Zalez looked worried and went up to Blap, motioning a away a few feet.

"You can't share a room with him." he whispered.

"Why not?"

"Are you going to stay in that suit all night?" Zalez asked, almost surprised Blap didn't catch on.

"If I have to. I only need a few hours sleep. I pretty much learned to sleep standing up."

"I worry about you, my friend."

"Trust me, Belhopsa, I'm good. Besides, I'm gonna find out more about wot his end game."

Zalez frowned, "What do you mean?"

"I don't trust his smug self no more than I can throw him. Nobody is that nice, no matter wot planet or galaxy you're from. Not even you, Chordattian."

Laterille walked into the Great Weta's chamber and saw he was sleeping in his throne. She stood there for a minute, not knowing what she should do. She never woke the Great Weta up before.

"Great Weta!" Narob marched in, standing next to Laterille.

The Great Weta woke up instantly, looking down at them. So much for being discreet, Laterille thought to herself.

"What is the meaning of this, human?"

"I have questions." Narob said seriously.

"I said to you before you never should come here in person. If anybody finds out..."

"I hired a private flight. No one is going to say anything."

"You have no idea what you're doing, boy."

"I killed for you, Cakerlak, innocent beings. Risked my life for the Order, did what you wanted... purchased Consolidated from Governor Jaboney for you. I did everything you wanted..."

"What I wanted? You did nothing that I wanted, human boy. You did it for the Order."

"The Order, yes, this mysterious Order that everyone knows about! What is this Order? Was my father a part of it?"

The Great Weta almost laughed, "Your father? The Galaxy President? No. He was not part of the Order. He wasn't strong enough."

"Then why did he have 'Blattodea' as his password on his home info-pad?"

"You don't know?"

"Don't know what?"

"Your father found out about the Order and was researching it. We had to take care of him before he started telling everyone in the Cabinet, boy. So we had to stop him."

“Stop him? Stop him how?”

“Poison.”

Narob’s eyes started to water. “Poison. But he had a heart attack. His doctor said nothing about poison.”

“You are such a naive child...”

“I’m not a child...”

“Yes you are, human child. We had to kill your father to stop him from talking about the Order.”

“No! I will not believe this!”

“It’s true, child. If your father only knew you were a member of the Order now... do you imagine what he’ll say?”

“I hate you, Cakerlak! I will finish this!” Narob cried out, literally crying, not knowing what he was going to do.

“Good luck, human child. It’s too late. The galaxy is in disarray, an invasion is going to happen and there’s nothing you or anybody can do about it.”

Narob clenched his fists and ran out the room, feeling alone and stuck.

***CHAPTER 16***

Like everything on Old Eborocum, the Inn Aptitude was dark and industrial looking, but the suite Blap and Allard walked into, led by the bell-robot who wore a red jacket and matching hat was very bright and welcoming.

"This is your suite, Galactic President. Have a good night and feel free to contact the front desk. Good night."

The bell-robot left, closing the door.

Allard looked around the space nodding his head.

"That robot did not acknowledge me once." he remarked, taking off his black jacket and tie. He went to the large windows, looking out at the city.

"Did your feelings get hurt?" Blap asked, standing in the middle of the room.

Allard turned to him and smiled, "My feelings never get hurt, Blaphaus. Do yours?"

"Not in a bloody long time."

"That's good. Tough skin, right?"

Blap frowned, "If you say so."

"So, are you going to stand up all night or do you want the bed?"

Blap made his way to the bedroom door, looking in to see one big bed.

"You have the bed." Blap said, "I'll be fine."

"Why don't you just tell me what you really are, Blap." Allard told him.

"I'm not telling you anything, Felipe."

"Man, you're one stubborn bastard." Allard chuckled, shaking his head. He opened up the minibar and pulled out a small bottle of voddy.

"You want some, Blap?"

"No. I'm fine."

Allard took the top off and took a swig.

"So, you're going to stand all night? How do you sleep?"

"That's none of your business."

Allard slumped down on the couch, drinking.

"So, it just must be tiring being you, am I right?"

"Look, I don't know who you are or wot your game is, but you're not getting me to open up to you... if that's your goal."

"I'm just making small talk, Blaphaus, don't get all strung out."

"You don't know wot strung out is. And yes, if you must know, it's tiring being me."

"So, why continue?"

151

"Because I was put in this bloody position. Why don't you tell me who you are and more about this Committee."

Allard sat up, taking another swig from the bottle.

"I told you what they are. They want to reveal what you really are, and my job is to make sure that doesn't happen."

"So, if they do 'reveal wotever I am really','' it's not good for the galaxy I take it."

"Nope. Which means they have someone in mind to be your replacement."

"That being could have this gig."

"Somehow I don't think that would be good for the galaxy, not like you're no better."

"Wotever. So, this Order business, that's still the bloody mystery..."

"That's up to your species and the Cakerlak originally, now I think it's a lot bigger deal. You can't deny knowing anything about it if you get approached by Fami or any other Committee agent."

"Why is that?"

"Because that will prove you're not really a Toob, Blaphaus." he stood, tossing the empty bottle in the bin. "Have a good night, Blap."

He went into the bedroom and closed the door. Blap muttered something under his breath and went to the couch. He counted to three in his head and fell backwards onto it, then rolled off and landed on his front on the plush carpet.

"Fornicate." he swore under his breath.


Narob got out the Ultra car in front of his house. The Cyrakuse driver waved at him as he went up to the front door. He unlocked it and went inside to be met by 1-4-3.

"Hello, young Narob, how are you? You don't look well."

"I'm fine, One. Where is my mother?"

"In the kitchen." One replied.

Narob went down the hall into the large kitchen where his sister Hoeka sat at a table eating with his mother.

"Where have you been?" Hoeka asked rudely.

His mother turned around to see Narob standing there, and before they knew it he started to cry.

"What's wrong?" Mrs. Traf asked.

Narob didn't know what to say... he broke down crying and gave his mother a big hug.

"What a baby." Hoeka scowled.

Peezle and Yerkal sat across the table from each other in the Launderington restaurant called the Plive Yard.

"So, Noj, I have to ask you something. It's really important."

Noj took a sip of his red merlot and nodded, "You know you can ask me anything."

"It's about Blaphaus. He's not really a Tooberosum, is he?"

Noj almost spat out his drink. "What makes you say that?"

"It's a hunch. We have not seen any other Toobs at all."

"That means nothing, Yerkal, and you know that."

"I do? I don't think so, Noj. If you can't be honest with your own husband..."

"It's not like that."

"When you were Traf's Assistant things were so different... and easy. Now with you a Governor, there's all these secrets. I don't like it."

"You're the one who went off to Cakerlak, disappearing, not saying a word."

"Yeah, I know. I regret that."

"Well, it's in the past."

"This woman named Fami stopped by the House when I was leaving it earlier, Noj. She asked for Blaphaus, said she met you."

"Yes, I know who she is. I met her once."

"Well, she said she knows the truth about Blaphaus, and said you and the Governors know." Yerkal looked at Peezle in the eyes across the table. "This is my last time I'm going to ask. Who or what is he?"

"I can't tell you, Yerkal. I'm sorry."

"So am I." Yerkal said, dropping his napkin on the table. He stood up and said, "Guess I have to find out myself."

He walked out the restaurant, not noticing he was followed by an older man in a dark red overcoat, wearing a green hat.

Peezle just sat there surprised, tears in his eyes.

The next day on Old Eborocum, Allard walked out the bedroom to see Blaphaus laying face down on the floor next to the couch.

"Blaphaus!" Allard exclaimed, thinking the Toob was dead. He knelt down to move him, turning him over. Blap's eyes opened and stared up at Allard.

"Stand me up." he demanded.

Allard struggled but pulled Blaphaus to his feet.

"You're not as heavy as you look." he told Blaphaus, "What are you?"

"Let go of me." Blap pushed Allard away.

"How the hell did you get on the floor like that?"

"Doesn't matter. Get your tie and jacket on so we can go get this thing over with."

Allard just nodded, thinking he knew definitely Blaphaus wasn't really a Toob.

At the Consolidated building, a crowd of employees stood in front of it. A stage was set up in front of the building with GNN robo-cams hovering about ready.

"On Old Eborocum at the Consolidated building my brother the Governor Kwoh Jaboney is going to make an announcement in a few minutes. The Galactic President Maximus is there as well, and Zalez Belhopsa, head of Dook Energy. I wonder what the announcement is going to be. This explains why they are on Old Eborocum. I want to ask the G.P. a few questions again... maybe I'll get a chance. Crisp Jaboney, GNN."

Inside the building behind the stage, Jaboney stood with Zalez and Nate and Rooboydau when Blap and Allard walked in through another door.

"I'm glad you're here, Blaphaus. The Traf boy is not here though."

"I don't think you invited him." Allard commented.

"I did this morning but heard nothing." Jaboney shrugged, "Oh, well. We should get this over with."

"Yes, please." Blaphaus muttered.

Jaboney said, "There's a ramp for you to get on the stage."

"Wotever." Blaphaus replied.

Zalez said to Nate, "Wait inside here with Mr. Allard. I'll be back in a few minutes."

Nate nodded, "I will, father."

They went through the doors, going outside to the stage. They climbed the steps except Blaphaus who went up the ramp. Four robot-cams hovered before the stage, broadcasting live on GNN.

"Hello, everybody." smiled Jaboney, speaking into the microphone, "Thanks for being here. Myself and the Galactic President Maximus would like to announce that Consolidated is now owned by Narob Traf as well as Dook Energy."

"Rooboydau will still be in charge of this building and Zalez Belhopsa will still be on charge of the space station... as far as I know. I don't know what Narob Traf wants to do, and I wish he was here. Anyway, that's about it. Anything you want to say, Galactic President Maximus?"

Blap replied, "Nope."

"Zalez, do you have anything to say?" Jaboney asked.

Zalez said into the microphone, "I just have to say Dook Energy is now called Narob Energy, but will do the same job as we have done for all the years, since the Dook Brothers founded the company."

"That's about it then, everybody." grinned Jaboney.

Roob whispered to him, "I don't think the crowd is too happy, Governor."

Jaboney said, "I can't help that."

Inside, Allard whispered to Nate, "So, what do you think about Bla...?"

He stopped when they all walked back into the building.

"We'll talk about it later." Allard whispered and winked.

"Are we done here?" Blap asked.

Jaboney said, "You could go, Blaphaus. I'm staying here to talk to anybody who wants to talk to me. Maybe the Traf boy will show up."

Zalez said, "I better take Nate back home."

"Awe, father! I want to stay here." Nate complained.

"You can come to this planet any time you want." Jaboney said.

Roob said, "Ummm... do you see what's going on out there?"

"Where?" Jaboney asked.

A Cyrakuse in a purple suit stood on the stage, talking into the microphone as the GNN robot-cams hovered before him.

"I want you to know that Galactic President Blaphaus Maximus is supporting the Cakerlak, funding them with weapons, and doing business with Narob Traf who is tied to the Cakerlak and the Order of Blattodea..."

"What is he talking about?" Jaboney asked.

"Bloody Cyrakuse!" Blap cried out, shuffling off to the doors.

"Where are you going?" Allard asked following him.

"To shut him up."

"This can't be good." Jaboney muttered.

Roob said, "Get someone to turn off the microphone."

Blap made his way up the ramp, ignoring the robot-cams who were watching him.

"Cyrakuse! Wot are you doing?" Blap demanded.

"Oh, hello, Toob... if that's what you are."

"You know wot I am." Blap said angrily.

"Yes, I do, why don't you tell the galaxy?"

"Why don't you bloody disappear again?"

"Do you hear that?" Joorg asked, "Blaphaus threatened me..."

Allard pulled the microphones plug out and put his hand on Joorg's shoulder.

"I really don't think you know what you're talking about."

"This is Crisp Jaboney, are you working with the Cakerlak?" a voice said from a robot-cam.

"Not any more. Joorg here is no longer a Governor and Cakerlak is not part of the House anymore." Blap replied.

"That's a lie." Joorg said.

"What about Traf being a member of the Order?" Joorg asked.

"I can't speak for him." Blap said.

"But you know he was..."

"I think you said enough, the public doesn't know what the Order is..." Joorg interrupted Allard, "It's about time they did, whoever you are." Blap said, "I'm done."

He turned to the back of the stage and walked down the ramp.

"I know the secret about Blaphaus, human, all the Governors do, and pretty soon every one will know. There's nothing you can do to stop it."

Allard glared, "Want to bet?"

"The galaxy will fall and it's all because of the G.P. Let that be a warning."

Joorg stepped off the stage and made his way through the crowd. Allard turned to a robot-cam and frowned.

"You can stop recording now."

Crisp Jaboney sat at the anchor desk, looking very serious.

"Well, I did not expect that. That's a lot to take in. Seems like one of the House Governors is not happy at Blaphaus Maximus, your G.P. Also, what's with this Order of Blattodea he mentioned? Also, who was that man in the dark suit? I don't know about you, viewers, but I kind of miss the quiet days in the galaxy when Traf was Galactic President."

## CHAPTER 17

Everything was going wrong, Blaphaus was supposed to bring unity to the galaxy, but now everything seemed to be falling apart. And not one Governor knew what to do. They all saw what went down on Old Eborocum the day before which was a big surprise. Pretty much *all* of the galaxy saw it, and Blaphaus' ratings were lower than ever, even lower than Traf's ratings ever were.

GNN had a field day talking about what happened, and how Blaphaus reacted. Buterdau Kooper wanted to defend the G.P., but he had no case. Crisp Jaboney made it obvious to his viewers he did not like Blaphaus at all, and this proved it. It didn't help that his brother the Governor was a member of the House.

All the Governors were in the conference room at the House, except for Peezle who just didn't show up, and Jaboney who contacted them and said he had something very important to do on Old Eborocum but never said what. They just figured it was to do with him selling his power company. They had no idea why he would do that, but he did and they figured he'd just explain some time.

"What the bloody hell is happening to use Blap's words." Noam said, standing on his chair.

"You have to pronounce 'what' like 'wot.'" Gillian commented.

Some of the Governors laughed.

"And sound a little more irritated." Haathee remarked.

"You're closest to Joorg, Haathee, what is his deal?" Zucaritas asked.

Haathee shrugged, "I don't know, but once again the Order was mentioned."

"It's very worrying." Gillian said.

Thaw added, "We are dealing with something none of us have ever expected. Do you think we should reveal the truth about Blaphaus?"

"Sure. Do that. Put me out of my misery." Blaphaus shuffled into the conference room followed by Allard.

"Blaphaus, Mister Felipe is not a Governor, he shouldn't be here again." Zeb pointed out.

Allard slumped down in Peezle's vacant seat.

"Then make me Governor."

Dawber glared at him across the table and said, "You know that was offered to you years ago, and you declined."

"Governor of what planet?" Thaw asked, sitting to Allard.

Allard shrugged, "Pick one."

"As Galactic President who do I answer to?" Blap asked.

"Yourself." Rüppell said, "I assume, as you're not married."

"Correct. You lot answer to me. From now on I'm in charge, not you lot. Do I make that clear?"

Southington said, "We'll do our best, Blaphaus."

"So, what happened on Old Eborocum?" Zeb asked, "Why was Joorg there running his mouth? He could be dangerous."

Haathee said, "I will try to reach out to him. He might talk to me."

"He's off his rocker." Blap said, waving his arm. "He talks big but nothing."

Dawber said, "I can have the GBI bring him in and talk to him. Is that okay, G.P.?"

"That was sarcasm, lady. Yes, do that."

Lluhdor said, "We still don't know what the Order of Blattodea is. Do we?"

Blaphaus said, "Back on my planet we had cults. Do you have them in this galaxy?"

"This is more than a cult." Kordiack said, "And yes, we have cults in this galaxy."

Sugden added, "We had a big one on Xenartha once, years ago. The Branch Jacksians were a big problem."

"I don't need a bloody history lesson." Blaphaus said, "Someone must know about the bloody Order. Someone that's not part of them."

"I'll ask Professor Phence." Thaw said.

"Well, thanks to Joorg everyone in the galaxy knows about the Order now. And if you remember, we never announced to the galaxy that Joorg is no longer a Governor."

"We need a press conference then." Southington said, "I'll contact GNN."

"I'm not talking to Jaboney's brother." Blap said.

Southington nodded, "I don't blame you. I'll get Kooper."

Blap then realized that Peezle wasn't there.

"Where is Peezle?" he asked.

No one had the answer.

"He better have a good answer for not being here."

Kwoh Jaboney strolled into the GNN space stations main foyer, puffing out his chest. He walked up do the reception desk that the blond human woman sat behind.

"Governor Jaboney, am I right? Welcome, sir. What could I do for you?"

"I'm here to see my brother... Crisp."

"He's broadcasting right now, but should be done soon. I'll take you to his office if you'd like."

"I appreciate it."

She came around the desk and shook his hand.

"My name is Brie Kanberra, and I'm a big fan."

She led him through the door and down a hallway.

"So, what do you think of G.P. Maximus, Governor?"

Jaboney shrugged, "I think he's great for the galaxy. He talked me into being Governor."

"Do you think it's a coincidence that the galaxy is such a darker place now?" she asked.

"I don't think it has anything to do with him." Jaboney said as they stepped into a lift.

Moments later they were out the lift and went to Crisp's office.

"Your brother should be here in a few minutes. Governor, I think you'll make a really good G.P. I wish it was you instead of a Toob."

Jaboney grinned and looked down at her cleavage.

"I think so too. So, are you married, Ms. Kanberra?"

She shook her head, "No, I'm single."

"Really? An attractive woman like you is single? Hmmm. Well, that's a crime. We need to fix that."

"Then let's do that, Governor." she winked at him just as Crisp stepped into the office.

"Brother, what a surprise? You're not flirting with Ms. Kanberra are you?" Crisp chuckled.

Jaboney smirked, "You know how I am."

Brie said, "I'll leave you two gentlemen to chat. Governor, hopefully I'll be seeing you soon."

She left and closed the door behind her.

"So, brother, what brings you to GNN?" Crisp went and sat down behind his desk. Governor Jaboney sat across from him. The Governor was older by a good ten years, and taller. It was unspoken that the only reason Jaboney was elected Planet Mayor was because GNN was behind him, and donated a lot of money to his campaign. The only reason that happened was mostly because Crisp made it happen.

"I have to talk to you about the Galactic President..."

"The big, ugly Toob? Man, I miss the days of the useless do nothing G.P. Traf. This G.P. is all over the Creator damned place. How do you even work with him, brother?"

"Crisp, Blaphaus is a good being, he means well, but your harassment on him, the slant you're doing, is making him look bad, which makes the Cabinet look bad, which makes me look bad."

"I think you're being brainwashed, Governor. You sold your business? Consolidated made you a feces lot of money. You handed it all over to a teenager. Did the Toob convince you to do that?"

"He had nothing to do with that..."

"But he was with you on Old Eborocum. Then that Cyrakuse arrived and it all went to hell. I'm telling you, Kwoh, he's not good for you, or the galaxy. I mean Governor Tostone is dead because of him, not to mention the other innocent beings."

"I'm not doubting any of that, Crisp, I just want you to stop making him look bad. Help to make him look good..."

"And lie? I don't lie, brother. And I don't make things up. Buterdau seems to like the Toob, but he's misguided."

"I'm telling you as your older brother to stop talking bad about the Toob."

"I'm telling you as a respected journalist I will not... unless positive things seem to happen. After New Galaxy Day all you Governors kept quiet, and didn't answer my call for interviews. Everyone thinks we are due for an invasion from another galaxy, and all because the Toob was chosen."

"There's not going to be any kind of invasion. Beings are paranoid."

"We'll see. By the way, the Cyrakuse who showed up at the Consolidated building mentioned the Order of Blattodea. Do you know what that is?"

Jaboney shook his head, "Not a clue, but I heard of it before."

"Well, you might want to find out, brother. I did some research, and I'm telling you, it's not good."


The Committee sat at their round table, sitting in the shadows.

"The whole galaxy knows about the Order now. This is not good." one female told them.

"No one knows what it means. I don't think there's going to be a problem."

"There's going to be beings that will look into it. We are going to have to be aware and prepared."

Another male said, "We are going to have to prove that Blaphaus is not really a Tooberosum to the galaxy really soon."

"Tapperdau is working on it."

"She's been working on it for a while now, and isn't getting anywhere." the female said.

"I trust her. I believe in her. It will happen."

"Well, it better happen quickly."

Joorg walked through the spaceport on Launderington, aware the GNN robot-cams were watching him. They weren't the only ones that was watching him. He was unaware that he was being followed by a blonde human female. Joorg walked outside where Rubyspears stood by his limo-vehicle.

"Gov... are you Governor? I'm confused. I saw you on GNN at Old Eborocum. What was that about?"

"I need to go to the House quickly, Chordattian..."

"I'm not Chordattian..." he grumbled, opening the back door of the vehicle for Joorg to get in. Joorg did and the blonde slid in next to him pretty quickly, before Rubyspears knew what was happening.

"Ma'am, this is for Cabinet members only... and friends."

"Shut up, Chordattian. Drive." Fami said firmly.

Rubyspears nodded and got behind the wheel of the vehicle.

Joorg stared at Fami as Rubyspears started to drive.

"Uhhh... who are you?"

"Someone that could be an ally. Nice stunt on Old Eborocum, putting yourself all over the news."

"It was what I had to do." he told her.

Rubyspears listened really closely to the conversation.

"What you wanted to do or what someone *told* you to do?"

"Does it matter?"

"It does matter, Governor..."

"I'm not a Governor anymore..."

"Really?"

Rubyspears quickly pulled over to the side of the road and turned to face his two passengers in the back seat.

"You're not a Governor? I'm a driver for Governors and the G.P. only."

"Shut up, Chordattian." she snapped, and turned back to Joorg, "You're not a Governor? Who is the Governor for Cakerlak then?"

"No one. Cakerlak is not part of the Cabinet anymore."

"It's not?" Rubyspears and Fami asked at the same time.

"No, which is not good." Joorg said, "I have to get to the House to tell the Governors to replace the G.P."

"Replace him? Why?" Fami asked.

"Because something is going to happen that's bad."

"You literally hopped up on a stage in front of a crowd and on GNN, Cyrakuse."

"I'm telling you, as long as the Toob is Galactic President, we, as in the whole galaxy is screwed."

"Do you know the Toob is not a Toob?" Fami asked.

"What do you mean?" Joorg asked, knowing the truth, but wondering why and how Fami knew... even if she did.

"I mean he's a man... a hu... man." she said.

If they could see Rubyspears' face they would've seen his jaw drop in shock.

## CHAPTER 18

Outside the House, Rubyspears parked the limo-vehicle where Allard sat on the House steps, eating a sandwich. Rubyspears got out and opened the door for his two passengers who stepped out.

"What are you doing here?" Fami asked.

"Having lunch. What are you two doing here? Going to cause another scene, Joorg?" Allard asked Joorg.

"No." Joorg said.

"I'm here to talk to Maximus." Fami told Allard.

"Sweetheart, that's the last thing you're going to do."

"Don't call me sweetheart. He can't hide from me forever."

Allard stood up and smirked, "He has no legs. He's not running anywhere."

He hurried up the steps and went into the House. He pointed at the robot in the foyer.

"Don't you dare let those two inside or I'll take off your head. Got it?"

"Yes, Mr. Felipe."

Outside Rubyspears said to the two, "So, Blaphaus is not really a Toob?"

"It's none of your business." Fami told him.

"Well, I'm late for picking him up at the hotel. I have to go."

"Wait. You're going to go pick him up?" Joorg asked.

Rubyspears nodded, "Yeah, I have to go."

"We're going with you." Fami said.

Inside Allard barged into the conference room.

"Wot are you doing?" Blap asked.

"We have visitors outside." Allard told them all, "Tapperdau and Joorg."

"Together? Wot are they doing here together?" Blaphaus asked.

"That Cyrakuse has a nerve showing up here." Noam remarked, standing on his chair, little fists clenched.

"I'm getting tired of you Cyrakuse." Blap pointed at Zucaritas. "One of your kind picked me for this position, another shoved me into a pool and hoped I'd drown and now this Joorg one. Wot is his deal?"

"That's not important right now." Thaw said.

"How are they both here together?" Lluhdor asked.

"Your chauffeur brought them here." Allard replied.

"Rubyspears? That's why that he didn't pick me up from the hotel? He's fired." Blap waved his hand, turning to the door to leave.

"Where are you going?" Allard asked.

"To have a word with him." Blap replied

"That's not a good idea, Blaphaus. Tapperdau is out there as well, she could be dangerous to all this."

"Dangerous? I never met a women who could be dangerous... except for the one who tried to drown me."

Haathee looked down embarrassed, wondering if Blaphaus was ever going to let that go.

Zucaritas stood up, "I will go and talk to them. Haathee, you know Joorg well. You'll come with me."

Haathee nodded, "I don't know him as well as I thought."

Rubyspears drove as the two passengers sat in the back again. He did his best to listen to their conversation but they were just whispering.

"Who do you work for?" Joorg asked.

"I cannot tell you. Not until you tell me who you are working for."

"Something that is far deeper than you can ever imagine..."

"I can imagine a lot." Fami told him. "You know the big secret about the Toob don't you?"

Joorg nodded, "Yes. All the Governors do. They are keeping it so secret."

"And you wanted to reveal it? Tell the whole galaxy?"

"No. But I might have to."

"Well, I'm going to." Fami replied, "I'm going to prove it that he's not really a Toob. The House will be all dismantled, and be put back together with replacements. This galaxy will be put back to normal."

They saw that the limo-vehicle and Joorg and Fami were gone before they walked through the glass doors of the House.

"Where did they go?" Zucaritas asked.

"Who knows?" Allard replied, "But it's not good."

"Can we contact Rubyspears in his vehicle to ask?" Haathee asked.

They went back into the conference room and Noam crossed his arms.

"That was quick."

"They're gone." Zucaritas told them.

"Rubyspears as well?" Gillian asked.

"Yeah, all three."

"Can we contact Rubyspears and find out where they're going to?" Allard asked.

Zeb nodded, "Of course."

The holo-call of Zeb appeared on the dashboard of the limo-vehicle, standing a foot tall.

"Rubyspears, where are you going?"

"To pick up the G.P., Governor. I'm very late."

"But he's he..."

Allard hit the info-pad quickly, shitting down the call.

"What did you do that for?" Zeb asked annoyed.

"Don't tell them he's here. They'll come right back."

Blap said, "Someone have the GBI meet those wankers at the hotel."

Dawber nodded, "On it."

The holo-call of Zeb appeared on the dashboard again.

"Sorry about that. I dropped the info-pad. Blaphaus is furious you're late, Rubyspears. You know how he gets. Head straight to the Icefence as soon as you can."

Rubyspears nodded, "I'm almost there."

The holo-call ended and Rubyspears hoped Blaphaus wouldn't be too mad.

"When we get there let me approach Maximus first." Fami told Zoorg.

Zoorg nodded, "Whatever you say."

The limo-vehicle drove up to the large u-shaped hotel and parked before the front doors. Rubyspears expected to see the G.P. standing outside the doors, looking annoyed. But he wasn't there. Fami got out the vehicle herself on the left side and Joorg got out on the right side. Fami couldn't believe it, Joorg ignored what she told him about her going first. She watched him go through the doors into the hotel's lobby.

"Hands above your head!" a GBI agent greeted him, pointing a weapon. Joorg saw other GBI agents were all over the lobby. He quickly put his hands up, standing there. Fami watched through the glass doors as Joorg was handcuffed. She quickly went to the limo-vehicle, getting into the backseat quickly.

"Chordattian, drive."

"Drive where?" he asked.

She looked out the window as Joorg was led out by the agents.

"Back to the House." she said urgently, "Drive now."

Rubyspears nodded and drove off. He had no idea what was going on, but it was pretty exciting.

Dawber told the other Governors, "It was a success... Joorg is now under GBI custody."

"Wot about the woman and Rubyspears?" Blap asked.

"No word. They didn't see them." Dawber replied.

"Bloody terrific." Blap complained. "I'm going to go talk to Joorg. Trunk face, you're coming with me. And you, Zucaritas."


A little bit later the limo-vehicle parked in front of the House once again and Fami stepped out quickly and hurried up the stairs. She went to go through the glass doors only to be met by Allard.

"Again, sweetheart?"

"I said don't call me sweetheart." she said, "Why was Joorg arrested?"

"Because he is causing problems... as you are."

"You haven't seen anything yet. You know the Toob is not really a Toob, right?"

"As far as the galaxy goes he is a Toob. Who cares what he really is. Or what?"

"You don't understand. None of you do."

"Then explain, darling,"

"Don't call me darling. I will tell Blaphaus."

"He's not here."

"Is he still at the hotel?"

"I'm not telling you where he is."

"Are any of the Governors here? Is Governor Peezle here?"

"Most are here, yes. But..."

"Let me talk to them." she said, "Please."

Allard sighed and nodded.

He went into the conference room where the others were.

"Tapperdau is here... again. She wants to talk to you all. She knows Blaphaus is not here."

"Bring her up then." Dawber told Allard.

"Is she human?" Bodie asked.

"Yes, she's human." Allard replied, before he walked out.


Jaboney stood outside the spaceport on Launderington, waiting for Rubyspears to pick him up. The House chauffeur had a reputation of never being late, and now here he was... over 45 minutes late. Jaboney wondered if anything happened to him. He pulled out his pocket info-pad and hit a button on it. Rubyspears' holo-call appeared, showing him from the chest up, which showed he was driving.

"Where are you, Rubyspears? You're late."

"I had a situation, Governor, a lot to take in. I'll be there real soon. I'm on my way."

Jaboney nodded, "I'll be waiting."

When he ended the holo-call he wondered what kind of situation happened.


The Governors watched Fami walk into the conference room and she sat in the chair on the right which was Peezle's chair. Allard went and sat in Jaboney's chair.

"Everybody, this is Fami Tapperdau, she works for the Committee." Allard told them all.

Thaw said, sitting besides her, "Why after all this time is the Committee getting involved?"

"Since the House chose a fake Tooberosum to be G.P., deceiving the whole galaxy."

"How do you know he's not really a Toob, love?" Rüppell smiled.

"Oh, please. I'm not stupid. Neither is the Committee. We know he's not really a Toob."

"Why do you say that?" Zeb asked.

"Because they were wiped out years ago." she said.

"We've been to their planet." Eastora said.

"Really? You've been to their planet? I hardly doubt that." Fami said getting annoyed. "You can lie to the whole galaxy but you can't lie to me or the Committee."

"Let's say, just for feces and giggles you're right." Ace said, "That the G.P. is not what or who we say he is. What about it?"

"The Committee will show the galaxy what he really is." Fami told him. "You will all be disgraced."

"What if you're wrong?" Southington asked, sitting directly across from Fami."What about if he is a Toob?"

"It's the start of another invasion."


Jaboney was happy to see Rubyspears drive up to the spaceport. The chauffeur got out and opened the back door for the Governor who got in. Moments later the vehicle was back on the highway.

"So, Rubyspears, what's been happening?"

"I went to pick up Governor Joorg from here and this woman got into the backseat next to him.

"Joorg is no longer Governor." told Jaboney, "Why would he be having you pick him up?"

Rubyspears shrugged, "I assumed he was."

"And who was this woman?"

"I don't know. She was cute though. And she mentioned the Galactic President was not really a Toob."

Jaboney felt a little uneasy. "Where did you take them to?"

"The House, then the Icefence Hotel and then back to the House. But Joorg was arrested by the GBI. Things are going crazy all of a sudden."

Jaboney looked out the window, a sinking feeling in his stomach. If only he was Galactic President.


Joorg sat in the interrogation room at the Launderington GBI building, waiting and tapping his claws on the table. Outside the room Blap, Haathee and Zucaritas stood with the GBI agents.

"I know the bloody routine." Blaphaus was saying. "I've done this kind of thing before."

The agent nodded, opening the door for the G.P. as Joorg watched as Blaphaus walked in with the other two, door closing behind them.

"Friend, what's got into you?" Haathee asked.

"Reality." Joorg replied.

"Being a Governor was reality." Zucaritas told him, sitting down across from the table.

"Is it your wife being with the Pachyderm here, or her trying to kill me, or her killing Tostone and his wife and those other victims?" Blap asked.

"None of it. All of it. She should've killed you. Tostone shouldn't have picked you." Joorg said.

"Well, no feces, but he did. So, explain that stunt yesterday... running your mouth on GNN." told Blap. "Wot do you want?"

"It's not what I want." Joorg replied, "The Toobs were an enemy of the Order of Blattodea and this galaxy. Now you're G.P., and..."

"You know very well I'm not really a Too..."

"Shsss." Zucaritas warned, "The GBI are probably listening."

"You know the truth about me." Blap told Joorg, "Whoever this bloody Order is I'd tell them."

"Do you really think that's what you want?" Joorg asked.

"If it stops all this mess and killings and feces then yes. I don't care. Tell them."

"You don't know how big the Order is." Joorg said.

"We don't even know *wot* it is." Blap replied.

"I will tell you... it's huge."

"It's the Cakerlak, right?" Zucaritas asked.

"The Cakerlak? Not just the Cakerlak. Cyrakuse like us, Pachyderm's like you, Haathee, humans like Narob Traf, you name the species, and they're in the Order."

"And the Gink?" Zucaritas asked.

"Not from this galaxy, but yes, a big part."

"And the Toob?" Blaphaus asked.

"No. Definitely not."

"Then not every species." Blaphaus snorted.

"The Order is because of the Toob."

"Terrific." Blap waves his hand, "I'm not a Toob."

"No, but with you here and G.P., the Toob will come back..."

"You said Narob Traf." Zucaritas remarked, "What does he have to do with this?"

"Do you know who killed those beings on Cyrakuse? The human who got away?"

"Who?"

"Narob Traf." Joorg said seriously.


Fami walked down the House steps followed by Allard, just as the limo-vehicle parked in front of it again.

"Allard, balls in your court. Talk to the Cabinet, you know what's the best." she was saying as Rubyspears opened the back door for Jaboney to get out.

"I don't think it's the best thing." he told her.

"You'll see. The truth about Blaphaus will come out soon."

She walked off down the sidewalk.

"That's her." Rubyspears pointed out.

"What's going on?" Jaboney asked.

Allard sighed, "I think the House needs to reveal the truth."

Jaboney nodded, smiling.


His brother, Crisp Jaboney stepped outside the GNN shuttle on Cakerlak, followed by two hovering GNN robot-cams. They were approached by Laterillel.

"What brings you to Cakerlak, news human?"

"Glad you asked. I want to talk about Blaphaus' trip here, and what did he talk about." Crisp Jaboney smiled.

"Follow me." she told him.


The GBI vehicle drove up to the House, and parked. Blap and the other two got out of it. Zucaritas and Haathee went up the steps and Blaphaus made his way to the lift on the left side. He went around the corner to come face to face with Fami... just as the two Governors went through the glass doors inside. They had no idea that Blaphaus was punched so hard in the eye it was shoved right into his head. Blaphaus has no idea what hit him but it didn't hurt.

## CHAPTER 19

Laterille led Crisp and the following robot-cams into the chamber where the Great Weta sat. Crisp, not being the tallest human, looked intimidated by the big Cakerlak who looked down at him.

"Ummm... hello, my name is Crisp Jaboney, I'm with GNN."

"What made you think to bring this human here?" Weta asked Laterillell angrily.

"He's on our side, Great Weta."

"What is it you want, human?" Weta asked.

"An interview. The Governor of this planet made a scene, getting up on a stage for all the galaxy to see and talked about how dangerous Blaphaus is. He also mentioned an Order of Blatto something or other. I take it you know something about that. So, what do you say Great Weta?" Crisp Jaboney grinned.

"I will do no such thing, human. But I will tell you this... the Order will protect the galaxy as we have done so before."

"Protect? Protect from what?" Jaboney looked confused.

"The invasion."

Crisp didn't know what to say. He needed to interview Joorg, if he could find him.


The Governors walked into the conference room, but Blap wasn't with them.

"Where's Blaphaus?" Southington asked.

"Did he pull 'runner' again?" Bodie asked chuckling.

Haathee replied, "He was right behind us."

Zucaritas added, "I assumed he was taking the lift."

"Tapperdau was just here, and you take your eyes off the G.P.?" Allard asked irritated, standing up.

"She's not going to do anything to him." Gillian told him.

"How naive. She's gonna deliver him to the Committee and they're going to strip him down, take him apart and reveal the truth about him. Then what? There's going to be no G.P. Is that what you want?" Allard asked frustrated.

"It might be best." Noam said under his breath.

Allard went to the doors and said over his shoulder, "It's not going to happen on my watch."

When he was gone the Governors all relaxed.

"I love you lot but this is not what I thought being a Governor was going to be fun, but it's not." Rüppell commented. "What do you think, Bode?"

Bodie scratched at his patch and nodded, "I have to agree with Rüppell, Blaphaus is a liability. And he made me wear this annoying patch."

Penya sighed, fingers crossed over his belly. "I like the Tooberosum but my fellow Governor's are right. I miss the more peaceful days."

"None of you are going to quit." Zucaritas said, "We have to stand by Blaphaus. We made this bed, we have to lie in it."

"I say let it go." Noam said, "Let this damn Committee do what they want with him. I think we all made a mistake in agreeing Blaphaus be Galactic President. Hell, Tostone is dead because he chose Blaphaus if that doesn't tell you anything."

"Stop this!" Bradypus cried out, standing up and slamming his hand down on the table. "We are better than this! We always have been! We never turned our back on each other... except Guoz and Joorg..."

"And wherever Peezle is." remarked Eastora.

Bradypus ignored him and continued. "We will not ever turn our back on Blaphaus! Man or Toob, from this galaxy or another! Do you all hear me?!"

Jaboney walked into the conference room just then and said, "I agree, Waydo. We will all work together to get his ratings up and protect his damn ass."

Southington smiled, "Where is he anyway? I hope he's okay."

Blaphaus was standing in the back of the GBI vehicle once again, with Fami sitting across from him. His yellow right eye was stuck inside his Toob head, making Blap pretty furious.

"I don't know who you are, lady, but you assaulted the G.P. by punching my bloody eye in. You could be locked up for this feces."

"You very well know that the eye doesn't do anything. And who is going to lock me up? The GBI?"

"I'll find *somebody* to lock your arse up."

She chuckled, "Good luck with that."

"So, wot's your deal? You've been wanting to 'capture' me for weeks."

"You deceived the whole galaxy. With the galaxy believing you're a Toob you could start an invasion... an attack. My people will make sure that won't happen."

"Yeah? Your people? This G.P. gig wasn't my choice, my dear."

"Don't say 'my dear,' I'm not your dear. It doesn't matter how you got the position, you still did G.P. work. You even went to Cakerlak and made a deal with them."

"I didn't make any deal. I was asked to fund the bloody planet with weapons and feces. Traf was the one who did business with them."

"And the Order?"

"I'm so bloody tired of hearing about the Order. Traf was involved with that as well."

"Do you know what the Order is?" Fami asked.

"Where are we going?" Blap asked. "Not the spaceport I know that. We would've been there already."

Fami frowned, "How do you know that?"

"Darling, I've been driving for months on Ceilingida. It's all the same. I'm good with directions."

"Is that how you got to this galaxy?"

"That was by accident. You sure are asking a lot of questions."

"It's my job. So, you didn't answer my question about knowing what the Order is."

"I have no bloody idea, but everybody is talking about it it seems."

"Well, if you were really a Tooberosum you'd know."

"Which you know I'm not?"

She nodded, "I know a whole lot about you, Blaphaus Maximus."

"Good. For. You."

Peezle had no idea how to contact Yerkal. Again his husband went missing, and it was starting to get old. There was a knock on the apartment door where Peezle sat in his kitchen playing the fob message Yerkal left before. He felt so sad that perhaps his marriage was falling apart. Things were so much easier when he was Traf's Assistant. The knock on his door continued. Peezle got up and went over to it, looking through the peephole. He didn't see anybody standing there but the knocking continued. He opened the door to see a short white furred Cyrakuse standing there, wearing a dark suit.

"Hello? Can I help you?" Peezle asked.

"Noj Peezle?" the short Cyrakuse asked.

Peezle nodded, "Yeah, that's me."

"You've been crying, sir." the Cyrakuse pointed out.

"Look, if you don't mind, I am trying to sort something out."

"Is it about Yerkal your husband?"

"Uhhh... yes. You know about him?"

"If you let me come in I can explain."

Peezle motioned for the Cyrakuse to come in. He closed the door behind him.

"Please sit." Peezle sat on the couch and the Cyrakuse sat in a chair.

"My name is Anegon, Mr. Peezle, Lyncon Anegon. I'm a member of the Committee. Do you know who we are?"

Peezle shook his head. "Not a clue."

"We are a group that makes sure the Cabinet stays in line. That's the best way to say it."

"Oh. And?"

"You have all been out of line picking Blaphaus as Galactic President. Blaphaus who is not really a Toob."

"What does this have to do with Yerkal? You mentioned him."

"Oh, yes. He's in good hands. We hope he'll tell us what he was doing on Cakerlak and what he knows about the Order of Blattodea. I'm hoping you'll do the same."

"I don't get it."

"Hmmm. You were Traf's Assistant, right?"

"Yes. So?"

"You were there when he slipped and fell and passed away?" Anegon asked.

"Unfortunately yes. I don't understand what this has to do with anything."

"Did Traf ever mention the Order of Blattodea to you?"

"No, he never did."

"Do you know what the Order is?"

Peezle shook his head, "I really don't know anything."

Anegon stood up and stood over Peezle with a smirk.

"Stand up, you're coming with me, Mr. Peezle."


When the GBI vehicle stopped, Fami stood up and opened the two back doors and walked down the ramp and Blap followed her. They were in some kind of courtyard with huge walls around it. GBI agents surrounded them, and Fami led Blaphaus towards a door. Just then a black vehicle drove through the large gate that led into the courtyard. It drove right up next to the black GBI vehicle.

"I don't believe it." sighed Fami.

Allard stepped out the vehicle and approached Fami who stood next to Blaphaus.

"What do you want?" Fami asked.

"Hand the Toob back over." Allard pointed to her.

"You know he's not really a Toob."

"Whatever. He's still the G.P., and you kidnapped him."

Blaphaus went over to stand next to Allard, watched by everyone.

"You know I had to bring him here."

"That woman punched my bloody eye in." Blap pointed to the black hole where his right eye was missing.

"Violence to the G.P., Tapperdau? That's not going to look good if that gets out in the press."

"You very well know no one is going to say anything."
"Ha! Have you met Blaphaus? He has a big mouth." Allard chuckled.
He went and opened the back door of his vehicle.
"Get in, Blaphaus
"I'm not going to fit in there."
"You will if you lay down." he pushed Blap down and shoved him into
the backseat and closed the door.
"You can't take him, Felipe. Not when I'm this close to bringing him
here."
"Sure I can. Better luck next time, my dear."
She glared as Allard got into his vehicle, backed up, turned it around
and drove back through the gate.
"This bloody hurts." Blap complained, squeezed into the back seat.
"Blap, I just saved your life."

Narob laid in his bed, wondering what he was going to do next. He
didn't tell his mother or sister why he was so upset, he had no idea how
they were going to take it. And he didn't trust either of them. Just then a
holo-call of a Cakewalk, the one that killed everyone in the store, appeared
from the info-pad on the bedside table.
"Traf, you are to go get Joorg out of custody from the GBI."
Narob sat up and shook his head. "No, I'm not doing anything for the
Order again. I'm done."
"I would think again, boy. You know the consequences."
"I'll run and hide."
"We'd fine you, boy. Go get Joorg. He'll know what to do."
The holo-call ended and Narob laid his head back down on his pillow
angrily.

Allard led Blaphaus into the Icefence Hotel lobby and towards the lift.
"You can go now, Allard. I don't need a chaperone."
"Blaphaus, I'm not letting you out of my sight. You don't know how close
you were to being revealed."
"I'm about to do that for them." Blap muttered. "I'm over this."
Allard led Blaphaus into the lift. A few minutes later they walked into
Blap's suite. Blap turned to Allard and sighed.
"You might want to sit down, Felipe."
Felipe sat on the couch as Blap took off his purple jacket, dropping it on
the floor. He pulled out his left eye and tossed it into Allard's hands. He
reached behind him and Allard watched as Blap pulled down his Toob suit,

and the other eye rolled out. The gray haired human Blap stood there with the data-pad strapped to him. Allard looked at Blap standing there.

"That's so not what I expected."

"Well, now you bloody know." Blap said, "Now get me a drink."


"Cyrakuse, you are free to go." the GBI guard told Joorg who sat in his cell.

"I am? Wow." Joorg said confused as he stood up.

Moments later he came face to face with Narob in the GBI buildings lobby. Narob shook Joorg's hand.

"Was it you who got me free?" Joorg asked.

Narob nodded, leading Joorg outside.

"Yes, it was me. I bailed you out."

"Thank you. You're Narob Traf, am I right?"

Narob replied, "Yes."

"Are you a member of the Order as well?"

"Yes."

"Well, I don't know about you, Narob, but I can't take this anymore. I'm going to drop out."

Narob looked Joorg into his eyes, "You can't walk away like that. They'll find you. There's no escape."

"There's always escape. Blaphaus got away from his planet and his galaxy even, and disguised himself as a Toob. I'll do the same."

"What do you mean Maximus disguised himself?" Narob asked confused.

"Oh, you don't know? Blaphaus is a human who is pretending to be a Toob. He's not from this galaxy. If he can 'hide' then so will I."

Narob thought for a minute Joorg had a point, but what about his sister and mother? And if Blaphaus was faking being a Toob then what? All this was for nothing?

## CHAPTER 20

Yerkal Peezle was laying in the bed with the worse possible headache ever. He woke up, and tried to focus his eyes. His normally perfect looking hair was a mess and he was unshaven. He felt that he was under some silk sheets that probably were expensive and he was still wearing his clothes, minus his tie, shoes and jacket. He sat up, rubbing the back of his head looking around. He looked around the room to see he was in some kind of suite. Across the room facing the bed was a transparent wall where he saw a hallway was outside the room. The last thing he remembered was he and Noj had an argument at a restaurant and he got up and walked out. That was it. Now he was sitting up in a bed, no idea where he was. Just then a short plump female appeared on the other side of the transparent wall, wearing a flowering dress with black hair and tons of make-up. The wall slid open and the short female walked in grinning ear to ear.

"Oh, you're up! I'm so glad!" she said cheerily.

Yerkal frowned, looking at the short female.

"Who are you? Where am I?"

"My name is Dwof. How are you feeling?"

"Ummm... I have a very bad headache. Where am I?"

"You'll see. Can you get up?"

Yerkal nodded and got out of bed. "Follow me, Mr. Peezle. Someone wants to apologize to you."

Apologize? Yerkal was thinking was Noj there? Wherever he was. He followed Dwof out the room and down the hallway.

"Are you a Smidge?" Yerkal asked.

"Yeah, how did you guess?" she chuckled.

Yerkal replied, "Ummm... it was a guess. Where are my jacket and shoes?"

"In the room where you slept... in the wardrobe. I'll get them to you in a bit."

They reached a set of doors and Dwof opened them, leading him in. Two men sat in the room, one was a bearded and a really skinny Chordattian, with a pink short sleeved buttoned shirt and the other was a human male, wearing a long red leather jacket with a green hat on his head. He was definitely older than the other two. Older than any of the Governors he thought, except Eastora.

"Mr. Peezle, this is Jackanapes, he's a Chordattian and this is Phedorra." she motioned to the two men.

Jackanapes stood up and shook Yerkal's hand. Yerkal couldn't take his eyes off Jackanapes furry arms.

"Hello, Solicitor."

Phedorra stood as well and squeezed Yerkal's hand really tight. He was pretty strong for an older man. He shook Yerkal's hand rapidly.

"I'm so, so sorry, my friend. You must have a pretty bad headache. I hit you harder than I thought. I hope you'll forgive me."

"Ummm... what's this about? Are you the Order?" Yerkal asked, gulping and feeling scared.

"Order? No, we're the Committee." Dwof chuckled. "Do you mean the Order of Blattodea?"

Yerkal nodded, "Yes, do you know who they are?"

"Oh, we know everything." Jackanapes replied, "We also know you're a member of said Order."

Yerkal looked at them in surprise. They had it all wrong.

At the House, Anegon led Peezle up the steps and into the front doors. The House-robot approached them.

"Hello, Governor Peezle. Is this a friend of yours?"

"Yeah, he's with me."

"This is Suwas Anegon, Governor Peezle, he's an enemy of the House. A member of the Committee."

"He's still with me."

"I am sorry, Governor Peezle, but he is going to have to leave." the House-robot said.

Peezle sighed, "I don't know what to say."

"Go get your other Governors, and the Galactic President if he's here." told Anegon.

Peezle nodded and marched off to the lifts.

Yerkal sat in the chair that Jackanapes was sitting in earlier.

"I've never been part of the Order."

"You met with the Cakerlak who tried to assassinate the Tooberosum, you went to Cakerlak with him. Am I right?" Jackanapes asked, standing over Yerkal.

"Yes. But it's not what you think. I was investigating. Neop said that a member of the Cabinet was a member of the Order. I had to find out what I could."

"Why?" Jackanapes asked, "You're not a detective."

"No. I'm a Solicitor. Someone had to find out what's going on, and I felt I should. But I'm not a member... I still don't know what the Order is."

"Does your husband?" Dwof asked.

"Does my husband what?"

"Know what the Order is." she smiled.

Yerkal said, "I don't think so."

"You know he was Traf's Assistant." Jackanapes told him, "And that Algar Traf was a member of the Order."

"I don't think so." Yerkal said.

"It's true." Dwof told him, looking serious for the first time. "As well as his son."

Yerkal shook his head, "I don't think this is true. You are all mislead."

"Do you know where the word 'Blattodea' comes from?" Jackanapes asked.

"No, I never found out."

"Do you know Lilly Traf's maiden name before she got married?" Dwof asked.

"I don't know a lot about the Traf family. Noj never told me too much."

Phedorra grinned, "You're a smart man, Solicitor. Think about it."


"Someone from the Committee is here?" asked Noam. "This can't be good."

Peezle stood at the end of the table and said, "I know. He showed up at my apartment. He's looking for Blaphaus. And he asked me about the Order."

"Why is he here?" Jaboney asked.

"He wants Blaphaus." Southington said.

"Where is he?" Peezle asked.

"We thought Tapperdau had him." Dawber said, "Allard went to get him."

"Well, apparently she doesn't have him." Thaw told them.

"Anegon is not coming up here." Zucaritas told them.

"The House-robot won't let him." Peezle said, "So I was sent up here to get you all."

Thaw said, "The Icefence Hotel, you will meet with him there. Tell him, Peezle."

Peezle nodded and sighed.


Fami sat in the room, facing someone who sat before her.

"I was so close." she pleaded, "But Allard Felipe showed up and just took the Toob back."

Doctor Siahl nodded, "I understand. I'm not worried about it. There's a lot more situations I'm worried about than the G.P."

"Okay. I hope the others feel the same."

Siahl gave a half smile, "They don't. But there's other things to worry about."

"Like what?"

"Like the upcoming invasion that's going to happen. Everyone is focusing on the wrong thing. The fake Toob is the least of our worries."


Allard sat on the couch in the suite as Dawber's holo-call was in front of him.

"Allard, I don't know where you or Blaphaus are but the Governor's are heading to the Icefence to meet with Anegon."

"I'm at the hotel with Blap. The Committee almost had him, Dawber."

"Well, get him out of there. We can't turn him over to the Committee."

"Sure. I'll get him off this planet..."

"Is he with you?"

"Ummm... kind of..." Allard muttered.

He threw his pocket info-pad down, grabbed his jacket and dashed to the door.

"Damn It."

Blaphaus sat at the bar, the same bar where he met Fami before, drinking some alcohol. Allard walked up to him from behind, putting his hand on Blap's shoulder. Blap was wearing a black jacket over a purple shirt. His gray hair was slicked back, and he looked relaxed. But that was going to end.

"Get your hand off me unless you're going to buy me a drink." Blap said, turning around to face Allard. "Oh, it's you. Wot are you doing?"

"How much have you had to drink?"

"Not enough. Why?"

"Anegon, someone from the Committee is on the way here. I have to get you out of here and off this planet."

"I'm not going anywhere. Wot do you think is going to happen?"

"You don't want to know." Allard said seriously. "We have to go get your Toob suit on."

"I don't care. " Blaphaus muttered, drinking.

"You don't understand..."

"Fine! Let's go! Pay the bartender-robot!"


Nekkod walked into Zalez's office on the now named Narob Energy space station.

"Zalez, our new boss is here."

Zalez looked up and frowned, "Our new boss? Narob Traf?"

Nekkod nodded, "Yeah. He'd like to meet with you."

Zalez sighed, "I can't imagine what it's about. Bring him to this office, Nekkod."

Nekkod nodded and walked out the office. Zalez sat back thinking, what could Narob want? He did not show up at the Old Eborocum press announcement which Joorg interrupted. Nekkod walked Narob into the office. He stood up, noticing Narob didn't look so good. He walked around the desk and shook Narob's hand.

"Hello, Narob, it's good to have you here on the space station."

Narob frowned at the Dook Energy overalls he was wearing.

"The logo still says 'Dook.'"

"It's going to take time, Narob. We'll get the logo and overalls changed. What can I do for you?"

"I was wondering if you could show me how you power the planets."

Zalez nodded, "Of course. I'll be glad to."

Narob smiled, which was rare for him.


Peezle and Anegon walked into the lobby of the Icefence Hotel.

"We can go to the conference room this way." Peezle told Anegon, trying to lead him away.

"Where is Blaphaus?" Anegon asked.

Just then Blaphaus walked out the lift, looking like a Toob again. Allard followed him, straightening his tie.

"Fancy pants, wot are you doing here?"

"I brought Mr. Anegon here to talk to you, Blaphaus. He is from the Committee."

"Another bloody Cyrakuse."

Anegon reached out his white furred hand to Blaphaus, wanting to shake Blap's hand.

"I'm not shaking your bloody hand, Cyrakuse."

"I was wondering if we could talk." Anegon said, "Somewhere more private."

"Wot? So you could punch my bloody eye in and drag me to your building?"

Anegon smiled, "No, I'm not going to do that. Ms. Tapperdau made a big mistake. Can we go somewhere more private?"

"Nope. Wotever you say you can say it here. No one is in the lobby but us four and the front desk beings over there." Blap pointed.

"Fine. The Committee knows you're not a Tooberosum, Blaphaus."

"So does the Cabinet. Good for you lot."

"You're dangerous. Being a Tooberosum could cause problems. The Order of Blattodea will be after you. You're not good for the galaxy."

"Ha! No feces. It wasn't my idea to be in the limelight. I was happy being unknown."

"And the Governor and Galactic President who picked you are both dead." Anegon said seriously.

"Not my problem. Not my fault. I never met Traf. And as for as Tostone..."

"Blasted down with his wife... because of you. Because of the Order... so many dead beings because of you..."

"Again I didn't ask for this..."

"No. But you are still in the position. Reveal yourself. Step down. Tell the galaxy you're not a Toob or we will do that for you."

"As much as I don't want to be G.P., I'm not a quitter. I will not reveal anything, or step down. You might want to tell Tapperdau to back off, as well any of your lot. This galaxy is a mess, more than my own galaxy was. Find the Order, stop them. And control your species. Stop focusing on me and focus on finding Joorg, who is obviously going off the deep end."

"Where is the Gink Governor?" Anegon asked.

"Oh? You don't know something? Ha! I'm not telling. But I took care of that. He was a bigger threat from another galaxy than I could ever be."

"There's going to be more." Anegon said, "There's worry there's going to be an invasion. What do you say about that?"

"I say bring it on. Now if you don't mind, I'm done. Go back to minding your own business, Cyrakuse, or help find the Order."

Blap turned to leave to the lifts then turned back to face Peezle and Anegon.

"Oh, Peezle, you're fired. Allard, we need to find another Governor for Ceilingida."

Allard said to Anegon, "You heard him, Anegon. Back off. The galaxy needs him."

"You know that's not true." Anegon said. "An invasion is going to happen in this galaxy and it's all because of him." Anegon pointed to the Toob who stepped into the lift.

On the Narob Energy space station, Zalez and Narob walked along what a platform, looking down at the beings working in a huge room at the top of the station. Large consoles and machines were being overlooked, each machine and large info-pad was dedicated to the plants that the company had power on, making sure the lights, air conditioning and everything else.

"We generate electricity from primary energy. Each planet has their own generator that convert mechanical energy into electrical energy in order to supply power to the electrical grid for the planet's electrical needs." Zalez explained.

Narob knew this, and was barely listening. He was only concerned about one planet and one generator.

"Where is the Xenartha generator?" Narob asked.

Zalez frowned, wondering why Narob would ask about that one of all planets.

"Over there." Zalez pointed to a generator on the far side, operated by beings from that planet.

"I want to get a better look." Narob said.

"Ummm... fine. We can go down there."

Minutes later they rode a lift to the work floor and made it over to the generator. Narob looked over the info-pad holo-screens that workers sat at, each one showing different areas of the planet.

"You can shut the power off for the whole planet?"

Zalez nodded, giving Nekkod who stood behind them a slight look.

"Yes, but there would be no reason to do that."

"Turn it off. Shut down power for that planet." Narob ordered seriously.

"What?" Zalez asked.

The workers turned from their consoles and looked at Zalez and Narob.

Narob reaches inside his jacket and pulled out a hand blaster, pointing it at Narob's chest.

"I said shut down Xenartha's power."

"Why?" Zalez asked. "What got into you, Narob?"

"Mr. Belhopsa, my father really liked you, I like you, I like your children. You wouldn't want them to grow up fatherless, would you?"

"Narob, put that down." Zalez said calmly. "You're not the killing type."

"Really? Tell that to the many I blasted on Cyrakuse. Now, turn off the power."

Zalez glared at Narob, feeling sick in his stomach. Nekkod started to sweat, feeling he was going to throw up. The Xenartha workers just sat there in shock. Just then Narob blasted Nekkod in the leg, making him scream out in pain and he collapsed on the floor.

"What the...?" Zalez asked stunned,

Narob pointed his weapon at Zalez again, "Next blast will kill. Turn off the power."

Narob had a crazed look in his eyes.

Zalez turned to the workers, "Do it. Shut down the power on the whole planet."

They all pushed buttons and flicked switches. The info-pads all showed the planets power was shut down.

On Xenartha the power shut down quickly, but it was day time, so nothing was dark. At the military base though, the solider opened the door to the room and went inside where the Gink's coffin was. It had a hard shell, and pinchers instead of hands. He opened the coffin's lid and Guoz instantly sat up, large bulging eyes open wide as always.

"About time. So, has the invasion happened yet? Are the Gink in this galaxy?"

The Cherlicereta shook his head, "No, we don't know what happened. They were in the galaxy but disappeared. The Order is ready to strike though."

"And the fake Toob?"

"The Galactic President? Fake?"

"He's still G.P.?"

"Yes. Fake?"

"Yes, but soon he'll be dead... then the Great Weta."

Before Narob knew it there were military soldiers, all armed, on the overhead walkways and on the work floor.

"Blaphaus made sure to put the Xenartha military on the space stations to look out for an invasion, Narob. I did not think you would be the enemy." Zalez told the teenager.

Narob was grabbed by two soldiers who approached him. One took the blaster away from him, the other cuffed him behind his back.

"Switch the power back on." Zalez told one of the workers.

"We are going to take him to the military base." a soldier told Zalez.

Zalez nodded, "I'll let the Cabinet know."

"The Order will stop the invasion." Narob said before he was lead away, "We are not the enemy."

"Your father would be so disappointed, Narob." Zalez said. "*I'm* disappointed."

Narob didn't say another word, he was led off.

Zalez knelt down next to Nekkod who laid there in pain still, the blast wound on his leg.

"Nekkod, I'll get you to the hospital on Ceilingida right away."

"I don't understand what just happened, boss." Nekkod moaned.

"I don't know, Nekkod. I really don't understand what's happening, and that scares me a lot."

The lights and power was back on Xenartha but the Gink was put on the military shuttle with Brigadier Harkouk.

"I'm hungry." Guoz said, "I've been in that tight box for days."

"You're free now." the Brigadier said.

Guoz nodded, "Yes. Free. The pilot knows we are going to Launderington, right?"

"The pilot is a robot-pilot and does know."

"Contact Governor Sugden and see if he knows where Blaphaus is. Tell him about the power going out on the planet."

The Brigadier nodded.

Zalez sat on the Dook Energy shuttle with Nekkod who was in a lot of pain. Zalez decided he wasn't going to call the company "Narob Energy," not after what happened. He looked out the portal window to see the other shuttle flying off to Xenartha with Narob. Zalez shook his head in disbelief. Nekkod moaned in pain, making a face of anguish.

"Mr. Belhopsa, you didn't have to come with me."

"Yes I do, Nekkod. You're my number one."

"Why did Narob do this?"

Zalez shook his head, "I have no idea."

"Do you think it's true he blasted those people on Cyrakuse?" Nekkod asked.

Zalez nodded, "Unfortunately I do."

"I don't get it, his father was the nicest person ever. What do you think made Narob so...?"

"Evil?"

Nokkod nodded, thinking there was no other word for it.

"I don't know. I wish I had answers. Now stop talking and rest. We'll be on Ceilingida real soon." Zalez put his hand on Nekkod's shoulder.

The holo-call of Brigadier Harkouk appeared on the conference table at the House, facing Governor Sugden.

"Governor, I have to report that for a few minutes power went out on Xenartha, on the whole planet."

"Did anybody get hurt?" Sugden asked.

"No, Governor, everyone is fine."

"And the military base where Guoz's body is being held?"

"It's fine. Like I said it was only for a few minutes."

Sugden nodded, "Thank you, Brigadier."

The holo-call ended and Sugden stood up.

"I think I better go to Xenartha and see what happened. I'm sure the beings on that planet were wondering what happened."

"What the Creator-damned." Zucaritas said, "Power on a planet doesn't just turn off. We need to contact Zalez and see if it's something to do with the Doo... Narob Energy space station."

"Let me know what he says." Sugden said before he left.

"Where's Peezle?" Zeb asked. "He knows Zalez pretty well."

Peezle was led into the room with the transparent wall where Yerkal sat alone. Yerkal did not recognize the Cyrakuse who was with Peezle. He jumped to his feet as the transparent wall opened and Peezle ran over to give his husband a hug. The transparent wall closed behind him.

"Gentlemen, I will let you two catch up. We will be with you soon. You both need to figure out together how you want things to end up. You could be the enemy of the galaxy or the opposite."

Anegon marched off and Yerkal frowned.

"What was that about?"

"It's a long story. What are you doing here, Yerkal? I haven't seen you since you got mad at me and left the restaurant."

"Well, I didn't get far." Yerkal said, sitting down. "I was knocked out somehow and woke up here in that bed, in this room." He motioned to the bed. "Whoever these beings are they think I'm part of the Order. They also seem to know the origin and what the Order is."

"I was with that Cyrakuse, who is the Head of the Committee which is this group. We came face to face with Blaphaus..."

"Peezle, Blaphaus is not really a Tooberosum, is he?"

"Hmmm. No, Yerkal, he's a human..."

"Why didn't you tell me?"

"As a Governor knowing certain things I cannot tell you. But it doesn't matter anyway, I'm not a Governor anymore."

"You quit?"

"No. I was fired."


Zalez's holo-call was in the middle of the table in the conference room.

"Zalez, can you explain why Xenartha's power went out? Governor Sugden is on the way to the planet." Southington asked.

"Yes, Narob Traf made a visit to the space station, pulled out a blaster and ordered the power to be turned off. He's now being taken to Xenartha by the military."

"Why would he do that?" Gillian asked.

"I have no idea. Luckily it was only out for a few minutes."

"Where are you now, Zalez?" Dawber asked.

"At the Jubilee Hospital on Ceilingida. Nekkod, my Assistant was blasted in the leg by Narob. That's not it though... he admitted he was the one who blasted the beings at the festival on Ceilingida."

"What?" Zucaritas exclaimed, "Why the hell would he do that?"

Zalez shrugged, "I don't know."

"Let us know if you need anything." Southington said, "I hope Nekkod is okay."

"Thank you. I'm sorry this happened." Zalez said before his holo-call ended.

"What in the galaxy is going on?" Zucaritas asked. "Narob Traf? Why?"

"His father would be devastated." Gillian said sadly. "His mother will be."

"Is Narob part of the Order?" Southington asked.

"Was the former G.P.?" Rüppell asked. "A member of this Order?"

"Who knows." Noam said, arms crossed. "I don't understand this galaxy anymore. I want to go to another."

Gillian gave him a dirty look, "We have to let Narob's mother know."

Eastora said, "What are we going to say? Mrs. Traf, your husband was a great G.P., sorry your dammed son is a terrorist and murderer and won't see daylight ever again."

"We have to be a little more tact than that." Dawber said.

"I think you females should go." Jaboney said, "Females can be more pleasant. Mrs. Traf might take the news better."

"I think Blaphaus should know what is going on." Lluhdor remarked. "And where is Peezle?"

"We'll go to tell Lilly, then we'll figure out how to announce it to GNN."

Jaboney said, "I'll talk to my brother. I cannot believe I sold my power company to that rotten kid."

"There's so many questions." Bodie said, "Once again this is not what I signed up for."

Thaw nodded, "None of us, Bodie. None of us. I'll let Sugden know what's going on. He can maybe ask Narob a few questions."

Southington stood up, "Someone contact Blaphaus and get his ass here. He should know what's going on."

Dawber added also standing, "And find out where Peezle went to."


Mal and Fadonna, the plump woman who worked at the Belhopsa Dance School were teaching a class, as Nate sat doing his homework on his info-pad. Romana was taking part in the class, jumping up and down. Zalez's holo-call appeared before Nate suddenly.

"Father! Hello!" Nate smiled.

"Nate, is your mother there? I need to talk to her."

"Yeah, she's teaching class. You don't sound good, is everything okay?"

"It's fine. I just need to talk to your mother."

Nate stood and took the info-pad over to Mal.

"Mother, it's father."

Mal took the info-pad and said, "Hi, honey, what's wrong?"

"I need to talk to you in private."

She nodded and went to the office at the back of the dance floor.

"Okay, what's up?"

"It's Narob Traf. He's gone crazy, he blasted Nekkod in the leg on the space station."

"What? Why?"

"Long story. I'm at Jubilee Hospital with him. Nekkod doesn't have a family, I need you to sit with him here. I have to get back to work. Stuff is happening that's not good."

"But I have another hour of teaching to do. I have another class."

"Have Fadonna teach it. Please, Mal, I need your help "

"Fine. But what about the children?"

"Don't tell them anything. Fadonna can watch them as well."

"Does this have anything to do with what happened on Old Eborocum, Zalez? I don't like this."

"I don't know. I will find out. I'll wait for you here at the hospital."

"Okay, I'll be there soon."

The holo-call ended as Mal did not look happy at all. She went out the office and over to where Fadonna was dancing with the kids.

"Fad, I need you to teach the next class, and bring my children home. I have to go somewhere quickly and meet Zalez."

Fadonna smiled, "Sure!"

"Everything okay, mother?" Nate asked.

Mal nodded, "I think so, Nate. I hope so."


A holo-call of Jaboney appeared before Crisp Jaboney in his office on the GNN space station.

"Hello, brother. If you're going to tell me to chill on the Blap stories I have to tell you we have not mentioned him lately. He's been rather low key."

"Crisp, I am not here to talk about Blaphaus. I have news on the Cyrakuse blastings... the first one. We know who it was."

"Really? And I take it you're going to tell me but don't want to report it?" Crisp asked.

"No, not yet."

"Then why tell me, Governor?"

"Because when time comes up to mention it you'll be the first to know."

Crisp nodded, "Fair enough. Shoot. Who was it?"

"Narob Traf."

Crisp just stared at the holo-call of his brother.


Allard waited in the hallway outside the suite at the Icefence Hotel. Blap, looking like a Toob again walked out, closing the door behind him.

"This better be good, Felipe. I'm not in the mood for games."

"Trust me, Blaphaus. The Cabinet called for you. They said it was an emergency."

"Wotever. Everything is an emergency to them."


Peezle paced back and forth in the suite as Yerkal just sat watching him.

"I have an idea, Yerkal, on how to get out of here."

"You do? I don't know if it'll work. We don't know how much power or what this Committee is."

"Exactly. But they're interested in the Order, and obviously Blaphaus... and Algar Traf. I'm no longer Governor, and member of the Cabinet and have no allegiance with anybody, but the Traf family. I'll do everything for that family. I also know the truth about Blaphaus. I'll tell them everything if they promise to let us go. What do you think?"

Yerkal said, "I think it's a good idea. But we still don't anything about the Order really."

"No, but when we are free you and I will investigate together. We will get answers, Yerkal. I promise."

Yerkal nodded, "Okay. So tell me everything you know about Blaphaus. No more secrets."

Peezle nodded and smiled. No more secrets.


Narob was led into his cell at the Xenartha military base. He faced the soldiers and clenched his fists.

"I want a Solicitor."

"That's not up to us." a soldier said.

In another part of the base, Brigadier Harkouk met with Sugden.

"Governor, did you get word on who we have as prisoner?"

Sugden frowned under the hard shell on his head.

"Prisoner? No. I'm here because the power went out for a few minutes. I want to see the room where the Gink is being held just to make sure everything is okay."

"Well, you'll be interested in the new prisoner, Governor. Follow me."

Sugden impatiently followed Harkouk to the prisoner area. They walked up to one cell and Sugden was surprised to see Narob sitting there.

"Narob Traf?" Sugden asked, "What did you do?"

Narob looked up to see Sugden standing there on the other side of the cell.

"I am not talking. I want a Solicitor. I want Yerkal Peezle."

"Well, I don't know where Solicitor Yerkal is."

"Isn't his husband a Governor? Ask him."

"Brigadier, why is Narob a prisoner on this planet?"

"He is responsible for the power going out. And he admitted to Zalez Belhopsa that he was the one who killed those at the festival on Cyrakuse. He also blasted a Dook Energy..."

"Narob Energy." Narob said seriously.

"He blasted a Narob Energy employee in the leg." Harkouk continued.

"Why?" Sugden asked shocked, "What's gotten into you, Narob? Your father would be stunned, shocked, saddened..."

"My father was weak. He knew about an upcoming invasion, and he didn't want to be G.P. anymore. I am doing the work he should've done."

Sugden shook his head, "You're so young, Narob. You are throwing your life away, and for what? The Order of Blattodea? Is that why you're doing all this?"

"Ha! The Order is the only thing that can save this galaxy. The Cabinet can't do feces. You even picked a damned Toob to be G.P., that race that wiped out so many before, that was stopped by the Order. But fun fact, Sugden, that Toob is not really a Toob... he's a human." Narob laughed a border line evil laugh.

"I know." Sugden said.

Harkouk looked confused, "What do you mean?"

"Long story." Sugden replied, "Narob, why did you have the power turned off on this planet?"

Narob chuckled, "You'll find out."


Rubyspears drove his limo-vehicle up to the large house again, through the gates. Again he had the three female Governors in the back seat. He parked the vehicle and turned to them.

"Want me to wait again?"

"Yes, please." Dawber said.

He got out and opened the back door for them. They got out and walked up to the house. Dawber buzzed the door buzzer and moments later the door opened to reveal the tall purple robot One standing there.

"Hello, Governors, welcome back."

"Thank you." Southington smiled, "Is Mrs. Traf in?"

"Yes, she's in the living room. I'll go get her."

One went back into the house while they waited. Lilly Traf showed up at the door moments later, One standing behind her.

"Hello, Governors, judging by the looks on your faces I don't think you're here with good news."

"Can we come in?" Gillian asked.

Mrs. Traf nodded and led them into the living room.

"Is it about Narob?" Lilly asked.

"Yes, how did you know?" Gillian asked.

"He came here a few days ago and broke down crying. He never said why though, and then he left again. Do you know what he's been doing?"

"Afraid so." Dawber said, "But we don't know why... yet. Currently he's held at a military base on Xenartha."

"Military base? Xenartha? That's not good. Did he kill anybody?"

Southington looked down sadly.

Blaphaus and Allard walked into the conference room where the Governors, minus a few, sat.

"Where are the bloody females?" Blap asked right away.

"How are you doing?" Eastora asked.

"I'm fine. I fired Peezle, he's working with this Committee, whoever they are."

"You fired another Ceilingada Governor?" Noam asked.

"I don't think Peezle is working for them." Zeb added.

"He was with one of them. A Cyrakuse of course..."

"Why are you here?" Thaw asked sitting next to Allard.

"You have to name another Governor for Ceilingida." Lluhdor remarked.

"Felipe for now will be Governor." Blap told them, "Now again, where are those three? And The Illicit? " he motioned to the empty seats.

"Sugden went to Xenartha. Narob is a prisoner at the military base."

"The Traf kid? Why?"

"He went to the Dook space station and blasted Nekkod in the leg, and ordered the power to be turned off on Xenartha." Zeb is explained.

"Xenartha? The planet with the bloody military? That's not bright. I knew something wasn't right with that family."

"It's not the family, Algar was good..."

Blap interrupted Thaw, "Keep believing that. I beg to differ. He made deals with the Cakerlak and probably was a member of the Order."

"Narob is not like his father." Zeb said.

"Wotever you say."

Zucaritas said to Blaphaus, "Blaphaus, Narob also was the one who killed all those beings on Cyrakuse at the festival."

"You know that for a fact?" Allard asked.

"Yes, he told Zalez." told Zucaritas.

"And to think you sold your company to that kid." Blap pointed to Jaboney. "He's a chip of the old block, that kid."

Lluhdor said, "Southington, Gillian and Dawber went to tell his mother."

"Bet that's not going to be a fun conversation." scoffed Blaphaus.

""Does GNN know?" Allard asked.

"No, not yet." Zeb said.

"Good. The less they know the better."


Sugden and Harkouk went into the room where the Gink's coffin was.

"I don't think the Gink would go missing."

"Why else would Narob have the power turned off here?" Sugden replied. "Open up there coffin."

The Brigadier did so and they saw the Gink Governor was gone.

"Why would anybody take the body?" Harkouk asked surprised.

"That I don't know." muttered Sugden.


Sugden's holo-call appeared on the middle of the long table in the conference room.

"Narob is not eating a whole lot, but he's not denying anything."

"Did you think of asking him why the bloody hell he would have the power turned off on the planet?" Blap asked.

"No, but I think I know why. Guoz was removed from the coffin." Sugden replied.

"What? Why?" Zeb asked. "Who would want it?"

"Maybe he's not dead after all." Allard told them.

Lluhdor replied, "We all saw him die. The King broke his neck."

"And you think that's what killed him? You have no idea." smirked Allard.

"Sugden, I want you to put military personnel on every planet."

"Blaphaus, I don't have enough soldiers for that. I already put a bunch on the stations."

"A fat good that did, Narob still managed to do wot he wanted."

"Do you realize that the Gink could be the ones to invade this galaxy?" Thaw asked.

"If so, we need to be ready." Allard said.

"You all need to think twice about wot mess you brought on yourselves." Blaphaus said, turning to the door.

"Where are you going?" Noam asked.

"To get my feces in order." Blap replied before he walked out.


Hoeka exclaimed, "Mother! I knew he was up to something. He was always going out, and when he was here he would lock himself in his room."

They all sat in the living room, Lilly in tears, crying into tissue after tissue.

"Alger would be so disappointed." she sniffed, "If he was alive still none of this would have happened."

"You don't know that." Dawber said, "Algar hasn't been gone that long... Narob could have been planning this a long time."

"I know you've been questioned a few times, Lilly, but did Algar ever mention the Order of Blattodea? We know he funded Cakerlak, and did some things we Governors knew nothing about."

"Nothing that would harm anybody. Algar was a loving man."

"But he did fund Cakerlak for weapons."

"To defend the galaxy probably."

"From what?" Southington asked.

"I don't know. Look, you went through his info-pad. Algar was innocent."

"And Narob isn't, mother." Hoeka said.

"A few day's ago he came home very upset." Lilly said, "But he didn't say why. I can't believe he would do this."

"I know." Gillian nodded.

"Does Noj Peezle know?" Lilly asked.

"I don't think so." Southington replied, "We don't know where he is. The Cabinet knows. We are not going to tell the press yet either. He just purchased Consolidated from Governor Jaboney and didn't show up at the announcement..."

"He did? How? With what dosh?" Lilly asked.

"I don't know." Southington shook her head.

"Did he break into your account, mother?" Hoeka asked.

"I don't know. So, he's on Xenartha? I want to talk to him... no, I want to kick his ass." Lilly said through gritted teeth.

"I don't know if that's a good idea." Southington replied, "Kicking his ass, yes, but seeing him. We'll see if you can."

Lilly nodded, "Well, feel free to search his room. You might be able to find some evidence... or what made him do all this. Or anything about the Order of Blatt... whatever they're called."

Dawber stood up from the couch and nodded, "Thank you, Lilly. We are so sorry."

Lilly nodded, "I know. I'm glad you told me. I just wish Algar was alive."

Blap shuffled into the Icefence Hotel's lobby. He made his way to the lift, pushing the button to go up to his suite. A hundred thoughts were going around in his mind... he so wanted to quit, to rip the Toob suit off and be done with it. The lift door opened and he went into it. The doors closed but not before someone joined him. Blap could not believe his fake yellow eyes.

"Hello, Maximus, we need to chat." Guoz grinned at him.

## CHAPTER 22

The lift door opened and Blap shuffled out, followed by Guoz, who was pointing his blaster at Blap's back. They made their way down the hallway.

"How the bloody hell did you walk into the lobby with a weapon?" Blap asked.

"They think I'm still Governor, remember? I have to defend myself."

"Governor of a fake planet." Blaphaus replied. "If you're going to kill me do it now."

"I want to kill you. But not yet."

They reached the door to Blap's suite. Blap pulled out the key card from the inside pocket of his purple jacket and waved it over a scanner. They both walked into the suite, Guoz closing the door behind him.

"Take off your Toob outfit, human." ordered Guoz.

Blap turned to face the Gink.

"No. I'm not going to do wot you say, Gink."

"Pop your eyes out, Blaphaus. Pull that costume off. I want to look at the human male, the real you."

"Again I'm not going to do that, Gink."

"Fine. You will eventually."

"Wotever."

"You claim you're from another galaxy... a planet called Phulfortha if I remember. Did you lie about that?"

"Nope. It's true. I'm not from this feces of a galaxy."

"That means there's two other galaxies at least, apart from this one."

"Terrific. You want to invade my home galaxy as well?"

"I'm hardly an invasion, Blaphaus, I'm one being."

Blaphaus pointed out, "How the bloody hell are you alive anyway?"

"I'm a Gink. We don't die easy. My neck healed in that coffin. I need to go to Cyrakuse and pay that King a visit. Break his neck..."

"Yeah, yeah, so, wot do you want? You're alive, you claim you were from this galaxy, I proved your arse wrong. Now wot?"

"The Gink are coming, Blaphaus, there's going to be an invasion. I am just a scout... sent by the Gink military when we discovered this galaxy from Traf. I learned about the Order... Traf knew all about it. He was fascinated by me, asked me if I'd be a Governor. Of course he also thought that moon was my planet. He knew of the Tooberosum, knew they were vicious and lethal. Knew the Order was formed by Blattodea, led by the Cakerlak who brought in all different species to combat the Toob invasion. They thought they wiped the Toob out, then you showed up..."

"Who is not really a a Toob so moot point."

"But not many know that... the Great Weta thinks you're a real Toob." the Gink smiled.

"So, who is Blattodea? A Cakerlak?"

"No, Blaphaus. A human."

"From this galaxy?"

"Yes, from this galaxy. No one remembers who he was... no one alone anyway. Apparently he was the Galactic President before Traf was."

"Beings here have a short attention span." Blap muttered.

"It was a long time ago. The Toob were very violent... and vicious. The Gink are going to come, Blaphaus, and we'll 'protect' the galaxy... and there's nothing you or the Cabinet *or* the Order can do. We will be the new Order."

"Good luck with that, Gink."

Guoz smiled, "You'll need the luck."

He made his way to the door, still pointing his blaster.

"Maybe we will invade your galaxy and planet next."

"Wotever. You survived now, you won't survive again."

The Gink opened the door to reveal Allard standing there. Allard grabbed Guoz, grabbing his sharp saw shaped nose which cut his hand. He yelped in pain, and stumbled back. The Gink laughed and matched off down the hallway.

"His nose cut my hand!" Allard said with gritted teeth.

"Have you seen his nose? Wot kind of security advisor are you?"

Allard went into suite and made his way to the bathroom to wash the cut.

"You have a lot to fill me in on!" Allard called out.

Blap went to the window and looked out at the city.

"Felipe, I think this bloody galaxy is in big trouble. But we are not going to tell anyone."

Allard walked over, face cloth wrapped around his left hand.

"You have a lot of explaining to do, Blaphaus."


The Ultra vehicle drove up to the mansion on planet Phytnes. The human driver got out of it, and opened the back door. Joorg stepped out and made his way to the front door.

"Have a nice day. You did a great job on Old Eborocum with that speech."

"Thank you. Just looking out for this galaxy."

The driver smiled and waved before he got back in and drove off. Joorg buzzed the door buzzer and moments later Enitittuk, the big brown haired Bovie opened the door and stood there.

"Oh... hello, Gov... Joorg... I saw you on GNN. What happened?"

"Is Haathee here?" the Joorg asked.

"No, he's at the House on Launderington. He hasn't been here recently. I've been very lonely."

"Well, you're not going to be lonely much longer, Enitittuck. Contact that Pachrydon and tell him to get here now."


Peezle stood in front of the transparent wall, tapping in it, waiting for one of the Committee brings to show up. Yerkal was laying in the bed, hands behind his head.

"They're not going to come here, Noj. They have bigger situations to take care of."

Noj turned around and faced the bed.

"Yerkal, you can't be thinking they're just going to leave us here alone to rot. Surely they're going to feed us, come and say something."

Yerkal shrugged as he laid there.

"I don't know, Noj. This whole thing is all messed up."

Just then Dwof walked up to the other side of the transparent wall and stopped.

"You should sit and relax, Mr. Peezle, you're going to be here for a while."

"Ma'am, I want to talk to Anegon, and make a deal with him. I will help with whatever you need. I have no allegiance to Blaphaus or the Cabinet."

Dwof frowned, "I'll see if he wants to speak to you. I wouldn't hold your breath though, Mr. Peezle, not too long. Right now there's more situations we have to deal with."

"What is going on now?" Peezle asked frowning, looking worried.

"Narob Traf was arrested and is on Xenartha."

"Arrested for what?" Peezle asked.

"You'll find out. Maybe your husband knows."

She then walked off leaving Peezle standing there looking really confused. He turned to look at Yerkal who was laying in the bed.

"I don't know anything, Noj. But it can't be good."

What possibly could Narob have done, Peezle wondered.


The female Governors got out the limo-vehicle and made their way up the steps. Rubyspears stood there, watching them. He had no idea what was going on, but knew it wasn't good. A few minutes later they went into the conference room just as Haathee was walking out, followed by Bodie.

"Haathee, are you okay?" Gillian asked seeing Haathee was looking worried.

"Enitittuck my servant contacted me and said I need to go to Phytnes right away. I don't know what's going on."

"I volunteered to go with him, love." Bodie smiled.

"Good luck." Southington said, "We'll fill you in when you get back."

They went into the conference room where the others were.

"When are we all going to be together at one time again?" Southington asked.

"You got me." Rüppell shrugged.

At the Jubilee Hospital on Ceilingida, Nekkod laid in bed, his leg wrapped up where Narob blasted him, hooked up to a robot-IV. Mal sat next to his bed, watching him.

"I really appreciate you staying here, Mrs. Belhopsa. I have no family to visit."

"It's all good, Nekkod. You can call me Mal. Zalez thinks highly of you."

Nekkod smiled, "And I think highly of him and your family. I have no idea what got into Narob Traf's mind, why he would do this."

"I agree. This galaxy all of a sudden is flipped in its head. At least my children are safe, that's all I can say."

Fadonna parked her little red vehicle in front of the Belhopsa house, and got out. The children got out the vehicle as well and they made their way to the front door. Their old robot O-U, with his head attached again rolled out through the little robot door to face them.

"O-U?!!!" the children exclaimed together.

"Hello, children, I seem to have missed a few weeks. Was I turned off? Hello, Ms. Fadonna."

"You don't remember what happened?" Nate asked frowning.

"One minute I was going to tell the Governors and your parents something and then everything went black. Was I turned off?"

"Not really turned off." Nate said, not knowing how he should explain it.

"Who fixed you?" Romana asked.

The front door then opened to reveal the multi-colored painted 10-E-C robot.

"O-U, were you going to leave the children outside all day?"

"Ten! How are *you* fixed?" Nate asked surprised.

"Can we go inside?" Fadonna asked.

"Of course. Come in." Ten told them.

They went inside to see an older human male sitting at the dining room table with a green hat on his head, wearing a dark red leather overcoat.

"Hello, children." he smiled standing up. "I had some time of my hands and fixed both of your robots. It's odd they were both headless. Someone must've been mad."

"I'm sorry, sir, who are you?" Fadonna asked, "Are you a friend of the Belhopsa's?"

"Not really. But I'm taking the children with me. You can come to if you want."

"Where are we going?" Nate asked. "I don't think we should go anywhere."

"You're just a child, young man, you shouldn't think at all. Well, ma'am, are you coming with us or staying here?"

"I can't let the children go anywhere without their parents knowing."

"Oh, their father will know, after the fact."

"Mister, I don't know who you are so we are not going." Nate said firmly.

Phedorra smiled, "Young man, you don't have a choice."

Fadonna pulled out her info-pad from her purse to contact Mal but Ten took it from her in a snatch.

"Hey!" she said.

"Shall we go now, children?" Phedorra asked.

Zalez got out of the Ultra vehicle in front of the House, as the human driver opened the door for him. He made his way up the steps and went into the lobby to be met by a House-robot.

"Mr. Belhopsa, welcome, can I help you?"

"I need to see Governor Peezle please."

"Governor Peezle is not here, Mr. Belhopsa."

"Then any of the other Governors or Galactic President Maximus. Someone. It's urgent."

"Please wait right there." the robot turned to leave.

Just then Allard walked into the House followed by Blap who was right behind him.

"Belhopsa, wot are you doing here? Don't you have a space station to watch over?" Blaphaus asked.

"That's why I'm here, Blaphaus. Nekkod was blasted in the leg, power was turned off on Xenartha..."

"And that bloody Gink escaped." Blaphaus said.

"Escaped? He was dead." Zalez remarked.

"*Was* is the key word, Chordattian, but somehow he's alive."

"Beings just don't come back from the dead, Blaphaus." Zalez said.

Allard held up his hand still wrapped up in the white flannel that was now blood stained.

"Zalez, he's alive, and his nose is as sharp as hell."

"Where is he?" Zalez asked, "You saw him?"

"Yup. He paid me a visit at the hotel, and Felipe right here stupidly grabbed his nose. Where he is now I don't know." Blaphaus explained.

The House-robot came out the lift and went over to where the three stood talking.

"The Governors said they will see you, Mr. Belhopsa. Hello Mr. Felipe, Galactic President Maximus." The House-robot said.

Zalez's pocket info-pad beeped and he took it out his pocket. A holo-call of Phedorra appeared above it, about six inches high.

"Phedorra." muttered Allard.

"Hello, Mr. Belhopsa, you don't know who I am but I'm a friend of your children." He bent down and picked up each child in his arms. He was stronger than he looked.

"Hello, father, we are okay, but Fadonna was knocked unconscious." Nate said.

Romana cried, "We are in a shuttle going somewhere, father. Please help!"

Zalez never looked so mad in his life.

"Where are you taking my children? Who are you?"

"I'm taking them to Launderington, I'm sure your friends can help you find out where. Come get them, Mr. Belhopsa, it's you we want to talk to, not the children. Ms. Tapperdau would be glad to see your son again though. See you soon."

The holo-call disappeared.

"What the hell? Who is this?" Zalez waved his info-pad.

"Phedorra Playce, a Committee agent. He is not very nice." Allard said, "But he won't hurt the children."

"Wot do they want with Belhopsa?" Blap asked.

"Considering he is someone else that knows you and is head of the energy company that shut off the power on Xenartha making the Gink escape probably a lot. Do you know Blaphaus' secret, Zalez?"

"Yes. But I'm not going to say what it is."

Allard smirked, "You don't have to. Now let's go get your children."

"Are you gonna let your wife know about this?" Blaphaus asked.

Zalez shook his head, "No, not yet."

Blap snorted, "Smart Chordattian."

***************************************************************************************

Dwof approached the transparent wall again, this time with two GBI agents. Peezle jumped to his feet from the love seat he was sitting in.

"Is Anegon ready to talk?"

Dwof shook her fat head on her squat little body.

"No, I did not ask him. Yerkal, can you stand up, please?"

Yerkal sat up in bed and asked, "Stand up? Why?"

"Because you're coming with us, That's why." she said seriously.

Peezle said, "Why? Where is he going?"

"That's none of your business, Mr. Peezle."

The transparent wall opened and the agents walked in, each grabbing Yerkal's arms, yanking him off the bed.

"Ouch! You're hurting me!" cried Yerkal.

"Not as much as what's going to happen." Dwof replied chuckling.

"Where are you taking him? What is going on?" Yerkal demanded.

"You'll find out if we choose to tell you later."

Yerkal was dragged out the room, the transparent wall closed and a shocked Peezle watched as Yerkal was dragged away. He angrily punched his fist on the transparent wall, making it shake. Just then the wall opened to his surprise. He hesitated for a minute then walked out into the hallway and went in the direction they took Yerkal.


"Where is Rubyspears?" Blap demanded, standing on the pavement outside the House with Zalez and Allard.

"It doesn't matter, I have my vehicle." Allard smiled.

"Wot? The one I have to lay down in?"

"Let's just go." Zalez said impatiently, "Do you think Phedorra is going to be going to the spaceport?"

"No, their shuttle will be going to the Committee building called the Capital. We are taking my vehicle."

Zalez looked up the sky wondering where his children were.


Peezle went through one door, coming face to face with a Cakerlak with a red shell with black spots.

"Ummm... hi..." Peezle did not know what to say.

"Governor Peezle I presume." the Cakerlak said.

"Ummm... Yes... no, I'm not a Governor anymore."

"You're working for the Committee?"

Peezle shook his head, looking around nervously.

"No, I'm not. I'm trying to get out, or find where they're taking my husband..."

"Yerkal. The human Solicitor."

"Yes, that's him."

"Follow me, Peezle. My name is Laterille, this galaxy is in big trouble." Peezle hesitated then followed the Cakerlak.

On the roof of the long building the black shuttle landed. The ramp went down and Phedorra walked down it, the children either side of him. He had his hands on their shoulders and led them to the door which was for a lift.

"I don't feel so good." Romana moaned.

"It's because you're on another planet." Nate told her, "You'd get used to it."

"You're a smart boy." Phedorra smiled, as they went into the lift. A few minutes later they stepped out the lift into the hallway to come face to an older lady with dirty blond hair, wearing a white pants suit.

"Phedorra, what is the meaning of this?" she asked.

"Hello, ma'am, I was sent to get them. Well, just the boy really but I couldn't leave this little girl alone."

"You're going to cause more problems than we want."

"Are you his wife?" Romana asked.

"No, miss Romana, I'm his boss. *The* boss. The one who is going to stop all this nonsense once and for all."

Laterille led Peezle through the door into the courtyard just as the black vehicle drove into it. The human and Cakerlak stopped as the car stopped and Allard stepped out, but not as quick as Zalez did. Zalez went right up to Peezle.

"Noj, what are you doing here? Where are my children?"

"Help me out of this thing." complained Blap.

Allard went around the vehicle, opened the back door and pulled the Toob out.

"Fancy pants, wot are you doing here?" Blap demanded, waving to Laterillell.

"And oh, look, hanging out with the enemy."

"I'm not the enemy." Laterille said, "The enemy is on their way."

"Where are my children?" Zalez said through gritted teeth.

"I don't know what you're talking about." Peezle said.

Just then the Chordattian Jackanapes walked out through the doors, looking worried. His furry hands were shaking as he took the scene in.

"Hello, your children are safe, Mr. Belhopsa."

Zalez turned to look at his fellow Chordattian, and approached him.

"I don't know who you are, but you have my children. Where are they?"

Jackanapes swallowed, "They just got here. They're safe. We just wanted the boy, and you."

Blaphaus stepped forward, "Take him to them, shaky."

"Look, I will. But she's here, if she knew you are here then you'd be done, Blaphaus."

Allard looked worried, "She's? What are you talking about, Jackanapes?"

"Allard, it's…"

Zalez grabbed Jackanapes by his pink shirt. "Take me to my children. Now."

Jackanapes just nodded.


On Phytnes, the Ultra vehicle drove up driveway to Haathee's mansion. The brown furred Enhydra got out, and opened the back door of the blue vehicle.

Bodie stepped out, followed by Haathee.

"It's a pleasure to be your driver, my dudes. I hope you'll have a great sunny day. Tell the G.P. I support him."

"Thank you." Haathee replied.

He walked up to the door which opened up to reveal Enitittuk standing there.

"Governor Haathee, I'm glad you're here."

Haathee walked inside followed by Bodie who shook Enitituk's hand.

"Nice to meet you, mate. I'm Governor Bodie." he whistled, looking around the mansions foyer and the big chandelier above them. "Haath, mate, you chose being a Governor over living here?"

"I was forced into it."

Enitituk motioned to the back of the mansion.

"You have someone out back waiting to speak to you, Governor."

They walked through the glass doors in the back to the pool area where Joorg, wearing just his underwear laid on a pool float in the middle of the pool, drinking some kind of alcohol drink from a glass with a small green plive in it.

"Hello, Haathee, my old friend. Come in, join me. Why is that Canis here?"

"Because I had no idea what to expect. There's already been one blastering on this planet so I didn't want to come by myself."

"And Bodie will protect you?"

"What's your story, mate?" Bodie asked Joorg. "I hope this is not a Cyrakuse versus Canis thing."

"It's an everybody versus the upcoming invasion thing." Joorg said, "Only the Order can stop it, if we all come together. Haathee, I know you you were having an affair with my late wife, but I'm not going to hold a grudge…"

"I wasn't having an affair, Joorg. She wanted me to join the Order, she warned me bad things were going to happen, and you and her were part of an Order to stop it. She mentioned the Cakerlak, she mentioned the Toob, and then Blaphaus arrived here and forced me to be Governor."

Joorg smiled, "It's true, my old friend. Bad things *are* going to happen. We can all thank Blaphaus and the Cabinet for that. So, which side do you want to be on?"

"I say we stop being Governors." Bodie replied. "And go back to my quiet nice life. So much drama."

The holo-call of Fadonna appeared in front of Mal who sat next to Nekkod's bed in the hospital. Nekkod slept, and was snoring pretty loud.

"Fad, what's up? How are that children?"

"Mal, I don't know how to tell you this but someone took the children... he knocked me out at your house and took them. I have no idea where they went, I'm so sorry." Fadonna started to cry.

Mal looked mad, glaring at the holo-call of her friend. She had no idea what to say.

"Father!" the children cried out, running into Zalez's arms as he squatted in front of them. Phedorra watched, standing next to the older woman. Jackanapes, Peezle, Laterille, Allard and Blaphaus stood behind watching.

"Children, are you okay?" Zalez asked.

"Yes, father, but that man knocked out Fadonna." pointed out Romana.

Zalez stood and glared at Phedorra and the woman.

"What is the meaning of this?"

"I apologize, Mr. Belhopsa. Phedorra here had no right to take your children and bring them here."

Just then Zalez's pocket info-pad beeped. He pulled it out the pocket of his overalls and Mal's holo-call didn't look happy.

"Zalez, Fadonna said..."

'Mal, it's okay... the children are here with me."

"Hello, mother!" Nate smiled.

"Mother, I don't know where we are but father is here!" Romana said.

"Zalez, what's going on?" Mal cried, "I'm sick of all this."

Zalez stood and nodded, "Me too. But we are coming home. I'll explain to your later. Everything will be okay." He turned to Blaphaus and the others.

"I quit. I am not going to put my family in any more harm. And I'm not going to be the head of Dook... Narob Energy or whatever it's called anymore." he looked down at the children. "Come on, children. We're going home."

Lilly Traf walked into the kitchen where the robot One was cooking dinner.

"One, Algar spent a long time talking to you. I know he told you a lot of things. Did Narob do that too? How can he be so bad? What is happening to my family? What's happening to everybody?"

One turned her head to look at Lilly and replied, "I was told by Algar only to reply to these questions if *you* asked. Algar was a good man, Lilly. He cared for the galaxy and he cared for you and the children. But he knew something bad was coming and he didn't know what to do."

"One, something else happened... Algar was in good shape, it's still so weird he had that heart attack. And what about Narob?" Lilly's eyes started to water. "How can he be so bad? There's so many questions..."

One put her purple metal hand on Lilly's shoulder and nodded.

"Follow me, ma'am."

She led Lilly out the kitchen and into Algar's old office. She closed the door and walked over to the desk and opened a drawer. She took out a holo-recorder fob and held it on her hand.

"You might want to sit down." One told Lilly.

Lilly sat in a small red leather chair in the office and before she knew it a full-sized Algar Traf stood in front of her, as a holo-recording.

"Hello, if you're seeing this, there's a good chance One is showing it to you. She's the only one that knows this recording exists. Not even Peezle knows. Not even Ten. I love all my Governors in the House but there's one I don't trust, and that's Guoz the Gink. First of all, he never went talks about his planet. I had the GBI watch him a few times, and he never leaves Launderington as far as we know. If you are wondering why I am Galactic President, as it seems I don't seem to do too much... well, about 30 something years ago I met by a man named Blattodea, who told me of a war between a bunch of different species, that he named the Order of Blattodea and this species that came from another galaxy, which I find very hard to believe, but they were called the Tooberosum. No one knows what happened to the Tooberosum species, but I believe they were all wiped out. There's a good chance if that's not true, and there's more out there they will come back, and do more harm."

Lilly looked up at One with a puzzled look on her face.

"Anyway, I don't want to say too much here. I would have you go and talk to Blattodea but unfortunately he has passed away. He should've been G.P., not me. I'm not cut out for this, at all. There's going to be another recording that I'm going to give to Ten, and in that I will tell you my plan for the future. I have no idea who is watching this or when, but if you know my dear, lovely wife Lilly tell her I love her, and keep an eye on Narob. When I get back soon I will have a conversation with him, he's worrying me. There's a lot that's worrying me. Bye for now."

The holo-recording winked and smiled and then disappeared.

Lilly looked up at One and said, "I have no idea what that all meant."

## CHAPTER 23

"Take off that ridiculous costume."

The older woman stood in the white walled room facing Blaphaus. To his right sat Allard, to his left Peezle who sat next to Laterille. Phedorra stood next to the woman, arms crossed.

"I don't think so, lady."

"I can have a few GBI agents here really quick to remove it." she said seriously. "Or I can have Phedorra here remove it."

"I'll break the old man's hands." Blap remarked.

"With those skinny arms?" Phedorra asked.

Blap grunted.

"I want to know where Yerkal was taken to." Peezle said, sitting forward.

"He's going to be taken care of." she said. "You might see him again. Now, Maximus, take off that costume."

Allard nodded to Blaphaus, "I'd do what she says if I were you."

"You're the worst bloody security advisor ever. When we get out of here you're fired."

Allard smirked, "That's the least of our worries."

Blaphaus grunted again and pulled off his jacket, then popped out one eye, then the other. They watched him pull of the Toob skin, revealing again the gray haired human he was, with the data pad strapped to his chest.

Laterillel's antennas stuck straight up. "You... you're not a Tooberosum?"

Blap motioned Peezle to stand up. "Fancy boy, get up. It's my turn to sit."

Peezle nodded and stood to let Blap sit down.

"Where are you from?" the woman asked him.

"Lady, I'm not answering any questions until you answer mine. Who the bloody hell are you?"

"My name is Rosecy Blattodea..."

"Blattodea? As in the fornicating Order? The ones behind the blasterings, the ones causing all these problems?" Blap stood back up, fists clenched. "You're lucky you're a female, old lady."

"It's way more complicated than that... it's more than you. I knew you weren't really a Tooberosum as soon as you were in the news."

"Good for you. The Cabinet losers had no bloody idea..."

"How did you know?" Allard asked.

"I met the real Tooberosum... not all of them, but a lot of them." she glanced over at Peezle. "I'm surprised you didn't, Mr. Peezle. Algar met some... before he was G.P."

"So, are you going to inform us who this species was?" Allard asked.

"I don't give a feces about the Toob... I want to know why the Order ordered all the blasterings." Blap pointed out.

"The Order is not the same as it was when my husband started it. The Order was supposed to stop the Tooberosum... the Order was the defense. The Cakerlak had him murdered, then went into hiding." She looked over at Laterillel. "I'm sure you knew a lot about that, right?"

"I don't know anything."

"You know about the Great Weta."

"He's some bloody figure head." Blaphaus remarked.

"He was the one who ordered the death of Blattodea, but we have no proof."

"And the Gink who are not from this galaxy?" Allard asked.

"No, they're from another galaxy."

"They also are hard to kill." Blap told her. "I figured out about the Gink, the planet you all thought was his planet was a moon. The King we thought killed him, but he escaped. In fact, I saw him again and he's out there somewhere." explained Blap. He motioned to Phedorra, "Why don't you send old man child kidnapper here to find him?"

"I have beings looking for him as we speak, Maximus." she replied.

"So, I was with Algar a lot, ma'am. He never mentioned Blattodea, or any of this." Peezle said.

"I can't speak for a dead man, Mr. Peezle, but it's good he didn't."

"His bloody son sure made a name for himself." Blaphaus muttered.

"I can't speak for him either." she told him. "He will be taken care of though."

"You do realize that none of this would happen if you weren't Galactic President." Phedorra spoke up.

"Again not my idea..."

Allard sat up, "You can't prove what you just said, Phedorra. The Gink was already here."

"You said he could be Governor anyway?" Blap asked. "With no research? The same lot that picked me?"

"I don't know. Traf chose him to be Governor."

"Well, I said it before and I'll say it again, you lot. This galaxy is really fornicated up. I thought my old planet and galaxy was bad enough. You lot take the crown."

"Speaking of..." Rosecy said, "You're not from this galaxy... we can't have you acting as G.P."

"He's not, but the Toobs are." Peezle told her.

"That's the whole point, right?" Allard said. "He admitted he's not from this galaxy, and just a cranky old man. But as far as the rest of the galaxy knows he's a Toob, good or bad. We need to prove the Toobs are not a bad species."

"How do we do that?" Phedorra asked.

"Stop making him out as the enemy... focus on the real enemy."

"Which are?" Jackanopes asked.

At the House, the few Governors that were there sat around the table as always.

"I have a nasty feeling that we are not going to see Maximus again." Zucaritas told them. "We definitely can't stick by him."

"What do you suggest?" Dawber asked.

"That we reveal we were all duped." Zucaritas replied.

Kaktovic said, "I am not going to turn my back on the Galactic President no matter who he is. We have to all stick together... in Traf's and Tostone's honor."

"No. Zucaritas is right." Zeb said standing up. "He's not even from this galaxy, and the Gink who sat in that chair..." he pointed to the chair that Rüppell sat in, "was not from this galaxy. I have a family back on Chordatta. I need to be with them. I have a feeling in my big gut this whole galaxy is in for a whole lot of hurt."

Southington nodded and also stood up. "I agree. I am going back home as well. I don't think I want to be involved with this any longer. This whole galaxy has gone nutso."

"So, you're just going to leave?" Noam asked.

"We have to remain strong." Jaboney remarked.

"I'm staying here but I agree with them. We need to think ahead. It's like a game of stabber, this political business is." Noam said, 'Right, Eastora?"

Eastora shook his head and stood. "No, my little friend. This is way too much than we bargained for. I'm going back to Burdernchurdettu."

Thaw leaned back and shook his head, "What have we all become? If the House breaks up and the galaxy beings find out..."

"Don't tell them. Keep it a secret like all the other secrets." Zeb said walking out.

"Southington, you can't go." Dawber said sadly.

"I have to, Dawber. I have to." she then walked out.

"I don't like this at all." Gillian shook her head.

On Cyrakuse, the King out of his palace's front door to see the green figure standing in front of the royal shuttle.

"Your highness." Guoz nodded to the King.

"Guoz, no one saw you get on my private shuttle, did they?"

"No, no one did. I wore robes to cover up. I'm not stupid, you know."

"And no one knows you're alive I take it?"

"Blaphaus does. I paid him a visit on Launderington at his hotel..."

"What? You said you weren't stupid, Guoz. You know he has a big mouth."

"King, you know he's not really a Toob."

"I had my suspicions from the moment I met him. Let's go inside, we can talk in there. I have a feast waiting. Is your fleet almost here?"

"Yes, King, they are very near."


Professor Phence studied his info-pads, staring through his spectacles. He spotted many white dots coming out from the planet they assumed was Tooberosum... from the other side of it. He got up quickly and made his way to his office. Someone had to know.


On Launderington, Noam walked down the steps of the House to see a fellow Smidge standing on the sidewalk waiting for him.

"Noam, I need you to come with me." Dwof told him in a slight panic.

"Who are you?" Noam asked her.

"You don't know who I am? We went to school together, Noam. We sat next together on the short bus. Remember the short bus?"

"Lady, all the busses on Homunculus are short."

"I wore less make up then."

"Oh, yeah, now I remember. You were the far annoying one... like now to be exact."

"Can I ask you where you're going?" she asked. "I know you're the Governor of Homunculus..."

"That is none of your business."

Just then Rubyspears drove up in his limo-vehicle.

"Noam, I am a member of the Committee. Something is going to happen to this galaxy... I think you and I need to go to Homunculus right away."

"I am not just going to take off and leave. I might not like Blaphaus but I have to play by the rules."

"Noam, where are your other Governors going? I know a few of them are not here. I'm telling you, Noam, this galaxy real soon will not be at the same."

"This galaxy hasn't been the same since Blaphaus came along, toots."

Blaphaus strolled out the Committee building, glad he wasn't wearing the  bloody Toob suit. Allard and Peezle followed him, carrying pieces of the suit. Jackanapes followed behind them, arms and fingers all twitchy.

"A vehicle will take you back to where you need to go. Is there anything else we can do for you?"

"Yeah, get off my case, twitchy. Leave me alone. In fact, all you losers leave me alone."

They reached the vehicle in the courtyard that was waiting for them.

"I hope we can all work together in the times coming up." Jackanapes told them.

"We'll let you know, Jacky." Allard told him.

Blap was already in the front passenger seat of the vehicle.

"Let's go! I'm done here." he called out.

Inside the building Anegon walked up to Rosecy and brushed his whiskers.

"So, how did it go? What's the verdict?"

"If the invasion happens, we are all screwed." she replied.

Fami sat across from Doctor Siahl in his office, high up in the building on Launderington.

"Doctor, I don't know what to say... I tried my best..."

"Fami, my dear, you did great. You did everything you could. The Cabinet fooling everyone in the galaxy that Blaphaus is really a Tooberosum is going to bring doom to everyone. I just hope I'll be able to help them when the invasion happens."

'Do you think for sure it'll happen, sir?"

"My dear, it has already happened."

"Oh my. I'll do everything I could to help."

He smiled at her and nodded, "I know you will, my dear. I know you will."

Blaphaus got out of the vehicle in front of the House building. Allard and Peezle followed him, each carrying the parts of the Toob suit. They hurried up the stairs before anyone noticed, not like anyone was there. They went inside to be approached by the House-robot.

"Hello, gentlemen. The Cabinet, what's left of them is waiting for you."

"Wot do you mean what's left of them?" Blap asked.

Allard was already at the lift, "Let's go, this suit is getting heavy."

Blap snorted, "Then put the bloody thing on."

A few minutes later they walked into the conference room and they put the suit on the table.

"You're not dressed as the Toob?" Zucaritas asked.

"Nope. That lady in the Committee wanted to see my body." Blap sat at the end of the table.

"Lady? What lady?" Dawber asked.

"Rosecy Blattodea." Allard told them, "Widow of Blattodea that started the Order."

"They are swearing up and down the invasion or something is going to happen soon." Blap said. "So, where are the others? Blondie? Shorty? Trunky? One-eye? That fat Chordattian..."

"They left." Kaktovic told him, "But I'm sure they will be back."

"That's good. That's a lot of Governors to replace."

Just then Phence's holo-call appeared in the middle of the table.

"Hello, Governor Thaw, other Governors, Galactic President Maximus, I discovered something you should all know."

"Terrific. Wot?" Blaphaus asked sarcastically.

"I believe my satellites picked up a fleet of ships coming around from the planet you call Tooberosum..."

"Castor. Not Tooberosum..." Blaphaus said matter of factly.

"Ummm... okay, Castor. The huge fleet of over a hundred ships is coming around from the back of the planet."

"And?" Jaboney asked. "The are coming?"

"No, not the Castor... another species that's been here before."

"The Gink?" Blaphaus asked.

"No, not the Gink..." Phence said.

"Then who?" Blaphaus asked.


The King smiled and watched as his shuttle took off again with the Gink inside it.

Inside the shuttle, the Great Weta's holo-call was in front of Guoz who sat.

"The invasion hasn't happened yet, Gink. I'm getting rather concerned."

"Calm down, my species' ships will be here soon. I'm sure they are going to invade this galaxy before we know it. I'm going to go straight to GNN and announce the invasion is happening and Blaphaus needs to stand down or reveal his true self."

"It better happen soon, Guoz. Laterillel reported back to me that Blattodea knows everything."

Guoz grinned his sharp teeth. "Like I said, we have nothing to worry about."

On the bridge of a bulky big ship a short squat Tooberosum approached the slightly taller one in the black military jacket.

"Commander, a small shuttle is approaching. What shall we do?"

The Toob Commander smiled and replied, "Destroy it. We will let this galaxy know the Tooberosum have arrived... again."

The King's shuttle approached the big green ship which opened fire, blowing the shuttle up with the Gink inside it. The Tooberosum have arrived.

*TO BE CONTINUED...*

9 7 9 8 7 0 0 6 1 3 4 6 0